Alpha
EXILED

LORIE O'CLARE

D1103643

ELLORA'S CAVE
ROMANTICA PUBLISHING

What the critics are saying...

৪৩

ELEMENTS UNBOUND

5 Angels and Recommended Read "Lorie O'Clare has crafted a well-paced, fabulous tale with charming characters that are bound to capture readers' hearts. *Elements Unbound*, is the first book in the *Werewolves of Malta* series by Ms. O'Clare and it's a great start to what promises to be a terrific succession of stories. Make sure not to miss this one!" ~ *Fallen Angels Reviews*

"Lorie O'Clare always enthralls when writing werewolf stories. *Elements Unbound* is no exception. [...] There are no punches pulled in Ms. O'Clare's books and the stark realities in the werewolf pack of her imagination is that the strong will survive. [...] Pick this one up for a short, but intense read!" ~ *Euro-Reviews*

LIVING EXTINCT

"This book has already been set aside for rereading; I found it that good." ~ *Joyfully Reviewed*

"I was hooked by the story and the characters from the very beginning and was sad to see this book end." ~ *EuroReviews*

"LIVING EXTINCT is a page-turner that will keep you on the edge of your seat from the first page. The character development is great and the plot is sensational." ~ *Romance Junkies*

An Ellora's Cave Romantica Publication

www.ellorascave.com

Alpha Exiled

ISBN 9781419957802
ALL RIGHTS RESERVED.
Elements Unbound Copyright © 2006 Lorie O'Clare
Living Extinct Copyright © 2006 Lorie O'Clare
Edited by Mary Altman & Sue-Ellen Gower.
Cover art by Syneca.

This book printed in the U.S.A. by Jasmine–Jade Enterprises, LLC.

Trade paperback Publication June 2008

ALPHA EXILED

ഔ

ELEMENTS UNBOUND
~11~

LIVING EXTINCT
~71~

ELEMENTS UNBOUND

Chapter One

そ

Bruno Tangaree pushed low-hanging tree branches out of his way. The cliffs weren't too far away, and the salty wet smell of the Mediterranean hung heavily in the air. Moist air clung to his skin, dampening his shirt. He moved silently through the trees, more concerned with whom he'd find than the nearby ocean.

Taking control of the pack hadn't been easy. Werewolves understood domination ruled. The strong prevailed. Their pack leader was old, beyond his prime. No one challenged his call to replace him. But Bruno wasn't pack leader yet. He would be in hours though — at midnight.

There was a simple matter to take care of before challenging the old alpha. The werewolves of Malta were headed in a new direction, a direction the old werewolf who'd lazily kept the pack together for decades couldn't master. Bruno would lead the pack, and he'd do it with his bitch at his side. Now was the time to claim her.

He stopped right before the clearing, camouflaged by the thick foliage surrounding him. Thick damp grass covered the open area before the cliffs. Just as he'd been promised, Renee Guarta stood at the cliff, staring toward the ocean. She'd run here to escape, knowing damned good and well that being out here alone was forbidden. Good little bitches didn't run by themselves. It gave them a bad reputation. And a tarnished female had a harder time catching a good mate.

Not that Renee would suffer from that age-old belief that still maintained conviction in their pack. He'd see to it. She was wild, as unpredictable as the elements, and she'd be his bitch. His mate. His woman. He'd made up his mind. There

11

was no other who possessed the grace, the intelligence, the willfulness to take on the unknown like Renee. Those were the qualities needed to be queen bitch.

Her reasons for running here were valid. Pack gossip washed over the town faster than a tidal wave. And he didn't blame her a bit for escaping to this private paradise to clear her thoughts.

Renee had her back to him, her long black hair falling to her ass and lifting slightly when the breeze kicked up from the ocean. Her simple dress, common to most females in town, whether human or werewolf, blew around her legs. The light yellow pattern showed off the dark glow of her smooth brown skin. None of the females in the pack compared to how fucking hot Renee was. They didn't even come close.

He sucked in the salty air, his cock hardening as he imagined stroking her soft flesh, feeling her mouth on him. God, he needed her more than he needed to breathe. Her hands fisted at her side, her long slender arms waving back and forth slightly alongside her. He knew she was pissed, knew she'd run for a reason. Her sire wished her mated with one of the wealthier, older werewolves in the pack. He used her to secure his den, make sure he was comfortable in his old age. The werewolf didn't give a rat's ass about Renee's comfort, or her happiness.

But Bruno cared. Every day that she walked this island, he'd make sure the elements parted for her, bowed down to her. She would be queen. Never again would she be wronged, used for her beauty and grace. Renee deserved happiness, her intelligence and sultry beauty admired and honored.

"If my sire sent you, you're wasting your time." Renee didn't turn around.

The wind blew against her and it impressed him she'd picked up his scent. Not that he'd hidden it from her. Her scent, on the other hand, wrapped around him like an erotic flower, sweet and intoxicating. Add that to the way her dress clung to her, pressing against her soft curves by the brisk wind coming off the sea, and his heart thumped harder, faster in his chest. A more carnal, raw side of him surfaced, eager and ready to claim what he wanted—what he would have.

"I'd be the last werewolf your sire would send."

Renee turned quickly, brushing her hair from her face when the wind captured it. She held it behind her neck, staring at him.

"Bruno." She whispered his name slowly. "What are you doing here?"

Her black eyes widened, her gaze traveling slowly down him and then quickly returning to his face. Unbridled curiosity, bordering on lust, hit him hard with the next gust of air. But there was fear too, uncertainty. He wasn't exactly what most dens would consider mating material. With no den of his own, a rogue werewolf, the old stick-in-the-muds in the pack wouldn't give him the time of day.

He worked hard at the plant, kept a den over his head, and always had. Not once had he sought out the pack for help. And when help was needed, he was there, as would be any decent werewolf. It was his lineage that didn't impress. There was nothing he could do about that. His line would start with him, with Renee. Together they would create a den that would go down in history—he felt it—he sensed it.

"I'm here because you are," he answered honestly, taking his time in narrowing the distance between them.

The late afternoon sun hit his arms and shoulders, adding to the warmth that already simmered inside him. The brightness shimmered in her hair. A rosy hue covered her caramel colored skin, brightening her cheeks while she studied him.

"Who betrayed me?" she asked.

He smiled, respecting the werewolves in their pack loyal enough to provide him with information. Catching Renee before her sire shipped her off to some overweight werewolf to drool over mattered more than anything. Enough of the pack stood behind him. Renee's whereabouts had been easy enough to learn.

"There was no betrayal." He moved in closer, inhaling her scent.

"Bruno, we're friends," she whispered.

"Yes."

"But I swear if you try anything, I'll kick your ass."

He chuckled, loving how her eyes widened, and then her tongue darted over her lips as he cleared the distance between them. He lifted a strand of hair, brushing his knuckles over the swell of her breast. She hissed, sucking in a quick breath.

"Tell you what, you may kick my ass if I try, and don't succeed."

Her lips formed a thin line and she slapped his hand away from hers. "Listen here, wolf man, your cocky attitude will get you in trouble."

"No one will get in trouble here," he assured her, grabbing her hair again and twisting it around his fist. "You have my word."

The wind lashed around them. Her hair flew around her face, while her dress twisted around her legs. Her nipples hardened and he got a wonderful view of her small ripe breasts pressed against the material of her dress when the breeze from the sea lifted her hair and blew it behind her. Even as the wind's direction changed, her scent remained wrapped around him, clogging his senses, filling him with hard pounding need.

She grabbed his wrist, her touch burning his skin. "Let go of my hair," she said under her breath, fire burning in her gaze.

"I'm not letting go of any of you," he hissed. Her defiance did a number on him, bringing out the better half of him, calling forward his more carnal side.

"You don't have any of me." She was angry, or at least that's what she wanted him to see.

Not many werewolves mastered controlling their scents, and at such a young age. In fact, most reeked of their own self-confidence, something Bruno found incredibly annoying. At a young age he'd taken on the elements, worked with the wind and the earth to hide his scent and keep others in the pack from knowing his intentions. The drawback was that many in the pack now didn't trust him. No werewolf trusted what he couldn't smell. But enough knew he'd make them strong, powerful, a pack all would fear and respect. And they would be rewarded.

Renee had the gift too. She managed to conceal her scent out of desperation, to keep her den from smelling her misery. But it lingered in her eyes, in the way she carried herself. Instead of despising her, since she was a young unclaimed bitch, it simply made a lot of the pack leery of her. Her sire worried she wouldn't mate, so took matters into his own paws. Bruno burned inside with outrage and disgust when he learned the amount her sire had paid to ensure her a mate.

His anger fueled his trek up the mountain in search of Renee. In daylight, changing and bounding up here in his fur would be a bit too dangerous. Their pack dominated the small seaside town, but there were humans here too. Humans who didn't want to be reminded how thick the coast was with werewolves. Renee wouldn't be in her fur. And he'd found her as he anticipated, tormented and hiding from the destiny her sire laid out for her.

Bruno had other plans for her—for them.

"At the moment, no one has you." He looked down at her small fingers wrapped around his fist. Her fingers didn't meet at either end. And she hadn't let go. "That's about to change."

"I'm not mating with that ancient werewolf." She did release him then, turning and tugging on her hair just above where he had a grip on it.

He let it slide through his fingers, the soft silky texture adding to the need that burned inside him.

"No. You're not."

She turned from him and he grabbed her, wrapping his arm around her and pulling her against him. Her soft round ass pressed into his cock. Need for her fought his rational thought, tearing into his human resistance. When she would have struggled against him, he reached around her, grabbing her chin and turning her head far enough so that she looked up at him.

"You will be my mate," he told her simply.

She swallowed, her neck moving under his fingers. He stroked the soft flesh, feeling her heart beat rapidly against his fingertips. A rich sultry smell, strong and sweet, floated around them. Almost like fresh flowers, cleansed after a spring storm, it grew stronger as he stared into her dark eyes. The rich scent of lust, sexual desire and yearning filled his nostrils. His muscles grew, everything inside him hardening in reaction to her sweet intoxicating smell that he guessed she didn't fight to hide. That or he'd caught her off guard enough that she was too surprised to control her reaction to him.

"My sire would never approve my mating with you. You are a den of one." She didn't look away, her lips barely moving as she spoke. "Not to mention what the pack leader would say. You're not exactly top alpha."

"That's about to change." He wouldn't add that only the old werewolves didn't have a clue what went on under their noses. Those too slow to run with the pack any longer, yet still led it. "By midnight I'll be pack leader, and you shall be my queen."

She stiffened and then suddenly struggled in his arms, twisting and finally punching him in the chest until he let her go. Her teeth pressed against her full lips, the only indication of her outrage.

"You think I give a rat's ass about being queen bitch? You're no better than the rest, Bruno Tangaree. I'm a fool to think that you were." She stormed away from him, heading toward the trees. "I don't need to be impressed by rank and prestige. Is it too much to ask to be loved?"

He lunged after her. She cried out, trying to break into a run, but he pounced on her. The two of them fell to the ground and she let out a very unladylike howl.

"I'm not offering you prestige, Renee. Our task won't be an easy one."

Her smaller body stretched out underneath him. He rolled to the side, pulling her up against him so that he cradled her in his arms. The rich smell of dirt rose around them. Earth at her purest state, hard and unyielding, yet able to provide and care for all who lived on her. Just as they would lead their pack. The elements guiding them, and them guiding the elements.

"And believe me," he added, his voice gravelly as he fought the change she brought out in him when her hot little body pressed against his. "You have my heart already."

"You're trying to buy my love by offering to give me rank if I mate with you," she accused. Again she'd hidden her feelings, stuffed them deep enough inside her that he couldn't smell them. Her hand slid up his chest, reaching his collarbone. Her fingers stroked his bare skin above his shirt, gently touching him. The fire it created was anything but gentle though. "Like what you have to offer alone isn't enough," she added quietly. "I wouldn't mind if you had no rank."

He combed his fingers through her hair, tangling them in her black locks and then tugging so that her head fell back. She didn't fight him, not that she could in the position he had her.

"We possess a gift, Renee. You know it as well as I do. This pack is old, stale. Its stench is annoying. The werewolves of Malta will grow strong again under our leadership. You and

I will call forth the elements and make all of Malta aware of how we are stronger, better than any other werewolf on this planet."

"I don't have any gifts." She shook her head as her lie filled the air between them with its foul smell. She wrinkled her nose, but pressed her lips together, silently challenging him to call out her untruth.

Bruno wouldn't argue with her. For too long he'd watched her, seen how she made the wind stop blowing when he'd hoped for a peek up her dress, noticed when flames jumped in the large fireplace in Freddie's *locanda* when she walked past it. Her gifts burned inside her, alive and aching to be drawn forth, educated and trained.

Not only were her gifts almost as strong as his, her beauty made every other bitch in the pack look plain. None of them grabbed his attention, made him hard. Renee was drop-dead, fucking gorgeous. More than once he'd walked past her, inhaled her lustful curiosity when he caught her eye.

He much preferred the sweet smell of lust on her than that of a lie. Stroking her cheek, he brushed his lips against hers then deepened the kiss. She opened to him, her lips parting and her tongue meeting his. She tasted like chocolate, rich and creamy. Yet smelled like lavender, her shampoo, soap, creams she might apply to her soft silky skin attempting to cover up her natural scent. Yet they failed. Her lust, her craving to explore, her desire to be taken, surrounded him. It was a rich sweet smell, thick and intoxicating. He dove deeper into her mouth, impaling her with his tongue, while he grew drunk on her scent.

Damn. He swore she'd be hesitant, unsure. He saw how she watched him during pack runs. He'd caught her sideway glances at pack meetings. But her den was protective, overly so. Renee never had a moment alone, until today, until all hell was about to break loose. The fever he'd been sure ran through her, burst forth with more energy than he'd anticipated. His cock flamed to life, hardening instantly and throbbing between them.

Renee would love it rough, hard and fast. Her quick submission let him know he could take her to places that would make her howl until she screamed. He'd work with her, educate her, make her his very own. She craved it, begged for it.

He grabbed her head, tilting it back while tangling his fingers in her thick black hair. His tongue swirled around hers. He explored, took what she offered, while he craved more. So much more.

All worries of what might happen today faded with that one kiss. The only thing that mattered now was being inside her, fucking Renee, making her his forever. She would see this was the right choice. That he was the werewolf for her. If he had to keep her up on this cliff until the challenge, he'd do just that. Whatever it took to convince her that life for both of them would be better if she ran by his side.

His cock throbbed violently. Every inch of him hardened fiercely. She tasted so fucking hot. Smelled so damned perfect. Every dream he'd had. Every fantasy he'd jacked off to. Nothing compared to how she felt in his arms, returning his kiss, with her lust and the smell of her sex fogging the air around them.

"Bruno," she cried out, breaking the kiss and panting so hard, for a moment he saw the change consume her.

Chapter Two

ော

Renee gazed into Bruno Tangaree's dark brooding stare. Every time she was anywhere near him he gave her the chills. And not in a bad way. Those dark eyes. His thick straight black hair that was longer than most werewolves in the pack wore it. His dominating, silent presence always unnerved her.

Bruno never tried to impress the other werewolves. He didn't join in on pack fights, trying to impress the surrounding bitches with brawn and no brain. The silent one, strong and dominating, standing to the side, he commanded the attention of everyone around him simply by entering the room. Every unmated bitch in the pack drooled over him. And Renee was no exception. But he was the werewolf she'd never have. The one she'd always dream about but would never be close to. Her den saw to it. If she even got close enough to inhale his deadly arousing scent, her sire or mother had grabbed a hold of her, leading her away quickly. As if being too close to him would somehow endanger her innocence. If they only knew how desperately she ached for him to do just that.

And it wasn't fair. She ran with the pack, had been allowed a small amount of freedom to enjoy time alone with other werewolves and bitches her own age. Hell, she was twenty years old, hardly a cub. There had been a romp or two in the cliffs with a willing werewolf. Like any of them would tell her no. But somehow, no matter how discreet she tried to be, whenever Bruno was around, someone in her den, or a close relative, managed to shoo her away from him.

How many times had she fantasized about what it would be like to be with him? Run with him. Lay her kill at his feet.

She knew it would never happen. Bruno had no den. His sire and mother had died when he was a teenager during one of the raids with the humans. He worked in the tobacco factory. She'd known him since high school, and she and the other females her age often whispered about him when he drove by on his motorcycle. A powerful alpha, he didn't run with the other werewolves. At least not that she'd heard. Any of the runs she'd been allowed to join, he'd never been present. No one knew him that well. But his incredible good looks, the way he seemed to stalk anyone he approached — every bitch in the pack wondered what it would be like to be sought out by Bruno Tangaree. But he was the rogue werewolf, someone all of them knew they could never be seen with. With no den, no history with the pack, her parents would have put a leash on her if she'd ever even mentioned his name to them. Bruno was a werewolf to fantasize about. Larger than most, strong with a deadly stare, he frightened and had her coming in her panties at the same time.

Yet here she was. In his arms. On the ground. His scent smothering her. And that kiss. That kiss almost dragged her soul right out of her body. His lips were so soft yet his actions so demanding. Her heart thudded in her throat. Hell, he'd thrown her to the ground and kissed her so aggressively, for a moment she thought the change would take over.

Remembering his words about her gifts sobered her enough to regain control of her senses. "We shouldn't be doing this," she whispered, barely able to make her voice work.

"We're going to be doing a lot of this." He stroked his rough finger down her cheek and then outlined her collarbone, stretching his fingers around her neck, tightening his grip, and then relaxing it.

Her nipples hardened painfully, while her breasts swelled. He was so aggressive, but then gentle, as if silently showing her he would have what he wanted, but encouraging her to want it too.

What she wouldn't do to experience his mouth on her nipples, sucking, nibbling. Her pussy swelled and got so wet there was no way she could hide the scent. Every inch of his hard body pressed against her. And his cock—hard as stone and pressing against her hip. She dared to stroke his arm. Muscle harder than steel brought forth her more carnal side. Her heart beat faster, pumping blood through her veins at a dangerous speed. Tiny hairs rose to attention on the back of her neck, down her arms, and her back. If she put on a bit of muscle, showed that she was strong too, she could take him on. Something told her fighting him would simply make him fuck her faster. It would get him so wound up he'd devour her, being rougher than he was now. Just thinking about how wild she could make him had cream soaking her pussy. God. Rough and out of control sex with Bruno Tangaree. The smell of raw untamed lust soaked the air between them. Fire burned her cheeks and neck. But it was too late. He knew she ached to have him.

His hand moved to her breast. She almost came when he stretched his palm over her, pushing slightly and then squeezing the soft flesh.

"You make it sound like you're mating with me."

"I just told you that I was." He pulled her closer, lifting her back off the ground so that suddenly her head was buried in that rock-hard chest.

Having sex bonded werewolves for life, or so tradition said. These days many of her generation defied that law, fucking secretly under a full moon. But never so that any of the elders in the pack would know. One-night stands—something to take the edge off. And although she'd tried it, Renee didn't run with the wilder werewolves that often.

Solid muscles pushed into her face. Her heart thudded so hard she couldn't hear anything else. Her sense of smell went on overdrive though. Every breath filled her with masculine domination, hard and raw and untamed. She shivered against his touch yet fire burned inside her.

Too much domination. He caressed her breast, squeezing it through her dress. His other hand moved down her back. It took a minute to realize he'd just unzipped her dress.

Oh God. He was undressing her. Out here. Alone. And good little bitches didn't run alone. Right now, right here, was exactly the reason why they didn't. Horny rogue werewolves would chase them down and have their way with them. This was not something she made a practice of doing. She'd been pissed, angry with her sire, and escaping the pack and their ridiculous laws and traditions for just a minute.

Bruno had found her. And he wanted to fuck. He claimed he wanted to mate, but maybe he just said that to get her to consent.

Not that she was fighting him.

And she should. Somehow she needed control. The way he touched her, seduced her, told her he'd make her his bitch.

Wait. His bitch. Did she want this?

One thing she did want—more than anything—was to experience Bruno Tangaree. Maybe he did a wonderful job of growling in a bitch's ear just to get a piece of tail. If so, she'd probably prove the easiest bitch he'd ever taken on. But to know what it was like to be fucked by him, to have that hard cock impaling her, even if it were just this once, damn, it would make life so much easier to have this memory to enjoy.

She sucked in a breath, turning her head too late to avoid filling her insides with his all male scent. He was like a drug, taking over her senses. And she'd spent twenty years of her life learning how to control and keep her senses from being detected.

And with that training, she'd learned how to read other werewolves better too. Bruno said they shared the gift. Right now, she swore she smelled every emotion running inside him. His need, his raw lust, the hard ache that pumped with the steady beat of his heart, and more. With every breath, Bruno smelled of lust and compassion.

Maybe she was a foolish bitch. Or maybe she read him right. But God, she believed him. He wanted her as his mate.

With a quick fluid movement, he grabbed her dress at her shoulders and pulled it down. It trapped her arms, pinning them to her side, while exposing her breasts for him. Her bra did nothing to keep her from suddenly feeling very exposed and vulnerable.

Two feelings she absolutely detested. Somehow she needed more control. She needed assurance what she smelled was right.

"You're making all these decisions without asking me?" She squeezed her eyes shut.

She controlled where she ran. No werewolf had her by a leash — not now, not ever.

"Renee," Bruno whispered, almost growled.

He moved quickly, faster than she'd anticipated. With fluid movement, as if he were already changed, he pushed her to the ground. She hit hard earth and all air flew from her lungs. Instantly he was on top of her. She couldn't fight him. Hell, she could barely move. The way he said her name put her entire body on edge.

His hands stroked her shoulders, moving her bra straps down her arms. "Look at me."

She opened her eyes, and met his gaze. Bruno always struck her as intense. Quiet and in control, the other werewolves respected him even though he'd never challenged any of them. He didn't have to. There was a powerful presence that swarmed around him. Thick-chested and well built, in human form or as a werewolf, he demanded respect without having to request it.

But the way he devoured her with his gaze, and crept deep into her inner thoughts as she drowned in his dark eyes, stole her breath. She inhaled quickly, knowing if she didn't fight him she'd go belly up and spread her legs without a thought to the world.

He didn't look away from her face when he slid her bra below her breasts. He cupped her bare flesh in his hands, tugging just enough to send jolts of electricity straight to her pussy. She pressed her legs together, feeling pressure build inside her.

"I won't be put on a leash," she said, speaking her thoughts, which was something she never did.

For some reason her words made him smile. "Do you need a leash?"

"No." Trying to carry on a conversation when he caressed her breast and twisted her nipple between his fingers was the hardest thing she'd ever done in her life.

No. Mastering the elements was the hardest. If she focused, she'd regain control here. It had to be. Nothing was stronger than the elements.

The ground. Blessed earth underneath her, pressing hard against her back. And air, at the moment saturated with the mixed smell of their growing lust, carried by the breeze from the sea. Water lapped against the rocks at the bottom of the cliff not too far from them. And fire, burning inside her like flames that coursed out of control.

"You won't make decisions without my consent," she managed to say. Damn, her voice was gravelly.

"Am I doing something you don't want me to do?" he asked, his breath torturing her flesh.

He lowered his head, running his tongue over the sensitive part of her neck. A low growl rumbled inside him and he moved down her, until he scraped his teeth over her nipple.

She arched into him, every inch of her going stiff while her body cried for release. He didn't play fair. But damn if she could stop him. Hell. She didn't want him to stop. For years she'd imagined being with Bruno, taking on the quiet alpha whom no one dared to challenge.

Now for some reason she ached to challenge him. He'd made a decision, chosen her. And announced he planned on fighting for position of pack leader. If he wanted it, Bruno would gain that position. Their pack leader was an old werewolf. Time was right for new blood to take over. Suddenly she was chosen to run alongside the werewolf who would draw that blood.

"You know what I mean," she said, practically panting. "And you aren't allowing me to think clearly," she added quickly.

Being queen bitch meant a lot of responsibility. There were tasks, things expected of her. At the moment she couldn't think of what one of them might be. Hell, she barely remembered her name. He threw a lot at her feet, and expected her to pick it up and run alongside him. She needed time to think. Damn it. Fighting off his skilled seduction so she could fathom a thought sure as hell didn't appeal to her at the moment.

He raised himself off her, his hard-packed body suddenly not touching her everywhere. His black hair looked a bit more ruffled than it had a minute before. His more carnal side, the other half that made both of them whole, ached to come forward.

Bruno pulled his shirt over his head and tossed it to the ground next to him. She got one hell of an eyeful of thick, black, curly chest hair spreading over muscles that rippled everywhere. It wasn't the first time she'd seen this much of him. The entire pack stripped down together when they went on runs. But never this close. Only at a far distance, with pack members moving between them, blocking her view. Now he was right here, all for her, every inch of him.

God. Could she control a werewolf like him?

The thought of it spurred new fire to life. Life would never be dull. Going after her kill, racing up the cliffs by his side, prancing alongside him under a full moon—life would be fucking great!

Her mouth went dry while her heart raced in her chest. Blood pumped through her veins too quickly. She about drowned in the smell of her own lust.

"Never lose control of your thoughts." He grabbed her dress at her waist and lifted her ass off the ground when he pulled on it, yanking it down her legs and then flinging it to the side with his shirt. "I know you can do it. You have the gift. Just like I do. Which is why you're destined to be my mate. I've seen you do it. You were ready to do it when I showed up here on the cliff."

If her heart pounded any harder inside her chest it would explode. He grabbed her underwear, almost ripping the small amount of material from her body when he pulled them down her legs and then lifted her legs until her panties were on the ground next to the rest of their clothes. He reached for her bra, wrapping his fingers around the material between her breasts, his fist pressing against her overworked heart. She clasped her hand over his, holding his hand to her chest, and keeping the one tiny bit of material on her body. Like it did a bit of good. She was naked underneath him.

"What are you talking about?" There was no way he could know.

No one knew. Not a damned soul. She'd stood at the edge of the cliff, her private sanctuary until today, and had cleared her mind, allowing her thoughts to leave her body. It was the most invigorating experience, and something she could get away with even during the day. When changing into her pure form, taking on her animal form, tearing across the island and running through the wild wasn't an option, leaving her body and soaring over the sea uplifted her, allowed her to think more clearly.

Bruno had interrupted her chance to flee from the torment her sire had laid out for her.

"You are fucking beautiful," he whispered, not answering her question. His cock pressed against his jeans, his shaft long and creating a hard thick line up to his belt.

She licked her lips and almost told him he was the most beautiful werewolf she'd ever seen too. That would sound ridiculous though. Beautiful hardly described Bruno. Impressive, deadly, manipulative. And breathtaking, absolutely breathtaking.

"You're not..." she panted, "answering my question."

With one quick hard tug he ripped her bra from her body. The material tore, scratching over her skin. She jerked from the abrupt action, a shriek escaping her. When he pulled it from her, it lifted her body from the ground momentarily. She fell against the grass with a thud.

"Oh shit," she cried out, his sudden roughness turning her on more than she ever imagined something like that would.

Her pussy throbbed, a dull, hard beat that swelled through her insides. Hot and wet, the sweet smell of her sex clung to her. Her breasts swelled, craving his attention. She needed him touching her, filling her, relieving the pressure that was about to fucking explode inside her.

"That's because you know what I'm talking about," he growled, and reached for his belt.

She struggled to breathe, her pussy swollen and absolutely soaked. She watched him remove his belt, and then unzip his fly. No way could she move. Every inch of her pulsed, the change aching to come forward. Her muscles twitched, while blood pumped too quickly through her veins. He stood, slowly taking off his pants.

She should do something other than simply gawk at him. He stripped, revealing perfection as he slid his jeans down his hard, muscular legs. Her fingers itched to touch him. There was a small hairline scar above one knee, and another on his right hip. What she wouldn't do to stroke his hard flesh, feel his coarse body hair under her fingertips.

Renee pushed herself to her elbows, unable to get up before he was on her again—this time completely naked.

"Don't assume anything about my thoughts," she told him, fighting to sound in control. "What do you think I was going to do at the cliff?"

He positioned his legs between hers, running his hands under her thighs and lifting her while he adjusted them so that his cock throbbed against her soaked pussy.

"You were going to leave your body," he whispered, and then slowly began kissing her. "And once we share our bodies, my little bitch, I'll show you how we can share our minds."

He nipped at her lower lip, sending so many sensations crushing through her that she couldn't focus on his words. She opened her mouth, ready to cry out but he impaled her with his tongue. His hand moved down her side, squeezing her hip. He braced himself with his arm, keeping most of his weight off her and giving her enough room that she could rub herself against his hard muscle. The coarse hair on his chest tickled her breasts, making them swell with need that matched the intense craving in her pussy.

She wrapped her legs around him, offering herself to him. His shaft brushed against the entrance to her heat. Her pussy was burning hot and wet, soaking both of them.

Renee turned her head to the side, gasping for air. His hard body over her, the sweet smell of lust, and his unique scent, a mixture of confidence and domination, overpowered her.

"Bruno, please." She'd never begged a werewolf for a damn thing. Not once.

His cock pushed against the entrance of her pussy. "You're mine, Renee," he hissed, thrusting hard and fast inside her.

"Holy fucking shit," she screamed, knowing damn good and well none of the few werewolves she'd been with in her life had ever been this big.

And not one of them claimed to be mating with her when they'd fucked.

She'd argue of the meaning of their actions later. Right now, it was all she could do to breathe. He thrust that cock of his clear up to her belly button. Her blood boiled, the ringing in her ears stealing her ability to think. Her senses heightened, her teeth growing enough to prick her lip as she arched into him, allowing him to go deeper.

She was out of her fucking mind. If she were sane, she'd stop him. But damn. Nothing had ever felt so good in her entire life.

Bruno thrust again, not hesitating to take what she offered. He fucked her hard and fast, pushing her over the edge too quickly. When she knew she'd explode, he pushed his arms underneath her, scooping her up, and pushed himself to his knees.

Not only did he manage to stay inside her, suddenly she straddled his thick thighs, her legs stretched out on either side of him. He grabbed her hair, holding her face close to his, and impaled her so that she almost choked.

"Fuck me, Renee. Fuck me while I fuck you."

"Damn you," she complained, on the edge of coming but having been robbed of her moment.

And now he wanted her to move, to think enough to fuck him. Damn him for suddenly offering her control. Something she wanted. And he gave it to her. Except her mind was fogged over with lust.

He grinned, sensing her frustration. "Prove we're equals and fuck me as I fuck you."

She couldn't look away from him. Not only because he had her face pinned, holding on to her hair, but she lost herself in his dark penetrating gaze. Once or twice in her life, she'd experienced more than the scent from another werewolf's emotions. Something allowed her to go deeper, feeling what they felt. Usually it happened when her own feelings were heightened. Staring into Bruno's almost black eyes with silver streaks, like lightning, showing her his more carnal side, she reached past the strong wall of domination that he had built around himself.

Slowly she managed to get her leg muscles to cooperate and she lifted herself off his cock. Before he was out of her, she sank on to him again. As she fucked him, his concern, his fear that he'd be able to pull off leading the pack, and his heartfelt yearning to have her by his side while he did it, filled her mind. She'd moved into his head.

Holy fucking shit! She read his mind, their thoughts mingling together as their bodies joined.

As she shared her body with him, he shared his mind with her. He needed her, was convinced without any doubt that what needed to be done could only be done if they ran together. He'd kill for her, protect her, and would love her.

God. She saw it all in a flash, dumped into her head. She picked up the pace, ignoring the burning in her thighs as she rode his cock. He moved his hands from her hair, stroking her back, holding her to him while she glided her pussy over his cock.

When the pressure burned out of control inside her, it flared to an exploding point in him. Renee knew that exact moment, as a tidal wave of pent-up need erupted inside, that she took him with her. He held her in a death grip, throwing his head back and growling as he filled her with his come.

They collapsed on the ground, both of them breathing too hard to speak. Which was fine with her. She didn't have words for what they'd just shared. And she wasn't sure she was ready to hear his explanation.

Chapter Three

ဢ

"Bruno!" Bernard Tangaree yelled from his bike as he zigzagged through the trees.

His motorcycle rumbled over the rough ground, the smell of oil burning suddenly filling the air.

"Oh God. Oh shit!" Renee struggled underneath him, panic taking over as she scrambled for her clothes.

"It's okay." He grabbed her dress for her, shaking it out before handing it to her. Her look was wild when she stared at him wide-eyed. He blocked her with his body and turned toward his cousin who approached quickly. "Wait there," he yelled.

"I've got to go. If I'm discovered," Renee muttered, struggling as she pulled her dress over her head.

Her slender body stretched before him briefly before the soft yellow material of her dress glided over it. She pulled it over her head and then lifted her long hair, letting it stream over her shoulders and down her back. The glow on her face was as beautiful as the smell of their sex.

He pulled his jeans on, holding her gaze as he did so. "You are protected with me. Do you understand that?"

"You were serious?" She frowned at him, and at the same time her smell faded. She fought to block her feelings from him. "You want to mate with me? Bruno, we don't know each other that well."

He didn't bother with his shirt. This was a hell of a lot more important. Cupping her face, he stretched his fingers through her hair. God. Just holding her like this warmed his insides. More than just great sex, knowing how linked they would be, that she was his other half, would make her the perfect mate.

He stared deeply into her eyes and used his mind. *You have the gift, Renee.*

She blinked, and the salty smell of nervousness swarmed around them. *What is this? Now you're in my mind?*

"When were you in my mind?" This surprised him.

She was more powerful than he'd imagined. Yet she hadn't worked with her gift, hadn't fine-tuned it. This would take time, and he'd guide her through mastering it. Together, they would make each other even stronger. No werewolf in Malta would surpass what they'd possess together.

A slow smile crossed her face and she backed away from him, glancing beyond him to where Bernard's motorcycle idled. She wasn't going to answer him. They would work on trust, it was imperative that it existed between them. Not to mention, he wondered what she'd found in his mind. More than likely she learned he wasn't as confident as he wanted her to believe. Damn. He'd have to fight for her after fighting for position as pack leader. None of this would be easy.

"Having a gift, as you call it, doesn't mean we're compatible as mates." She didn't look at him, but stared past him toward Bernard.

Bruno took her arm, pulling her to him until he had her attention. Her hand brushed over his chest, her fingers spreading over his thumping heart.

"You've watched me for years, and I've looked out for you since you were a pup. Are you turning down my offer to mate?" He had to know.

A mixture of scents hit him, none of them strong enough to label. She licked her lips, searching his face. "I'm not sure the offer is sincere."

Something stabbed his heart with piercing accuracy. He stared down at her. Bernard revved his motor behind him, letting him know he grew impatient. Bruno ignored him. This was more important. He reached into Renee's mind, searching for the hesitation she claimed existed.

His thoughts mingled with hers. God, she was warm. Creeping into her mind was like finding a sanctuary that was hot and sensual. She wrapped around his soul, embracing him with steamy, sultry need. He almost forgot why he was in there.

Not once had he explored a mind so open, so content and relaxed. There was no manipulation, no intention of deceiving anyone. Renee detested trickery. She wouldn't run with scoundrels. She was young, just now twenty, and she wasn't sure what she wanted to do with her life. But she did know she wouldn't waste it mated to some old werewolf who would parade her around on a leash like a souvenir.

Suddenly she pushed him away, a wall shutting him out of her mind. She straightened her dress and long strands of silky black hair fell over her face.

She brushed them over her shoulder, her dark eyes growing black as she looked up at him. "And I'll know it's sincere when you speak your mind and quit trying to probe mine."

"It's sincere." He grabbed her wrist, pulling her hand from her hair. "And that's fucking amazing that you feel me inside you."

She blushed, her cheeks taking on that rosy hue that contrasted so beautifully with her dark skin. God, she was sexy as hell — breathtaking.

"I still feel you inside me," she whispered, and then looked down at the ground quickly.

As if deciding being shy didn't appeal to her, she lifted her head, straightening. Standing a few inches shorter than him, she almost met him eye to eye. Something spicy, like anger, filled the air between them.

"Your friend is waiting for you." Her tone turned serious, guarded.

He wouldn't have her holding back from him. Not now.

"Yes. He is." He looked over his shoulder at Bernard, who leaned over his handlebars, watching them. "He's here to tell me where the challenge will be."

"You're really going to challenge Alberto?" She looked at him in disbelief.

Her support was imperative, along with her trust.

"You doubt me," he said.

She hesitated. "No. I think you'd be an excellent pack leader."

That surprised him, and pleased him. Pleased the hell out of him.

He grabbed her hair, needing to taste her. He wanted her on his lips, her scent filling his nostrils when he entered the field where he'd fight the older werewolf who'd led their pack for most of his life—until one of them died.

She almost squealed, her emotions suddenly flooding him, when he took her off guard and slammed her body against his. Holding her head, he tilted it back and nipped at her lower lip then ran his tongue over her teeth. She submitted to him, collapsing against him. She ran her fingers over his shoulders and he thought he'd explode again right there, holding her.

Their tongues swirled around each other, exploring, probing. He loved her hesitation that mixed with determination to be strong. He'd seen these qualities in her before, but they came forward when she'd run from her sire, refusing the mating he'd planned for her. Some day, after the ordeal of securing his title as leader of their pack was over, he'd ask her if her refusal had anything to do with him. The curious looks she'd given him over the years had branded her image in his brain. He'd prayed she longed for him as much as he'd ached for her.

He ran his hands down her hair, over her shoulders, and then down her arms. Grabbing her waist, he pushed her from him as quickly as he'd grabbed her. She panted, her teeth longer than they'd been a minute ago. She was one hot little bitch.

And she wanted him. He knew that. Her hesitation stemmed from doubts regarding his sincerity. His words weren't good enough for her. She needed actions.

"Stay here while I go talk to him," he told her.

She simply nodded, taking slow breaths. He'd give her that moment to calm the beast that ached to surface inside her. Without her bra, her small breasts pressed eagerly against her dress, her nipples harder than stone. He let his gaze drop, devouring them before turning from her and heading toward Bernard.

"Taken a mate?" Bernard asked quietly, leaning his head to see past Bruno.

Bruno growled, grabbing his cousin's attention. "What do you have to tell me?" Unmated werewolves would chase after the single bitches in their pack until a claim was announced.

Bernard snapped to attention, Bruno's silent warning to quit staring enough for the other werewolf to show respect. "The challenge is at midnight, just like you asked. Alberto wasn't too happy." Bernard chuckled, his breath smelling like onions and beer. "He agrees to the location, the isolated meadow just south of town. Word is running thick through the pack."

"I'm sure." Bruno wouldn't mourn the werewolf until he was dead. Then he'd personally see to it that the previous pack leader had a glorious funeral.

It was their way.

"Setting fire to the pack grapevine doesn't take a lot of effort. Most dens are in favor of your leadership. They speak of new strength and aggression that will make us stronger."

Which was exactly what he wanted them talking about.

"Word should reach everyone by nightfall." Bruno wanted the entire pack there. They had to be. Once he killed

Alberto, the entire pack would belly up to him, or be killed too. "After I've gained rank as leader, I'll announce my mating to Renee."

"You've made a good choice." Bernard leaned a bit to look at Renee again, but this time his expression remained chaste.

Bruno wouldn't tell Bernard how perfect of a match it was. No one knew his strengths. For now, it would stay that way. In time, he'd teach others his gift. It would make the werewolves of Malta the strongest and most powerful in the world. The small island of Malta would be seen with new reverence.

"We'll meet you at Freddie's *locanda* at eleven thirty," Bruno told him.

Bernard nodded. "Sounds good, *fratello*. See you then." He revved up his motorcycle then turned it around and headed back down the mountain toward town.

Bruno turned, and froze as he stared at Renee. She'd walked away from them, respecting their privacy. At the distance she'd been, if she'd been quiet, she could have overheard their conversation. Werewolves had heightened senses even in their human form. But she hadn't tried eavesdropping. Instead she'd walked back toward the cliff.

Renee wasn't a snoop. She didn't itch to get her nose in other werewolves' business. Soon she would learn that his affairs were hers too. She honored his privacy. That in itself was a level of trust he respected. There would be no secrets. They would always run together. But he gained even more respect for her seeing that she made no effort to learn firsthand what he'd share with her as soon as he could.

He drank in her beauty. As he had when he'd first seen her. Black silky hair lifted with the breeze and blew along her back. It almost reached her ass, but not quite. Which was a damn good thing because that ass of hers was breathtaking. Her pale yellow dress hugged the slight curve of her hips, showing off the soft roundness that he'd love to slide his cock into. Just thinking about bending her over, her hair falling over her face and shoulders, while her soft ass was on perfect display for him, was enough to send all blood rushing to his cock.

The change hardened every inch of his body. For a moment, movement was impossible. He clenched his teeth together, feeling them grow against his lips. His vision grew more acute, and the leaves rustling in the trees around him made his ears ring. He fought the sensation that gripped him. The more carnal, more primitive side of him cried to come forward. Fuck her in her fur and she'd be his for life. Some traditions held strong and true no matter how modern the pack became. And those traditions ran thick in his veins. Some would call it old-fashioned. But the ancient laws of the werewolves remained intact for good reason.

Pack law and tradition were what had her running up here to the cliff in the first place. He wouldn't do anything to force her into mating with him. Bruno knew he didn't have to. Even though he'd tried searching her mind for proof of her desire for him, he hadn't found it. But he knew — somehow he knew — even without the gift.

His legs were stiff when he walked through the trees toward her. Renee wanted him as much as he wanted her. Possibly the ways of packs made it a bit tougher to date, get to know a bitch before mating with her for life. Even if his head remained curious, the pain in his heart wouldn't throb this strong for a bitch who wanted nothing to do with him.

"Soon I will head into town." He needed to make a presence in the pack. Word was out. Werewolves would sniff for trouble — it was the way of their kind. He'd be there to help build strength, make sure they knew they'd have a strong new leader.

Renee nodded, not turning around. She still kept the wall around her mind, shielding her thoughts from him. But her scent wrapped around him, adding to the throbbing in his cock. He inhaled deeply, her rich sexuality, the creamy scent of her skin, the mixture of soap and shampoo and lotions that mixed to create her own special smell. But there was something else—fear, no—anger.

He grasped her shoulder and turned her around. That's when he realized she shook with rage. She slapped his arm off her shoulder.

"You come to me, seduce me, offer me what I've always fantasized about, and then announce you are going to challenge our pack leader." She barely whispered, her body shaking more with fury with every word. "It's a fight to the death, Bruno. How dare you!"

He'd offered her what she'd always fantasized about? The wall of worry that had grown hard and rough inside him shattered quickly, almost making him dizzy. He grabbed her hand that had just slapped him, holding it between them. He squeezed when she tried to pull free.

"There are always dangers in life," he told her, pinning her gaze. She'd hear him, and stand by his side. It had to be like this, or their mating would never hold. "I will not die in this challenge. We'll be triumphant and the werewolves of Malta will grow strong and gain respect with me as their leader."

"So now you see the future too?" She quit trying to pull her hand free. "Bruno, I understand that you wish to lead the pack. You've made that clear. I guess it's sinking in now. You've offered me what I've always dreamed about—having you. The thought of that dream being yanked away if you don't survive the challenge…"

Her anger faded to fear. Fear for him. He'd given himself to her. And as he'd thought, she'd wanted him. Now she worried she'd lose him. She breathed heavily, her lips parting, full and dark like her caramel skin. Long lashes fluttered over her black eyes, and he sensed the change growing inside her as she fought to keep strong emotions from taking over.

Her pain. Her newly accepted love for him shattered the wall of resistance she'd put up around her. It tumbled to pieces, exposing so many emotions to him that he almost teetered from their power. She wanted him. She'd howl for him. She'd lay her kill before him. And now she feared losing him.

"I see you and me making this pack strong enough that new respect will be given to Malta. You need to see that too, Renee." He yanked on her arm so that she stumbled forward, her free hand bracing her against his chest. Her feelings let off powerful scents, aromas she was too upset to conceal from him. He lifted her chin, letting his fingers glide down her slender neck. "My queen bitch will be strong, a leader to her pack. Have no fear that I'll lose. That won't happen. I will not die tonight. You and I will mate, we'll run together, we will hunt together, and be strong together. Tell me that's what you see too."

She slowly licked her lips, her gaze hooded. She wouldn't look at him. He held her tightly, making it impossible for her to move. They wouldn't leave this spot until she knew in her heart that they returned to their pack mated, and ready to take on all the challenges they would create.

"I came here to figure out how to handle my sire. With that in my head, you dare to throw a bone at me that might be larger than I can chew."

"I have a feeling you could handle any bone I give you." He had no doubts.

She sucked in a breath, her anger fading but her fear still lingering in the air. "I don't want you to die," she whispered.

"Then the feelings I've suspected you held for me are real."

She did look up at him then. Slowly, her hand moved up his shoulder. Her touch was like fire, erupting inside him. And the way she stared at him, hungry yet worried, stirred the more primal side of him to life. He let go of her wrist and moved his hands over her hair, holding her head so that she wouldn't look away. He could drown in that sultry look of hers. God. He swore his little bitch was ready to fuck again. If only there were time to fuck her right now. He'd seal their fate so that all doubts disappeared.

She nibbled her lower lip, focusing on his chest. "Mating is for life. Just because a fantasy exists doesn't mean it will grow into love that will last a lifetime."

"Yet you were ready to attack with tooth and claw at the thought of me endangering my life."

She didn't answer right away. He brushed his lips over her forehead, simply wanting to taste her. Filling his lungs with her scent would give him the strength he needed to win this challenge. He'd known he needed to mate with her before he attacked for position of pack leader. Now he saw why. In spite of her claiming to be unsure, she was the strongest bitch he'd ever known. Willing to take on her own sire, unafraid when Bruno had taken her on alone on the cliff, Renee possessed power that matched his. No other werewolf would do for either of them. And with that knowledge in his head, he'd be triumphant, knowing that together they could have anything they wanted.

She lifted her face, offering her mouth, which he greedily accepted. Nipping at her lip, he then ran his tongue over the spot he'd just bitten. She gasped, relaxing against him, submitting to him.

"Go do what you must do," she whispered into his mouth.

He ran his hands down her back and gripped her ass. Shoving his hard cock against her soft belly, he growled. His body screamed that what he must do right now was fuck her again. But he needed to walk among his pack right now, assure them that their new leader was strong and not hiding.

"You will be by my side." His voice was gravelly and his teeth pricked his gums when he tried speaking.

"Yes," she said.

Chapter Four

ରେ

Renee followed Bruno into Freddie's *locanda*. She almost drooled staring at his broad shoulders, the casual way he sauntered into the locally owned werewolf establishment. Muscles rippled in his back under his shirt. His thick black hair fell past his collar. Buns of steel would distract any bitch who saw him, and with a quick glance around the *locanda*, more than one of them turned when he strolled past tables, as if he owned the place. Silent and in control, moving like a predator claiming his pack, he commanded the attention of every werewolf there.

She met the gazes of nearby females, fighting a rumble in her throat to claim her territory, let them know he wasn't available. She glanced at the clock hanging behind the bar — less than an hour until midnight and the time when her life would change forever. Little bolts of electricity shot off inside her. Her palms got too wet and she rubbed them down her dress as she stared after Bruno. They would do this. Together they would make her pack stronger and more powerful. The nerves didn't go away, but a chill of excitement tightened her muscles.

"Renee, get over here." One of her packmates she'd grown up with, Maria, hollered from her bar stool at the counter.

Maria's mother, a widowed bitch who looked about the same age as Maria, turned and let her gaze travel down Bruno. He turned, just as a couple of werewolves walked toward him, ignored them, and grabbed Renee's neck.

"Remember who you belong to," he whispered in her face, and then pulled her to him for a hot, quick, possessive kiss.

It almost threw her off balance. Curiosity and lust clogged the air as every pack member, she swore—every last one of them—turned and paid heed to the aggressive, dominating act. He released her while his dark brooding gaze undressed her in front of everyone. She blushed as her nipples hardened, her pussy swelling with need so quickly a soul would have to be on the edge of death not to smell it. Growling at him, it was impossible to regain composure. He'd made his point to the pack. Now she would have to answer all the bitches' questions. The cocky son of a bitch. Part of her wanted to clobber him, while her other half craved grabbing him, returning the kiss, and eliminating any doubt anyone had whom he belonged to.

He tapped her nose with his finger and then turned before she could let loose a few choice words as to what she thought of his openly public domination before a mating had even been announced. Hell. Her sire would catch word of this before the challenge even took place.

"We heard your sire agreed to a mating with old Giovanni." Maria watched Bruno walk through the *locanda*, mingling with other werewolves.

Testosterone escalated quickly around the werewolves as they laughed and punched each other. That, mixed with the thick smell of beer, almost made her stomach turn. She was still lightheaded from his aggressive kiss.

"And I can smell Bruno's mark on you," Maria's mother, Anna, leaned forward and hissed, her breath smelling of whiskey.

"Mama," Maria scolded, but she grinned when she met Renee's gaze. "So tell us everything."

Renee never claimed to have a best friend. But she and Maria grew up together. Whelped almost at the same time, the two of them, along with other bitches their age, were grouped together on pack runs, and had huddled and played at the meetings. It was hard not to smile at her friend's enthusiastic grin.

"Bruno asked me to be his mate," she confided, it suddenly feeling a lot more real as she shared it with the two bitches.

Not to mention both of them would spread the word faster than they'd talk about the challenge, as soon as they walked out of the *locanda*.

"I'd take him faster than I'd go for Giovanni." Maria made a show of leaning around Renee and hummed her approval as she stared at Bruno. "Hell, yes. Buns of steel."

"And what does your sire have to say about all of this?" Anna took the role of the concerned mother, her gaze dropping down Renee as if with a glance she could see everything Bruno had done to her.

Heat traveled through Renee. Her body tingled anxiously, the thought of being with him soon, possibly after the challenge, when adrenaline would be high and sex would be rough, made every inch of her pulse like an overworked nerve ending. Both women's faces beamed. It wouldn't be hard for either one of them to smell her sexual anticipation.

"I haven't told him yet. Bruno says he'll announce it once he's pack leader."

"And you'll be queen bitch." Maria clapped her hands together, laughing out loud. "There is less than an hour until the challenge. God. This is too fucking exciting."

Obviously neither of the bitches doubted Bruno's ability to take down their current pack leader.

A hush fell over the *locanda* when the door opened. Anger and hostility flooded the air and Renee turned to see their pack leader walk into the place. He was a large werewolf. With a big pot belly and silver hair combed straight back over his wide forehead, she'd always thought he looked like a black bear in human form. His shiny black skin glistened with sweat.

She smelled his outrage, but moved beyond the obvious emotions and read his fear. What he hid from the pack, she saw clearly. Glancing from him to Bruno, she thought Bruno had to sense what she did. Alberto had no confidence in winning. Her heart constricted when she realized he'd come to terms with his death. But he held his head high, a proud werewolf who'd led their pack for years.

He ignored the bitches, moving across the length of the *locanda* in several long strides. No one spoke when he walked right up to Bruno and grabbed him by the shoulder. He stood taller than Bruno by an inch or two, but where their pack leader was large from weight, Bruno was packed with steel muscle, in his prime, and more agile.

Both of them looked very deadly as they stared at each other, aggression dripping thicker than syrup through the air. Renee held her breath, aching to put a leash on their leader, do anything to ensure Bruno would win the fight. She watched the fire in his eyes, the way he glared at their leader, and knew the strength of desire that pulsed through him to take the title of pack leader.

Bruno was aggressive, dominating, and his silent presence demanded the attention of everyone around him. No matter that he didn't shout to the pack promises of how life would be better — talk was cheap. Bruno would run with actions. He would move quickly, pouncing on opportunity with tooth and claw. Nothing and no one would stand in his way to make sure the werewolves of Malta were respected and honored by every werewolf on the planet.

And she'd run by his side. She'd put her kill at his feet. They would mate, and together they would keep honor and strength alive and strong in their pack. With their gifts, they would aid the pack the way no other pack leader could. She stared at the two werewolves. Her surroundings faded. The emotions of the werewolves around her receding. She saw their success. Staring at Bruno, her heart knew they'd be happy, be successful. She didn't know how she knew, but Bruno was right. The werewolves of Malta would go down in history because of them.

She straightened, watching the werewolves exchange quiet words. Even the bartenders stopped what they were doing and gave wary heed to the two large werewolves who quite possibly might not wait until midnight to start the challenge. It wouldn't be the first time a fight broke out in the *locanda*. Alpha males often didn't get along. Put a bit of whiskey in them, and you were guaranteed a few broken tables and chairs before the night ended.

A glass shattered to the floor, their pack leader's voice booming through the room.

"You fucking little punk! It takes more than brute strength to lead a pack."

Once his roar had terrified Renee. Her heart pounded and she sniffed the air, while fighting through too many emotions to pin down Bruno's.

Freddy actually jumped over the bar counter. "Not in my *locanda*," he yelled, running toward the two werewolves and jumping between them.

Their pack leader growled at him, looking for a moment like he'd send him flying. Bruno, however, stood tall and calm—almost too calm. Like the unnerving calm and silence before a deadly tropical storm. Muscles bulged over his entire body though. His clothes looked ready to split and tear from him. And his teeth bulged against his lips. Renee didn't have to climb into his mind to know he fought the change. Hell, her insides quivered with anticipation, anxious for the challenge— anxious for it to end and to enjoy the hot sex that would happen afterward.

"More than one cub will be conceived tonight," Anna whispered from behind her.

Renee's insides almost exploded as she thought how rough and demanding Bruno would be after the fight. She hurried to put up her mental wall, keep the bitches around her from smelling the lust that seeped from her pores. Her pussy swelled, eager and excited to take her werewolf in her arms, love him and fuck him until they both howled.

Would he take her in the field after the challenge? He'd be sweaty, bloody, and wound so tight he'd be almost violent. Or would he give the pack attention first, howl with the werewolves, keep her close, her body tingling in anticipation, until they were alone. Possible scenarios almost had her teetering with dizzy need. She gripped the side of the bar, relying on its real hardness to keep her thoughts at bay and stop herself from coming as she stood there watching him.

* * * * *

It wasn't until later that evening, when the pack began assembling outside town at the old ruins that marked where communal runs often started, that Renee caught sight of her sire. His old truck rumbled over the uneven ground, and she watched him climb out and her mother get out on the other side.

Quite a few pack members already lingered in the dark rocky area. Old ruins reached for the inky black sky, as if pointing toward a place free of all the worries and stress that surrounded each one of them. Their strong, age-old strength seemed to soothe her, and she focused on the old formation, before glancing again in the direction of her parents.

Surprisingly, her sire didn't approach her. Instead, he exchanged a few words with Giovanni. Her mother stood quietly behind her mate, and glanced toward Renee. She wore her black hair piled high on her head as she always did. In simple jeans and a sweatshirt, her mother had never been a bitch who stood out. She was quiet, reserved, the perfect mate. And the kind of mate her sire hoped his daughter would be. Renee smiled at her mother, and the smile was returned.

Warm and reassuring, the softly spoken bitch who'd raised her offered her silent support. That warmth filled Renee. She had her Mom's blessing. Her sire's would come in time, even faster once Bruno was pack leader. She loved the werewolf who'd raised her but knew he viewed the strength of a werewolf on what he had to offer. That would never change in him.

Cars pulled in, parking at different angles. Pack members moved around her. Renee heard the whispers. They tickled her ears and put butterflies in her stomach. As she'd guessed, the pack grapevine was as strong as ever. Right along with the buzz of the challenge, word was out that they'd have a new queen bitch within the hour.

Apparently everyone had confidence in Bruno winning.

Large rocks stuck up from the ground. Cubs began climbing them, fighting among themselves. Renee ignored them, glancing over to where Bruno stood with werewolves surrounding them. Already he had his shirt off, the glowing moonlight accentuating the rippled hardness of his chest. The werewolves growled and laughed, taking potshots at each other, and wrestling to the ground. Energy sparked in the air. Adrenaline, excitement and waves of testosterone charged the area around them. It made her skin prickle.

Blood would be drawn. A life would be lost. It was the way of their world. They were as violent as they were compassionate. Traditions laid out for them centuries before would be honored tonight. Renee clasped her hands behind her back, lowering her head while quietly wishing the best for the souls that would leave this Earth, and for the souls who would lead the pack. The wind blew around her, lifting her hair off her back. For a moment the earth trembled under her feet, not strong, and it was over so quickly she might have believed it never happened. But she knew—understood. The elements were on her side—there for her—for them. For her and Bruno.

Without notice, their pack leader bounded through the crowd. He charged into Bruno, screaming obscenities that were garbled due to his half-changed body.

Renee almost jumped out of her skin. She opened her eyes, lifting her head barely in time to see the older werewolf lunge at Bruno. "Shit. Isn't he supposed to wait until it starts?" she asked no one in particular.

"Pack leader says when it starts." One of the older woman who'd washed her scrapes and pulled her out of trees more than once as a cub, put her hand on Renee's shoulder and pulled her back toward the rocks.

Renee's stomach jumped into her throat. Not fair! What if Bruno wasn't ready? She'd never thought of her pack leader as a cheat. He was an old man, but he hadn't ever treated anyone unfairly.

Yet now he bulldozed into Bruno, knocking him off his feet. Howls tore through the night while werewolves scattered and the two of them rolled over the uneven ground.

Renee sat down on cold stone, barely noticing it chill her ass through her thin dress. She pulled her knees to her chest, wrapping her arms around her legs, and stared at the two werewolves who attacked each other ruthlessly.

One of them would die tonight. The challenge wouldn't end until a neck broke.

Her heart forgot to beat. Chills attacked her skin so hard, rushing across her flesh while she hugged herself. The smell of blood filled the air. Pack members screamed, jumping out of the way while the two werewolves made the change, and brutally tore at each other with daggerlike teeth.

The two werewolves were like a giant black mass, long, thick, shiny hair and white teeth, bodies rolling on the ground. Their growls curdled her blood. They screamed, lunged at each other, two ferocious creatures, large and deadly as they attacked and ripped at each other.

She wanted to scream at all of them to be quiet. She fought not to jump from the rock and try to stop the fight. Bruno didn't have to lead the pack. They would be happily mated even if he weren't leader. She'd wanted him always. He'd made it more than clear that he wanted her. This didn't have to happen.

"No," she whimpered, knowing no one around her heard her. "No one has to die."

Everyone watched the fight. Tension was thick enough to cut with a knife. The deadly brutal screams from the two alpha werewolves made her skin crawl.

And then a silence hushed the area. A soft breeze carried the smell of blood and sweat through the air.

"What's wrong?" Why had they stopped?

She'd never been to a challenge before. Maybe there were rounds, or something. She jumped off the rock, ready to hurry to Bruno and beg him to reconsider. He didn't need to risk his life, or someone else's, for them to be happy.

The breeze carried something else to her. Or maybe it came of its own volition. Satisfaction, complete and fulfilled. She didn't smell it. She felt it. In her mind. Frozen where she stood, a cry on her lips that wouldn't leave, she watched Bruno slowly take his human form. He straightened until he stood, and then threw his head back, his thick long, shiny, black hair flowing in the breeze behind him, and howled at the night sky over their pack leader's dead body.

He was cold. His thoughts mingled with hers. Sweat covered his human flesh, chilling him. And he was happy. Happier than he'd been when he'd fucked her. Warmth traveled through her when something else hit her. The silent promise that she'd be howling with that same happiness later that night. Need and desire hit her so hard she almost fell over.

Looking around quickly, she hurried toward two of the younger bitches in her pack who sat on a blanket in the grass.

"Please. I need your blanket," she told them.

She barely heard one of the older bitches snap at the young girls to honor their new queen bitch. Her head spun when the blanket was quickly thrust in her hands, and she almost stumbled over rocks as she hurried to Bruno.

My queen bitch. His garbled voice tore into her thoughts. He hadn't spoken. Her pussy throbbed and if he read anything in her brain at all it would have been gobbledygook.

She shook out the blanket and wrapped it around his shoulders. Bruno smiled down at her, his hair tousled and messy. Blood and sweat trickled down his face. But the satisfaction, the intense domination that coursed inside him, made her straighten. He was her new pack leader—her mate.

He gripped the blanket at his chest, and wrapped his other arm around her. His body was hot, damp, his heart pounding hard enough that it matched the throbbing that pulsed inside her. Slowly he moved them through the pack. Werewolves around them began howling, showing their respect and loyalty to their new pack leader. Females lowered their heads, acknowledging her new rank as queen bitch. She shivered, her legs quivering hard enough she almost couldn't walk. If Bruno held her a bit tighter, keeping her steady, she didn't notice. His thoughts flooded through her mind, like a fast roaring river, bombarding her with sexual promises he'd fulfill later.

Every inch of you, every hole, will be claimed and completely satisfied.

He let that thought float in her head, her stomach twisting in knots as she ached to disappear with him right now, and at the same time thought of running to a safer haven. She didn't realize they stood in front of her parents until Bruno paused and straightened. It took a minute to make her legs work when he let go of her and shook her sire's hand.

The pack leader didn't ask permission from a sire to take his daughter. And damn it if her sire didn't look like he beamed with pride. Renee met her mother's gaze. Tears streamed down her wrinkled cheeks and she grabbed Renee, hugging her fiercely while whispering how proud she was — as if Renee had done all the work in achieving this moment.

There would be time later at the official ceremony to chat with all the bitches. Bruno put his arm around her again, leading her toward the edge of the clearing where his motorcycle waited among all the cars and trucks of the pack.

"Wait," she whispered when she spotted an older woman at the edge of the crowd.

Standing alone, her hands clasped in front of her as she held her head high, Renee couldn't stop the tears as she approached the only queen bitch she'd known her entire life. How many times had this woman been there for her? As a cub with scraped knees, or a young teenager, confused with too many hormones surging through her. Juanita had been a pillar all the women in the pack could lean on. And she stood now, alone, tormented, her mate dead and her rank stripped from her.

Renee swallowed the lump in her throat when Juanita's pain wrapped around her. But the tears streamed down her cheeks nonetheless when she moved from Bruno's grasp and walked past the other pack members toward the older woman.

Without hesitation, Juanita opened her arms, pulling Renee into her plump arms. Juanita didn't hold back her pain. Her ample body shook as emotions tore through her and she clung to Renee as though suddenly the older bitch was the cub.

"May you have as many wonderful years as I did before this happens to you," Juanita whispered.

Renee knew her blessing was heartfelt and sincere. Juanita upheld the laws of the pack, was an example to everyone her entire life. Even in mourning, with her sudden widow status, she remained strong and accepting of their ways.

"You will be cared for and honored always," Renee promised her.

Juanita nodded, letting her hands fall to her side, and then graciously lowered her head honoring her new queen bitch.

Chapter Five

ഇ

Bruno opened the door to his den. He wasn't even sure what time it was, but the entire pack would sleep late the next day. They'd drunk and heard the loyalty promised to them from every pack member until he'd been able to sneak his mate out of Freddie's *locanda*. His cock had raged with need all the way home.

Now, watching her look around his quiet and simple home, she found it lacking. He sensed her reaction, knew she wondered how the two of them would make a den out of his small one-room quarters.

"A bachelor doesn't need more than a place to crash after a hard run," he told her, running his fingers over her long silky black hair. "We won't be here long before we move into the home of the pack leader."

She was suddenly jittery and stepped away from his touch.

"No." She turned around quickly, surprising him with her sudden attentiveness. "I won't have Juanita taken from her den. It's all she's known for forty years."

"She lives in the pack leader's den. That is how it's always been. Whoever is pack leader, lives in that den."

"Bruno. I don't care. Her loss is great. I felt it. It tore through me. I won't take her home along with her mate, and her rank. We can stay here until we build a new home."

She was determined about this. He smelled it on her, and saw it in the hard gaze she gave him. He nodded, approving. Her heart was big enough to care for an entire pack. And still she had enough to love him too. They would honor the older bitch who'd always been kind to him when the rest of the pack watched him warily. Juanita would know a peaceful existence with her widowed rank. He smiled, seeing how strong his new mate was.

"You will be the greatest queen bitch the werewolves of Malta have ever known."

She didn't say anything but turned again, her nervousness quickly replacing her determination now that the matter was settled. She walked the length of his large one-room studio to the opened windows that looked over the quiet downtown. Living over one of the shops had been convenient since he'd moved into his own den. For now, it would work for the two of them, although there wasn't a lot of space for her to make the den her own. He'd worry about her need to decorate later. Right now, he needed her.

Her mind spun with many emotions. He latched on to her more primal ones, sought them out, wrapped his own lustful thoughts around hers.

She grabbed the end of his bedpost when she sensed him in her mind.

"You are mine, Renee."

"I know." She faced him slowly, her breaths slow and deep. He watched her small breasts stretch the material of her dress. "And you, Bruno, are mine. Our hearts are one now. We'll run together for life."

Werewolves didn't have marriages like humans did. Many had argued over the years that such a ceremony should take place. Werewolves were stuck in their ways though, and change happened slowly. Bruno saw no reason to have such a lavish party to announce a mating. Right now was the time that mattered, where they would get to know each other, learn every inch of each other's bodies, and explore each other's minds and hearts.

"Your clothes are here?"

She nodded. "My parents had them dropped off earlier." She pointed to two boxes he hadn't noticed in the corner by the door. "I have furniture too," she offered.

"We'll get all of it," he told her, knowing her possessions mattered to her.

All that mattered to him was her. He grabbed her dress below her shoulders and pulled hard enough that the fabric tore. It ripped down her body, separating as he tugged it into two pieces. Her beautiful dark skin glowed underneath the fabric.

"Oh shit," she cried out, falling toward him as he ripped the dress clean off her.

She fell into him when he continued pulling until she stood before him in panties. There wasn't a more beautiful sight on the entire island of Malta.

He pulled her hair from her face, grabbing all of it until he held it ponytail-style at the back of her neck. Tugging slightly, her head fall back, her chest rising and falling quickly while she gasped for breath. Her breasts were full, round, small yet so perfect. And her nipples, puckered and hard, pointed toward him until his mouth watered.

"Our minds are powerful, Renee. I will show you what they can do. Did you see how quickly I defeated our old pack leader?"

She nodded, licking her lips.

He hadn't mastered everything, but focusing on his thoughts, stilling his craving for her, he thought about her body—its size, its shape, its gentle curves.

"God. Oh damn." She struggled to grab a hold of him when her feet floated off the ground.

Bruno held her in his mind until he'd moved her over his bed. Then he released her, watching as she fell onto her back.

"How the fuck did you do that?" She struggled to move to her knees.

Bruno crawled onto the bed, moving over her until she was forced to fall onto her back again.

"I'll show you sometime. And when we have the loyalty of our pack, we'll teach them together. I told you the werewolves of Malta would go down in history."

She stared at him, dumbfounded, and for the first time her mind seemed blank, in awe, too shocked to form a thought.

He lowered his head between her breasts and called forward the change, his more primal side, the beast always lingering that made him whole. Every inch of him burned as strength ached to take over his human form. Strength and power so deadly it would eat him alive. Make him whole. Controlling it took every bit of his concentration. But he allowed a partial change. His teeth lengthened, tearing through his gums. He scraped the tips of them over her skin, smelling her, tasting her.

His heart beat too hard for his human body. What made him better than a mere animal was the power, the ability to control his actions. He craved letting pure instinct take over, but Renee wouldn't stand a chance against the energy that throbbed inside him. He ran his mouth over her flesh, feeling its softness, tasting its sweetness, and a growl tore through him. Unbridled energy tingled inside him when she shivered underneath him. God. Controlling his needs, which were raw, hungry, demanding he take more, take it hard and fast, made his head pound as blood surged faster inside his veins.

Renee gasped for breath, grabbing the blanket on either side of her and fisting it in her hand. She arched into him.

"God, Bruno," she cried.

He ran his tongue over her flesh, scraped his extended teeth against her skin. She shivered underneath him. The smell of her sex, her ripe pussy, drowned him as he inhaled. When he reached her panties he grabbed the material, tearing it with his teeth.

"You better not do this with all of my clothes," she told him, her laugh bordering on nervous.

But she was excited. Her body tingled with it, glowed from the energy that washed over her. Her breaths came hard. Those small, perfect tits of hers rose and fell while her tummy hardened and she gazed up at him. Moist lips, eyes so round and dark with small silver streaks lacing them, showing off how aroused she was. Her long black hair streamed down her sides, covering her slender shoulders and shrouding her dark skin. What an image of fucking perfection!

Bruno growled, his mouth changed too much to speak. Not that he cared to have conversation at the moment. Her dripping wet pussy appeared before him. He tossed her panties off the bed then sank his thick long tongue into her hot cream.

Renee almost jumped off the bed. She grabbed his hair, holding his face to her pussy while she thrust with her hips and forced his tongue deeper inside her.

His tongue was longer in his partially changed form. By her reaction, he guessed she hadn't experienced this before. Knowing her sexual knowledge was limited pleased him. There were so many things he would teach her.

He rubbed the thickness of it over her clit, across her soaked hole, and then down to her ass. She tossed her head, her hair tangling over her face, while her orgasm tore through her. She got so wet he almost came from her wonderful thick odor. She was hot, so fucking hot, and she was all his.

He'd waited so patiently for this moment, but now all that patience drained out of him. If he didn't mount her, he'd explode, ruining the moment for both of them. Grabbing her hips, he flipped her over then pulled her up so that her ass faced him.

His cock was engorged, hard and enflamed as it throbbed heavily between his legs. Also larger in his current state, he grabbed it with his fingers, feeling his pulse beat wildly in his shaft, and pressed it into her soaked cunt.

"Oh my fucking God," she screamed, her long hair gliding over her back as she took him deep into her heat.

He couldn't take it slow, his animal instinct to mate was too strong. Riding her hard and fast he held on to the soft curve of her hips, keeping her in place while he pumped himself faster and deeper. Her pussy muscles crashed in around him, soaking his cock, caressing and teasing him.

She wanted him, loved him. Her thoughts screamed what she could no longer put into words. More werewolf than human, one thing was on his mind.

You are mine!

She cried out, attempting to assure him she was, as her own mind took on a more primal state.

He didn't want to come yet. Every inch of her had to be claimed. Pulling out of her was almost an impossible task. Her come soaked his shaft. Thick and swollen, it glistened with her sticky wetness as he looked down at the incredible sight before him.

Her ass was so perfectly shaped. White come clung to her dark flesh. Moisture glistened over her pussy and her ass. He moved his cock to her smaller, tighter hole.

She stiffened, tossing her head and fighting to look over her shoulder.

"Bruno," she said, her voice garbled and close to a growl.

"Relax. Give me all of you."

"Yes," she managed to say although it appeared a challenge to get the one word out.

Energy quickened inside him. He'd give her a taste of the most incredible sex she'd ever experience. But he knew she was a virgin here, and didn't want to hurt her. Even in her submissive posture, her willing state, she was small, tight, and his cock was engorged. His own orgasm was so close, he knew this wouldn't take long. But he had to know what that hot tight heat would feel like wrapped around his cock.

His body cried out in pain when he bent over and once again licked at her pussy. She collapsed on the bed, screaming.

"I wasn't expecting that," she managed to quickly utter.

Her words wouldn't have made sense to a human. Her hair was wild and long, her muscles, although small, thicker than usual. And her pussy tasted better than anything he'd ever had in his life. Stroking it with his tongue, he moved to her ass, circling the small puckered hole with his tongue.

Breathing her in brought out the animal and left the human half of him to the side. He trembled as he fought the change. There would be time later to mate in their fur. But here, in his small apartment, changing fully would destroy everything in the room. Werewolf sex could get rather wild.

"Come here," he growled, doubting she understood the command.

She knew the actions though. He grabbed her hips, his fingers knotted with muscles that craved to change him over completely.

Lifting her back up, he thrust his tongue into her ass and then lapped again at her pussy before straightening. When he pushed his cock into her tight hole, it was wet from her come and his tongue. Even so, her skin stretched slowly, taking him in with hesitation. He closed his eyes, clenching his teeth together as her tight hot muscles strangled the life from his cock.

Barely halfway in her, he swore he'd die if he didn't move a bit faster. Her muscles twitched around him furiously. He let his head fall back, taking in every sensation, and fucked her ass quick and fast until she screamed. She howled along with him as his orgasm hit so hard and quick he almost passed out.

For a long moment, he lay on the bed next to her, listening to her soft breathing, sure she'd fallen asleep. Tomorrow he'd start focusing on matters of running the pack.

Right now, all that mattered was his mate. He pulled her to him and was pleased when she blinked and stared up at him.

"The sun won't be up for an hour or so," she whispered.

He raised an eyebrow, skeptical that she had that much energy left to do it again.

"Let's go for a run."

Bruno grinned. They could change and move through the sleeping town unnoticed if they were careful. Pulling her up with him, he held her hand and then brought it to his lips.

"Whatever makes you happy, my love," he told her.

Renee had the most adorable smile. "I'll race you to the sea."

They left his small den. Once outside, two glorious werewolves, dark as night, their thick black hair long and glistening under the moonlight, ran side by side, the night submitting to their power as they headed toward the sea.

Chapter Six

The smell of the Mediterranean engulfed the variety of aromas from town. Damp pavement, dumpsters, bakeries starting their days with mounds of dough, all faded as the rich salt water consumed her senses. That and the pungent scent of fish and wet wood filled with harvests of tobacco smelled like home. The docks were never quiet, even before dawn. Ships docked, the busy market of tobacco and fish keeping their community alive and prosperous.

Renee stayed behind Bruno, captivated with how his large muscles glided underneath shiny thick long black fur. No one noticed them. The humans moving around down by the bay were preoccupied with their work.

She smelled them, but they were the furthest thing from her mind. Every inch of her tingled from hard satisfying sex. It amazed her that she wanted him again, in their fur, a more carnal, simple method of lovemaking, the true mating of werewolves. She'd make Bruno hers forever.

He held his head low, sniffing out any danger, his large head strong and beautiful. His ears twitched, taking in every sound. She heard them along with him, but nothing bothered her. Happiness and contentment made her heart pound in satisfaction.

She trotted behind him, realizing he took them back to the cliffs, to their private sanctuary where hours before her life had been so different. His black long hair glowed under the moonlight. She watched his long tail flow between his legs. He jumped onto the rocks. Their trek to the cliffs would be so much easier in their fur.

In minutes the secluded clearing appeared where they'd been earlier. Instantly he circled her, instinct taking over.

She laughed, wagging her tail and pranced around him. *You did it! We did it! Everything you said was right.* She wanted to celebrate, run through the waves below. The sea cracked and roared against the rocks below them, calling to her.

Bruno pushed his head between her hind legs, almost knocking her over. *Submit to me, my queen.* His need for her filled the air around them. Intoxicating, breathtaking — she was instantly dizzy from it.

Her body pulsed, shivers attacking her, although with her long thick coat, she was anything but cold.

Bruno's wet nose pushed against her sensitive pussy. *Damn, wolf man.* He wanted her — and he wanted her now.

In their fur there would be no foreplay, no tenderness. Werewolves moved on instinct, the intelligence from their human side even more acute while in their fur. They were here to bond completely. She realized that. She wanted it. Her insides swelled, growing wet, craving him. Bruno brought her up here to complete their mating, tie them together for life. Ceremonies would come later. But the uniting of werewolf and bitch was a private matter. Unlike humans, what happened between two mates was a personal issue.

He shoved his head into her backside, knocking her over. She rolled to her back, spreading her legs, going belly up for her mate. He stood over her, his barrel chest bulging with muscle. Powerful and dominating, he gazed down at her while his lips parted. Daggerlike white teeth appeared, and he ran his thick red tongue over them. Her pussy exploded, need hitting her so hard she couldn't breathe. Not once had she fucked in her fur. This more primitive form of sex had strong meaning among their kind. This was more than sex — this was a statement of their love for each other — of their commitment to run together until death.

His wet nose pressed against her swollen cunt, and then he ran his rough tongue over her sensitive flesh.

Oh shit! Bruno! She wasn't ready for the many sensations that tore her insides apart. Her head fell back, and she relaxed while he slowly licked her soaked entrance, preparing her for him, loving her most intimate areas. God he was so damned good!

He caressed her, stroked her flesh, sent fire roaring to life inside her. She whimpered, needing him so badly her body pulsed with anticipation. When he climbed over her, held her in place with his front legs, she couldn't control her breathing. All that mattered was that he fill her, take care of the hard throbbing that consumed every inch of her.

He almost squeezed the life out of her. Her heart raced when she looked up into his intense silver eyes. Glowing like two rare gems, he was at the top of the line of predators, powerful, intimidating, deadly.

She wasn't afraid though. Her pussy swelled, dripping with need. She parted her legs, offering him her belly the best she could as he held her tightly. When his giant cock appeared, growing and stretching, dark and menacing looking against his long black fur, her mouth went dry. She started panting, a craving stronger than anything she'd ever experienced fogging her senses.

Fuck me! God. Yes! Fill me with everything you have. She wanted him more than she wanted to breathe. His cock was big enough that it looked like it could fill half of her insides but she wasn't scared. An ache for him grew inside her and tore away at any rational human thought that lingered inside her.

He pressed his swollen cock against her soaked entrance. Long daggerlike teeth glowed in the darkness and his intense gaze hypnotized her when he thrust.

Oh my fucking God! She howled, more like screamed, when he shoved his giant cock deep inside her. She didn't want gentle, which was a damned good thing. Bruno was one hell of a powerful werewolf, and he didn't hold back with that strength when he started moving. Fast and hard, impaling her again and again. He gave her all he had, held on to her so that she wouldn't slide away as he pushed further, deeper, filling her, hitting sensitive areas inside her that had never been touched before.

She cried out again, her howls echoing against the cliffs. The sea roared below them, answering her screams of passion. Nothing had ever felt better—more perfect. No dream, no fantasy came close to matching the sensations that tore her insides apart. Hard and fierce, Bruno offered her every inch of him, giving himself to her completely.

She exploded, letting her head fall back as waves rushed inside her with more intensity than the bay below could match.

And when he grew, locked inside her and truly making them one, a fire erupted, the elements greeting them. Wind blew through her coat. Water crashed against the rocks below. The hardness of the earth underneath her kept her grounded.

He growled, fierce and hard, opening his mouth so that deadly teeth glowed over her head. God. He fucking split her in two when he exploded.

Cubs will be conceived tonight. The foretold prophecy she'd heard earlier today took new meaning inside her.

She had no doubts. Lovemaking this powerful would generate life. The two of them had mated, and they'd created another life. She looked up at him, loving him, while his engorged cock continued to pump his fluid inside her.

Time passed, she wasn't sure how much, but the most incredible sunrise glowed on the horizon when she opened her eyes. Its beauty hardly compared to the satisfied and dominating expression on Bruno's face. She raised her head, in spite of her exhaustion, and licked his thick coat. He growled, the rumble vibrating through both of them, as he smiled down at her. Slowly, he slid out of her, leaving her throbbing, soaked, and more satisfied than she'd ever been in her life.

His face contorted, his wide jowls altering, shifting as his hair slowly receded into his flesh.

Anxiously, she allowed the change to shift inside her too. Her bones popped, contorted and altered in size while her muscles changed. Her heart thudded too heavily in her chest and it took a minute to catch her breath. As she took on her human form, her pussy started throbbing and burning with an intensity that made her eyes water. God. He'd fucked the living hell out of her. She'd be lucky if she could stand for a week.

But she was happy. So damned happy. The wind rushed around her, and she closed her eyes, reaching out to the elements, praying that they still and allow her a few moments with her mate. She wanted comfort, peace, and the perfect surrounding to enjoy quality moments with her mate before they returned to town and settled in to sleep until nightfall when he'd make his first speech as pack leader. But with the sun rising, they'd have to return soon before humans awoke and noticed them in their fur.

"We've created life," she told him, feeling the tiny addition to her body settle deep in her womb.

"Are you sure?" He moved to a sitting position, pulling her into his arms and wrapping her up with the heat of his body.

"I've never been more sure of anything in my life," she whispered, more than awestruck that she could tell. Most bitches were at least a few weeks along before any signs of life became obvious to them. "Our love is so strong that life already grows from it."

Bruno grinned, staring over the cliffs at the endless sea that glowed against the morning sunrise. Never had she seen a werewolf look more smug, more satisfied, and her heart jumped with excitement that she'd put that happiness there.

"Your gift is stronger than I realized. Our cub will be even stronger than both of us. We will shield her and nurture those gifts in her. She'll be the most glorious bitch who ever walked this planet." He hugged her closer to him. "Imagine our love growing even stronger, Renee. We are truly perfectly mated."

"She?" Renee closed her eyes, trying to focus on the minute embryo that pulsed quietly inside her. Acknowledging out loud their love made focusing on anything else impossible. "I can't tell whether I carry a bitch or a male."

"She will be female. I feel it. And as beautiful as you are." His expression sobered, and he looked down at her, brushing damp strands of hair away from her face. "Our job won't be easy, Renee. Many will fight us."

She closed her eyes, willing herself to see what he saw. The future didn't lay itself out for her. She shook her head, squeezing her eyes shut harder, aching to know what lay ahead for them.

"I can't see it," she complained, experiencing a sensation of being left out that it all seemed so clear to him yet nothing more than a dark cloud that she'd approach one day at a time.

"I don't see events that will happen." His sharing that knowledge made her feel better. His hand was hot, soothing as he caressed her neck, brushed over her breast, and then stretched his fingers over her flat belly. "But we will use our gifts, share them with the pack, show them how to be stronger."

"There are many werewolves who don't show any signs or understanding of the elements." She walked among them daily, looking through them as if they were an empty page. In a way she pitied them, knowing they would never know life as fully as she did. "We will have to take care of those who simply can't learn."

"They will learn. The gift is strong, and can be taught. And with our strength, we will show the Werewolves of Malta how to be better and more superior than any other werewolf on this planet."

She gazed up at her mate, at his strong jaw line, at the way his black hair glistened against the growing light. There wasn't a more beautiful creature on Earth. And he was hers. Her heart leapt with excitement. This werewolf was her soul mate. He'd found her, given her more happiness than she knew possible, and she'd run by his side, enjoying every minute of their future together.

LIVING EXTINCT

෨

Prologue
ಬ

Renee stepped out of the warm water. Droplets trailed down her body, tickling between her breasts. Bruno watched, looking as alert as he would if entering into a fight. She loved the slight streak of gray in his black hair. A day's worth of stubble on his jaw looked almost silver and made her skin tingle. She imagined its roughness against her body, in between her legs, torturing her inner thighs and pussy.

"This will be our last day together like this." His deep, sultry baritone still made her hot even after twenty years.

Her heart constricted, suddenly too heavy in her chest. "Maybe it won't be like you say."

He raised one eyebrow in that all-knowing look he usually saved for a disobedient werewolf. "It will be like I say."

She sighed, knowing he was right. Life as they'd known it would end soon. She saw it too. Bruno accepted it, seemed almost excited for the next stage of their existence, and she burned for a way to change it.

"You can't change destiny, my sweet bitch," he whispered. "All we can do is plan for it."

She nodded, walking into the thick towel he held out in front of him. Bruno dried her with meticulous care, slowly caressing her shoulders, her arms, her front and back and then lower, between her legs. The roughness of the material scraped over her tender flesh, igniting need deep inside her. The pressure only grew when he backed away, taking the towel with him. A chill settled over her heated body.

"We must make sure Moira is safe — I need that assurance, Bruno." She followed him into their room and stood before him when he sat on the side of the bed.

"Our daughter won't die. Her future won't be an easy one at first, but she is no longer a cub. She can handle Dante Aldo." The strong smell of his confidence mixed with his enticing, lustful scent.

"If she agrees to be his mate," Renee said.

"They are perfect for each other."

Renee nodded and looked down at his cock, which was hard and smooth, stretching between his legs as if it tried on its own to reach up and touch her. She knelt before him, brushing her finger down its length. Bruno hissed, sucking in a breath while he tangled his thick fingers in her hair.

"How many packs seek to destroy us?" she asked, cocking her head and wetting her lips while delicately stroking his cock.

"I know of four. The gift scares them. That we've been so successful experimenting with pack members, showing them how to use the gift, terrifies them."

"If only we'd known." All she and her mate ever wanted was for their pack to enjoy the special powers, the gift, that she and Bruno had. "Showing them how to move things, how to mix with each other's thoughts seemed so clever when we first started."

"Do you have regrets?" He stroked her hair as gently as she did his cock.

"Not one," she told him honestly, looking up into his brooding expression. She kept her gaze on his, tilting her head to do so, and ran her tongue over the tip of his cock. "Not every member of our pack picked up on the gift, but many have. And Moira is a natural."

"Our daughter will be fine," he growled, sounding like he willed it to be so.

"And thanks to the gift, our pack will be safe." She ran her fingernails down his thighs. His muscles quivered under her touch, giving her a sense of power. "If Bernard hadn't moved into the mind of that werewolf from the Comino pack, we might never have known they planned to attack."

"They are here sniffing us out. But now we know they'll attack during the night, and we'll be ready." His worried expression unsettled her. Without going into his mind, Renee knew her mate feared too many of the pack would die.

"We're as prepared as we can be. Within the hour, all the dens will have been notified. Then we can move to help them leave before it's too late." The thought of leaving Malta tore at her heart. But for her mate, she'd be strong.

Renee stretched her mouth over his cock, tasting her mate's saltiness. Her pussy swelled, eager to be fucked. She would enjoy every moment of today. Their last day. After so many years mated to her werewolf, helping him lead their pack, the end stared them in the face.

She loved the sound of Bruno's growl. Her nipples puckered painfully and she purposely brushed them over his rough leg hair while sucking as much of him into her mouth as possible.

"Damn. Come here." He lifted her as he spoke, not waiting for her to obey his command. "Tease me with your heat and you know I'll just want more."

Bruno picked her up as if she weighed nothing.

"That was the plan, wolf man," she whispered and quickly nipped at his lip.

His skin was still hot and flushed from bathing and he hadn't taken time to dry himself as he had her. She pressed her fingers into his shoulders as he adjusted her on his lap.

"Scheming little bitch," he teased, and held her in place while thrusting upward with his hips.

Quick and hard, his cock spread her open, impaling her fast enough to steal her breath. She pushed him backward and he lay back on their bed willingly. Pressing down on his shoulders, she took over, riding him slow and easy. He swelled instantly and she leaned into him slightly, shifting the angle. His cock hit a new spot and sent spasms exploding deep inside her.

His gaze was on her breasts. She loved the way he looked at her, like he would devour her, eat her up with an eagerness of a cub given his favorite dessert. His usually hard expression now flushed with raw lust, with a need she loved drawing out of him.

Intent on how sexy he looked, on his cock moving in and out of her, she fought not to drool as she ran her hands down his hairy chest. Muscles twitched under her touch. His heartbeat was strong and steady, determined and powerful just like her werewolf. Renee arched into him, again altering the way he fucked her, taking him deeper yet.

"Oh God. I need it hard—fast." She'd brought herself so close to the edge.

Bruno chuckled. "Through using me? Do you need me to satisfy you now, little bitch?"

"Shut up." She laughed, although she quivered inside at the roughness of his tone. Her pussy trembled while his cock stroked it. She was so damned close to getting off. "Fuck me, wolf man. If you still got what it takes."

He yanked her off him so quickly she yelped, and then tossed her onto the bed. Just as quickly he pulled her legs up, positioning her ankles on his shoulders and thrusting deep inside her. She slid forward on the bed and howled at the intense pleasure he offered.

Bruno fucked her so hard and fast she couldn't breathe, couldn't think, could barely see his massive frame above her. When he swelled, filling her, every muscle inside her threatened to explode as her own orgasm tore through her.

"You are so incredibly wonderful," she cried out.

Her eardrums almost exploded with a loud boom.

Bruno crushed her, pressing his entire body on top of hers. It took her a moment to realize the booming sound had nothing to do with their sex. Something outside had exploded. Heat surrounded them so quickly, she couldn't breathe. She stared into the face of her mate, the only male she'd ever loved.

Come with me, he spoke in her mind, pulling her out of her body.

Their spirits fled the room as it burst into flames.

Chapter One

ഇ

Screams tore through the air.

"Fire!"

"Damn it! We're on fire!"

Moira Tangaree coughed, covering her mouth against the dirt and smoke clogging the air. Too many scents surrounded her, confusing the situation, and she fought to get her bearings. She whirled around, attacked with bewilderment. A car raced down the street, barely missing her, the whoosh on her back indication that it had been way too close.

The entire city had gone mad.

"We're all going to die!" Screams echoed off the buildings on either side of the street.

None of this should have been happening. Everyone was insane. Her world turned upside down as flames ignited everywhere. Confusion turned to anger, biting at her. Tight pain stabbed at her gut and wormed its way deep inside her, rising into her throat until she wanted to gag. Jealousy and ignorance had caused this. Stupid werewolves terrified of what they didn't understand. They should have offered their bellies to her sire, not destroyed him.

He offered all of them the gift. The ability to move things, to reach into other's minds and have their spirits leave their bodies and travel across land. It worked differently with each werewolf. Bruno Tangaree believed all werewolves had the gift inside them. Moira barely understood what her sire offered. What she knew, she'd learned by listening and watching.

And her mother was the kindest, most beautiful queen bitch any pack had ever known. No matter the hour, she'd hurry out of their den to help any of the pack in need. Her gift was strong and she'd helped Bruno long into the night, their quiet voices often lulling Moira to sleep. Neither of her parents shared a lot of what they did with the experiments with Moira—especially toward the end. She'd smelled their nervousness, knew something was up, but also knew questioning either of them would get her nowhere.

"Enjoy being a cub. Play and have fun." Her mom's voice in her head made her heart ache even more. "Once you are grown, I will show you how to use what is already inside you. You won't need to undergo any experiments for the gift to be part of you. Moira, you are a natural—just like your sire and just like me."

What she wouldn't do to have her mom next to her right now.

She fisted her hands, furious and unsure which way to run while the only world she knew was engulfed in flames. Her parents were nowhere in sight.

Sirens wailed, the emergency vehicles hurrying to block traffic. The stench of panic filled the air, billowing toward her like the dark smoke from the fires. Mixed with anger and fear, it clogged her senses. Too many emotions. Too much confusion.

There was no way to put the fire out. Flames spread faster than she could run. Frustration pissed her off even more. Nothing was worse than being unable to control a situation.

Heat burned her skin. The sky had disappeared, dense clouds hanging way too low. Tall limestone buildings seemed to dance in the thick smoke.

And flames. Everywhere there were flames.

She jumped when someone ran into her.

"Where is your papa?" Bernard Tangaree, her oldest cousin, grabbed her arm so hard it hurt.

She stared up at Bernard, dazed, fighting to make sense of the violence exploding around her. God. He needed to quit screaming in her face.

Something needed to be done. They needed to save their pack. Yet all she did was stand on the sidewalk, staring at the quick destruction and death. Feeling like a ditz, fighting to make sense out of a nightmare, an overwhelming emptiness attacked the anger inside her.

"Where is he, Moira?" He shook her fiercely. "Where is your sire?"

Moira pointed toward the fire, knowing without seeing that her father had burned alive along with the rest of them. Her mother had died in his arms, the two of them leaving this Earth in the same breath. The moment they'd gone, their souls leaving their bodies forever, everything had crashed in around her. "They're all dead." She knew it, no matter that she had no official training with what the gift offered. "I saw them die in my head, Bernard. I couldn't get to them in time."

Whoever had done this would die a slow and torturous death. Her body shook with fury, with intense pain that tore her apart. Her teeth grew slightly until the tips of her canines pricked the inside of her mouth. She wanted to run, to destroy, to allow the change and rip their attackers wide open, spreading their blood over the devastation they'd caused.

Bernard didn't question her. He shook his head, his sorrow briefly drowning out the smell of the smoke. "And with them dies the knowledge," he muttered.

Nothing would right the wrong she was witnessing. After all her pack had done for the other packs on the surrounding islands, throughout Europe, this was the appreciation they got. Paybacks were hell and if it was the last thing she did, every one of the motherfuckers who'd caused this would suffer. Suffer with pain and humiliation. She'd kill each of them with her own claws and teeth. No law would protect them.

Motorcycles rushed past them, the drivers' angry screams ripping through the air. Bernard almost yanked Moira's arm from her socket when he pulled her out of their way.

"Death to the werewolves of Malta!"

Even through the dense smoke, the disgustingly sweet smell of hatred, like bad fruit, turned her stomach. Well, now she'd learned to hate too. Now she could destroy just as they had. Taking out her pack would be the last despicable act any of these wasted pieces of flesh, these poor excuses for werewolves, would ever commit.

A handful of her pack members screamed and ran while the werewolves on motorcycles chased after them.

Sirens wailed down surrounding streets, but the firemen wouldn't save them. Once again, history repeated itself and a pack was burned out due to superstition and hatred.

"Get your ass to the sea, Moira. Move it now!" Bernard screamed in her face.

"I won't leave!" This was her home.

She didn't want to run from it, abandon it. Heat burned straight to her bones, making her want to tear the clothes from her body, change so that she could move faster, save any den still alive. Their wailing howls for help tore at her senses.

Primal instinct was taking over pack members around her. Billowing smoke made day look like night. Friends, dens she'd known all her life, werewolves who normally were civil, let the change take over and fog their ability to think straight. Werewolves raced down the street while others of her pack ran on two feet, half changed in their hysteria. Indifferent to who might see them. It was a horrific nightmare. Children, their tails bursting free from their clothes, cried as they hurried toward protection.

Nowhere was safe. All sanity had been ripped away. Too many emotions to think.

Moira's bones popped even though she fought the craving to grow, to master the power needed to retaliate against this hideous crime. A crime no one else would punish. Her lungs burned and her mind was in turmoil as human thought battled something more carnal, growing stronger the longer she dwelt on it.

Losing control was a sign of weakness. Werewolves didn't change form in the middle of the street during the day. Even if the day was streaked with blinding smoke, turning it black as night.

Bernard gave her a shake. "Get the fuck out of here!"

"I won't run with my tail between my legs," she hissed, wishing she could fight but not having a clue how to defend her pack.

She heard more screams and the sounds of motorcycles as the surviving members of her pack were hunted down and killed.

"You'll do as you're told. I want to know that you're safe. Get going!"

Whatever it took, Moira would see her sire get his revenge. Being his only cub, his closest blood, there had to be duties to take on. Muddled emotions made it impossible to figure out what all they might be. All she wanted to do was destroy those who'd wiped out her life.

Although barely eighteen, Moira knew more than she was supposed to. What surprised her was that they would take out her pack in the middle of the day. Men were so stupid, whether they were human or werewolf. Members of some unknown pack, or maybe members from several packs—she had no clue but she'd sure as hell find out—cruised the streets on their motorcycles, chanting their mantra of hatred toward the Malta werewolves. They chased them down on their bikes, dragging them or jumping from the bikes and fighting in the streets. All the while buildings and cars burned around them. What fucking idiocy!

Her father and uncles had led the Malta pack with iron fists, never hesitating to bare claws and teeth when needed.

Negotiation, discussion of pack law, had never been an option on this island. The surrounding packs had stayed on the smaller islands, but the time had been coming. She heard it in the whispers that weren't meant for her ears.

The other packs feared what they didn't understand. They didn't want a pack with the ability to control the elements, to do "magic" as it was so often misnamed.

Bernard hurried with her down the street, pausing at the corner and sniffing the air. All Moira smelled was burning rubber. It fucking stank too.

"Okay. Go. Run to the bay, Moira."

"But what about you? I can't bear it if you left me too." Moira grabbed her cousin's arm, seeing outrage on his face that matched the feelings that burned through her heart. "Come with me."

Bernard shook his head, peeling her fingers from his arm. "I said to get going. Now go!"

Her legs were still, pain and fury radiating through her as the screams trapped in her throat threatened to rip past the shock that still held her in its grip. Her legs stung from the heat of the fire, her lungs burned from the smoke and in her soul a wound was forever branded into her very spirit.

Please let everyone be safe. Let my den already be by the sea.

With a rough shove, Bernard almost threw her across the street, toward the shore, toward safety.

He didn't follow her. It didn't surprise her. His stubbornness pissed her off. Bernard would die with the pack—just like her sire and her mother. The humans wouldn't lift a finger to save him. And the attacking packs would hunt him down. Moira's heart weighed heavy. As if the smoke didn't make it hard enough to breathe, the pain that ripped through her over the den mates she would lose today was unbearable.

Another motorcycle turned the corner, rumbling down the street toward her. Moira took off running, cutting through the alley, her human legs no match for the speed of the bike. Turning on the bike, baring claws and teeth, would make her feel so much better. Even if it were just one werewolf. Attacking, showing those mangy mutts they wouldn't go down without a fight sounded a hell of a lot better than racing to her death. But she wouldn't change in broad daylight. Common sense remained in spite of her pain and outrage. Werewolves didn't change in front of humans. With the smell of everything burning, she had no idea who might be on that bike.

If only she could get one good, clean whiff of what was going on around her, she'd know what the hell to do.

She ran faster than a human could run, her heart pounding, blood rushing through her while muscles ached to change, bones alter. Cubs were taught to control the change. Moira used that control now, nipping at her lip, using the pain to help keep her brain alert. After several blocks she knew the motorcycle followed, matching her pace.

She wouldn't make it out alive. Overwhelming fear gripped her, seizing rational thought. Panic threatened to take over, giving her the shakes while she fought to keep going.

Willing herself to move even faster, she cut across the next street, wishing the Mediterranean would just reach up and grab her. What was left of her pack would be there, waiting at the bay. All would be fine if she could just outrun her pursuer for a couple more blocks.

The engine revved behind her, the smell of oil and gas filling her lungs. Moira made the mistake of looking over her shoulder, spotting the driver hunched over on the bike. Before she could make sense of what happened, she tripped, flying headlong into the ground as a scream of fear escaped her lips.

"Shit!" she howled, attacking her long black hair with her hands when it briefly blinded her.

The pavement tore at her skin, jolts of pain streaking up her arms and legs. Her short dress did little to protect her flesh. If she could just change! Her bones stretched stubbornly while her muscles twitched throughout her body. The urge to become so much more than human, to allow the sweet pain to course through her, enable her to protect herself, filled her. It would make escape so much easier.

Strong arms grabbed her and lifted her, pulling her into the air and onto the bike.

Instinct took over. Fight! These barbaric werewolves wouldn't kill her today!

"Let go of me, you fucking lousy mutt!" She twisted frantically, giving the bastard everything her human body could muster.

She kicked. She scratched and jerked her body. Her hair flew around her, making it impossible to see.

"Be still," a baritone growled at her. "You're going to get us both killed."

"Better to take you with me than surrender to your renegade pack. You are nothing!" Hair stuck to her mouth as she yelled at her captor. "Wiping us out will only destroy you too!"

Moira almost screamed when the motorcycle skidded around a corner, hauling her along with it. She pulled her legs up quickly, digging her fingernails into the werewolf's steely arms. Sirens pierced her ears, shooting pain through her brain like lightning attacking a fierce night sky. The wind slapped at her face. Too many scents slammed through her system— violated her, made it impossible to think rationally. Strong arms pinned her against solid muscle.

"You better start thinking I am something," he hissed in her ear. "I hold your life in my hands."

The last thing she needed right now was a pompous werewolf demanding that she beg for her life. Moira twisted furiously, almost capsizing the bike. Her captor was forced to let go of her, to grab the handlebars and fight to keep the bike upright.

Let him know right now who he was messing with. It would be a cold day in hell before she bellied up to some lame excuse for a werewolf.

He hadn't slowed as much as she'd like, but she wouldn't die. Not today. Not at the paws of the enemy who killed her pack. She closed her eyes as tight as she could and pushed off the bike with all her might.

Airborne for mere seconds, she hit the ground, knocking the wind out of her and scraping exposed flesh. Intense, acute pain shot through her arms and legs with piercing heat. She rolled, feeling her dress tear, the rocky, uneven road scraping deep into her skin.

She wailed in pain while her eyes watered so furiously that she couldn't focus. All she could do was continue to roll.

"Get back here!" he roared, the bike's motor whining furiously in protest as he came around toward her.

The sound of it drew nearer, its loud engine and the weight of it vibrating through the ground.

Every inch of her body hurt from her head down to her toes. She'd lost her shoes. Her dress was almost torn from her body. Now wasn't the time for modesty. Her life was on the line. All she could do was believe Bernard and have faith that safety lay with the sea.

"You are one fighting little bitch." The man on the motorcycle pulled up alongside her.

More sirens flooded the area, their varying pitches killing her ears. She winced from the loud wails of the trucks as they hurried past them, indifferent to her plight. The humans would put out the fires but then ignore the casualties. Knowing that the werewolves ran thick along the coast of Malta, they'd turn a blind eye, refusing to help what they didn't understand.

Moira ignored the scrapes and cuts on her arms and legs. They'd heal before the mental pain would. She bolted in the direction of the bay. Holding one hand to her chest to keep her torn dress from falling to her knees, she pushed her strength to its limits, sprinting faster than she'd ever bothered to before in human form.

No matter that the sidewalks were full of gawking people, none of them would help her. The humans scattered, their attention and buzzing conversations focused on the massive fire just a few blocks away.

"Get the hell away from me," she screamed, her heart nearly exploding in her chest when the biker jumped the curb and followed her between the buildings.

The crowded street was a normal scene along the coast. Burning buildings and almost naked women being chased by motorcycles were not. Humans were strange creatures, though. They ignored her, their semi-panic more focused on ensuring that trouble didn't come their way.

All werewolves avoided humans, and the humans managed to stay clear of them as well. But for once, Moira wished the police would notice this law-breaking renegade and detain him — anything to allow her to escape.

He whipped around in front of her, his bike skidding sideways while rippling muscle bulged against blue jeans. Large boots scraped along the ground, his heels leaving black lines on the pavement. She almost slid into him.

For the first time she took notice of her dark, dangerous predator.

He was dressed all in black with sunglasses too silver for her to see his eyes. She stared at him, frozen like a dumb animal realizing she was about to die.

He was a large man with a thick torso and powerful long, thick legs. Raven black hair fell straight, blown back from his face. Creamy white skin was uncharacteristic of native Malta werewolves, but at the moment she didn't give a rat's ass about his heritage.

"You don't need to run from me, Moira." His voice was deep and oddly calm considering the chaos surrounding them.

"Like hell I don't. Forgive me for wanting to live."

His lips were full, surrounded by a day's growth of dark stubble against the contrast of his white skin. That straight black hair of his brought out the color. But she noticed the broadness of his cheekbones, the hard contour of his jawline — signs that he was on the verge of the change. There was no way to tell specifically where he was looking with those silver sunglasses blocking her view of his eyes. All she saw was her own damned reflection in those blasted glasses. She fisted her torn dress in her hands, feeling her heart thud furiously against her palms while doing her best to keep herself covered.

"You will live. I'll see to it. Just quit jumping off my damned bike."

His expression didn't change. Not one muscle in his face moved. "You destroy my pack and then expect me not to fight you?" She let go of her dress with one hand and shoved her hair over her shoulder. When she took a step backward, the bike lunged forward toward her.

"There is no fight. The Malta werewolves are extinct as of today." He looked over her head at the burning buildings, his expression not giving any indication whether he cared or not.

"They aren't as long as I live," she argued. "Maybe I'm just a girl, but I'll fight to keep my pack alive."

When he looked back at her, the corner of his mouth curved, possibly a warped attempt at a smile. There was no way to smell his emotions with so many distracting scents surrounding her. "You're hardly just a girl," he said, his tone turning gravelly.

Heat sparked to life inside her. If he tried to rape her, she'd kill the son of a bitch. It sucked not seeing where he was looking. She'd grab those glasses off his face and toss them to the street if she thought she could get away with it.

"Werewolves like you give our kind a bad name." She let her gaze travel over his broad shoulders, keeping her expression stern. No way would this asshole catch her admiring ripples and bulges and a body that was harder than rock.

"Like me?" He revved his bike and it jumped closer to her, stopping before he ran into her. "You don't know a damned thing about me, little bitch. That was your sire's choice. But you will."

"I know everything I need to know about you," she hissed, needing to stay angry so he wouldn't smell lust as she drooled over the most perfect body she'd ever laid eyes on. "How dare you imply you knew a thing about my sire."

"Then you know that I care. That I've just saved that sexy tail of yours." He lowered his voice. "And I knew your sire very well."

Of course he didn't care. He wasn't part of her pack. She'd remember a werewolf as large and deadly-looking as this one.

"Liar. Don't play games with me." Her heart pounded loud enough she bet he heard it.

A powerful werewolf like him wouldn't give someone like her—a bitch who was barely grown—the time of day. Let alone call her sexy. First he destroyed her pack then he made fun of her. He was heartless. Sexier than any werewolf she'd ever laid eyes on, and cruel. With every breath he filled her insides, giving her insight to his raw, dominating nature. As much as she wanted to challenge him, accuse him of being shallow for hating packs he didn't even know, that would get her nowhere. The tension running through him while he glared in the direction of the fire was enough for her to know he wouldn't hear any argument she had.

"This is no game, little bitch. Bruno and Renee weren't perfect, although they damn near created perfection with you. Your sire couldn't stop the other packs from destroying him. But I've made a promise and so has your sire. You will get off the island today. You'll live. I promised Bruno and it will happen."

She wished to hell he'd get rid of those sunglasses. So much could be told by staring into a werewolf's eyes. Her mother always said they were the path to a person's soul.

Her mother…

Moira's eyes burned. Pain tore her insides apart. Her parents were gone. She'd never see them again. And what the hell was this werewolf saying?

"You came after me so you could kill me just like you did my parents," she yelled at him, almost raising her fist to attack but her dress slipped down and she grabbed it before her breasts were exposed to him.

"No," he said simply, quietly, his mouth barely moving.

The spicy smell of anger mixed with another scent, something a bit too sweet, clogged the air between them.

"Don't lie to me, wolf man. You say my sire made promises. That you made promises. What the hell are you talking about?"

He looked away from her, staring at the fire still burning a couple of blocks away. He had a strong jawline, straight and fierce-looking. Again, she wondered where he came from. She would have remembered if she'd seen him before. His strong presence, his obvious alpha attitude, was compelling, distracting.

"I'm not lying," he said without looking her way. "In return for helping your sire, he promised me his most cherished possession."

"And what's that?"

"You."

She stared at him, dumbfounded. No way in fucking hell would her sire give her to some stranger. Her mother would never go for it either. She'd heard the story of how her mother fought not to be shackled to a mate she didn't love. Her parents believed mating was done out of love, not obligation.

"Now I know you're lying." She jumped around him, ready this time when he moved his motorcycle closer to her.

She braced herself to run and froze when he spoke in that calm, smooth, deep voice.

"Moira, I'm not lying. Your sire insisted we not meet until after you turned eighteen. But he couldn't stop the destruction of his pack. He sent me to save you."

Would her sire have entered into such an arrangement? Why did she want to believe this stranger? Just because he was sexier than any werewolf she'd ever laid eyes on, that was no reason to accept his outrageous claim to her. She fought the urge to touch him again, to feel that raw power that had pressed against her body.

God. She was out of her fucking mind.

Distance. She needed distance.

Taking advantage of the brief moment when he looked past her, Moira darted around him, disturbing a group of human children who stood gawking at them and whispering among themselves. More than likely it wasn't every day they saw a lady in a torn dress arguing with an oversized brute on a motorcycle. They screamed obscenities at her in Maltese. Ignoring them and the cuts on her feet that shot pain clear up to her thighs, she raced to the bay—to safety—and her freedom.

I live! Moira refused to look over her shoulder to see if the mysterious werewolf followed. *As long as I do, the werewolves of Malta will never be extinct.*

Dante Aldo turned his bike and accelerated. She raced onto the wooden docks that lined the bay, immediately lost amongst the crowd of human fishermen. Satisfaction barely crept through him. Knowing she escaped the fire was enough for now. Bruno had asked him to ensure her safety and he'd done that. The only ships leaving today would take her to Italy. It wouldn't be hard to track her.

She wouldn't escape him. Her scent lingered in his senses. Her touch had affected every muscle in his body. Fire burned inside him, the carnal instinct to claim and possess running hard through his system. Catching a glimpse of her when she hurried around the people clogging the docks, he kept her pinned with his gaze. She grabbed hold of one of her pack members. The two of them moved closer to the water.

His cock throbbed to life, demanding he chase after her, possess what was his. He wouldn't think with that head though. Moira escaped Malta today, her pack officially destroyed. She would need time. And he'd give her that. But he'd watch her. She would never be too far from him. Patience wasn't always his strong point, but waiting for something as sexy and fucking perfect as Moira would be worth it.

Bruno Tangaree had left his mark on Malta, mastering the elements that so few understood. Dante knew and understood what Bruno had discovered. Every werewolf had the ability to tame the elements. It just took some training. With their experiments, they'd helped willing werewolves learn how to focus their minds, to use the elements so they could be even stronger, more powerful.

Moira had no clue what her sire's knowledge had done to werewolves. In spite of Bruno's efforts, his gift had been abused. The talk had spread throughout Europe, and from what he heard, news had reached the United States as well.

Monsters. The Malta pack had turned werewolves into monsters. He'd heard it all. Turning werewolves into wizards. Bending the elements while they changed, contorting powers that made them invincible killers. Lies and half pieces of information brought the Malta werewolves down.

Applying the brake, Dante let the bike idle for a moment while staring down the coastline. Malta was an overpopulated island with humans hurrying everywhere. Their distracted lives were an advantage to him. He allowed the bike to coast forward and then parked it along the curb, climbing off while satisfied that no one around him gave him more than a passing glance.

He began a slow stroll toward the harbor, the glare of the aqua sea intensified by the setting sun. People brushed against him, focused on where they headed. There were no werewolves on the crowded street, the stale smell of clogged emotions surrounding him typical of humans.

Nearing the harbor, he noted the many boats docked, the majority of them fishing boats. He sniffed the air, knowing there had to be werewolves in the area, and worked to stay focused. So many different smells made it harder to track—but not impossible.

Unclipping his phone from his belt, he pushed the button for the preprogrammed number.

"Where are you?" he asked when the familiar voice came through the line.

"On board. You ready to report the task as complete?" Juan Anthony was hard to hear.

Wherever he was, there were a lot of people talking around him. Dante squinted, his protective sunglasses not helping enough against the glaring sun and the bright water, shimmering as if the light source came from underneath the almost aqua sea.

"I've tried saving as many as I could." Pain bit at his insides over the loss of those who didn't make it. "I just wasn't good enough to help them all."

"Well, you got one. If you're looking for the girl, I've got her in sight."

Muscles hardened inside him. "Don't lay a fucking paw on her."

Juan chuckled, the sound scraping against Dante's over-alert nerves. Juan might be his brother by birth, but he could be an annoying son of a bitch.

"She's fucking hot as hell. You ask a lot of a werewolf."

Dante growled, wanting to wring Juan's neck. "Try to think with the head on your shoulders for a change. Just keep an eye on her, don't let her know you're watching her, and I'll get hold of you in a couple days."

Juan might be a horny werewolf but Dante trusted him. Juan respected another werewolf's property.

Chapter Two

ഇ

God, she was sick of this life, always jumping from one part of the world to another. The minute she'd landed in Grand Junction, Colorado, she'd smelled the worry and fear.

Another assignment that someone had fucked up. Werewolf Affairs sent her in to play cleanup. The agency had no compassion, no sympathy—just do the job, make everything better and then on to the next mess.

For five years the agency had used her, although she knew that she used them too. Ever since leaving Malta, running from the only pack, the only home she'd ever known, staying alive was all that mattered.

The gift she possessed made her a hot commodity. A gift from her sire—Bruno Tangaree. All she had left to remind her of him.

Her being more than a werewolf made Global Werewolf Attack and Reconnaissance—GWAR, an elite section of WA— keep a tight leash on her. And for a while she'd been grateful. Anonymity, never staying in one place too long, was necessary. They'd saved her hide more than once. And she'd bailed them out of more than one embarrassing situation.

"You're going in alone." The GWAR agent looked past her at the plane on the landing field. "You'll report in after you've located the target."

"What's the mission? What target?" Another thing Moira had grown tired of—being called out without having a clue where she was going or knowing anything about the mission profile until she'd arrived.

A cold wind followed Moira through the glass doors of the airport terminal. The strong scent of pine filled her senses. She ignored it though. It wasn't the smell she was after.

The agent was an American werewolf, his red hair cut short and freckles sprinkled over his skin. He shrugged, giving her a sympathetic look.

"Your instructions are on the disc. There's a car waiting for you outside. I'm sorry I don't have any more information." He looked like he couldn't wait to get out of there, already turning toward the door. "There's a laptop in the cabin where you're going. Read over your instructions there."

Moira nodded, worrying her lower lip as she flipped the disc over in her fingers and pushed her way through the glass doors to the waiting car.

Tension rippled inside her while she inhaled the strong smell of waxed leather. The driver never looked back at her, and his stifled emotions stunk from lack of use. A different life called to her as she stared out the window. Members of her old pack were scattered around the country. And somewhere out there was a werewolf who watched her.

She smelled him, sensed him, over the five years she'd been with GWAR. Not once had she seen him though.

Their drive was a short one, and the car labored up a narrow mountain road with dark green trees and undergrowth crowding them in. The car came to a stop, the driver still not looking at her but pushing a button which unlocked her door — her sign to get out.

"Just drop me off and leave like you couldn't get out of here fast enough." Moira glared down the narrow mountain road as the car drove off, leaving her. She looked around, trying to orient herself.

Usually the smells of the night were consistent.

The glow of the moon cast long, dark shadows over pines and the small cabin in front of her. Moira forced her body to relax. With slow, deep breaths her senses gained control, adjusting to the thinner air and taking in the many smells surrounding this dark place. A chill of unease rushed through her. Caution weighed heavy in the breeze.

Someone watched her, not moving but observing. They were far enough away that they were relaxed, satisfied she couldn't detect they were there. She grinned, lifting her face to the icy chill in the air. Her long black hair slipped behind her shoulder. They didn't know who they messed with. Damn fool hiding from her thought she was just another werewolf. She inhaled deeply and smelled a male werewolf, a bit too cocky for his own good. Someone wanted to play her for a fool.

There had been no time to get accustomed to the high altitude or enjoy the magnificent mountains that filled her view no matter where she looked. Even now, with some of the most beautiful scenery right in front of her, she ignored it. Something wasn't right here.

Moira stood on the edge of a narrow gravel road, staring down the side of the mountain, the view of the twisting road blocked by thick pines and fir trees. The car that had brought her here was no longer visible, its rumbling motor fading along with its intrusive smell of gas and oil in this otherwise isolated area.

I could take off — find a new life. It wasn't the first time she'd thought of bailing on GWAR. The desire to have her own den, a pack to call her own and live a normal life hit her quite a bit lately. Her superiors would frown on her trying to reunite the Malta werewolves, but she craved doing just that. How to do it was the question.

Gripping the disc in her hand, her bag that held pretty much everything she owned hanging from her shoulder, Moira whipped her waist-length black hair over her shoulder and stared at the isolated cabin.

"Well, isn't this just lovely?" A person could be forgotten in this isolated spot buried deep in the Rocky Mountains.

She sniffed to get a feel for her surroundings and unease washed over her. Her heart accelerated, thumping against her rib cage and making it harder to breathe the thin air. The sweet smell of the trees and the crisp, cold air drenched with fragrances of wildflowers drowned the other scents. There should be mountain lions, smaller animals, varieties of squirrels and birds. She didn't smell any living creatures anywhere nearby. Something higher up on the food chain than any enemy they'd faced before had descended on the place before she got here. And now he watched her.

She could smell him, feel him. But where the hell was he?

Moira knew next to nothing about Colorado, USA. Her brief visits to many different parts of the world over the past few years had helped sharpen her instincts and made it easier to quickly adapt to different climates and cultures, but she didn't rely on that as she stood within a dozen meters of the cabin along the edge of the rough road.

Turning the disc over in her hand, she stared into the thick trees that ran deep up the mountain past the small cabin. Blood pumped through her veins and her bones stiffened while the tiny hairs at the back of her neck stood on end. Something lingered deep in the dense trees. Very few things scared Moira, yet something out there put her senses on edge.

She tugged on her sweatshirt, feeling the chill in the air wrap around her bare legs. This wasn't the climate for shorts. Nice of someone to tell her how to dress!

Taking in a deep breath, tasting his scent, her skin prickled with nervous anticipation. Everything inside her flip-flopped, responding to the carnal domination that hung heavily in the cold air. She sensed aggression, but no anger. His calm confidence grew stronger the longer she stood there.

"Who the fuck are you?" she whispered, although she wasn't asking the werewolf who hid from her. She tugged at her senses, demanding the elements work for her.

Let the gift surge through me – pump through my veins.

She closed her eyes, feeling new strength burning through her.

Grant me the power to see who watches me without them seeing me.

Suddenly lightheaded, she fisted her hands while her muscles hardened around her bones. She braced herself. Blood pumped so hard that her chest tightened as the sweet pain that indicated the change made her so much more alive. Now wasn't the time to run over the mountain in her fur. There was a mission to get out of the way. But she would take a minute to learn who her unseen company was.

"Show yourself to me," she whispered, her lashes fluttering, blurring her vision.

She was in danger. There was no doubt about that. Challenging the unknown made life so much more interesting, though. Her breath caught in her throat. Suddenly she was too warm. The cold chill no longer bothered her. Her heart pounded, pumping blood through her veins painfully. Every inch of her throbbed, ached, cried out to meet this unknown challenge, this alpha male. The urge to change consumed her.

He watched her. The urge to grow, to allow the strength to ripple through her, distracted her. The thought of seeking out such raw strength turned her on. Her pussy throbbed, swelling with the excitement of an unknown predator. She suspected—no, she knew—that he didn't hide out of cowardice. His reasons weren't clear. But too much power and hard, dominating strength surrounded this werewolf. The longer she stood there, the harder her pussy throbbed.

Her skin tingled when the gift pulsed inside her, coming to life, working with the air to make her part of it. The best thing to do at the moment, although incredibly dangerous, was leave her body standing where it was. It stood there, a mere shell, vulnerable and unguarded. She couldn't risk more than a few moments. She soared out of her body, using her mind to explore her surroundings quickly, thoroughly and before anyone approached her body. Moira found the heartbeat so similar to her own. A masculine scent closed in around her, calling her to him.

God. She needed to get a grip on herself.

Taking a deep breath, she commanded the elements to work with her, to help her seek out this powerful werewolf. Searching the woods around her, she found him. Eyes so pale she couldn't tell if they were blue or green stared at the wilderness around him. He didn't blink. Not once. The male werewolf stood perfectly still, undetectable in the thickness of the trees. In his human form, clothed, there was still something about him powerful enough to steal her breath.

Over the years, the few werewolves she'd allowed between her legs never measured up to the memory of him. His rich scent, muscles of steel, an overwhelming sex appeal — all of it stole her ability to focus. He was the werewolf of her dreams, the male whose image she conjured up on those lonely nights when she'd masturbated her way to sleep. He was the one she visualized when she'd grabbed relief and fucked another werewolf.

And he appeared even more dangerous than he had five years ago.

She didn't know whether to run like hell or seek him out.

She thought of the simple rhyme that her mother taught her as a cub. *One with the elements, carry me. Show me all and all I will see.*

The gift, raw and untamed, attacked her soul like fire sparking to life. Not pain, but life, a true gift so few would ever experience. Enlightening, showing her every detail surrounding her, it charged her with power more brilliant than fireworks filling the sky. Every leaf, every insect that crawled on the ground, every creature that had darted for safety, every movement became so easy to see.

Anticipation, excitement, a thrill of tracking a much-coveted prey heightened his senses, made him easier to detect. The emotions that ransacked Moira terrified her and excited her at the same time. This werewolf was stronger than any enemy she'd ever encountered. Something about him tore at her soul, grabbed hold of her senses and attacked them with raw, aggressive emotions. He was excited, anxious and horny. Damn it. He smelled fucking better than any werewolf she'd ever smelled before. That overwhelming all-male scent that she'd fantasized about way too many times was now alive and stronger than ever.

She retreated into her body and sucked in a deep breath of mountain air.

Needing to keep her thoughts in gear, to not act before thinking, she stared at her rugged surroundings, wishing she knew his intentions. Cold sweat soaked her skin. Her hair clung to her shoulders, stuck to her back. The sweatshirt she wore did nothing to protect her from the vicious chill around her. Her teeth chattered so hard she almost bit her lip. Her legs wobbled, every muscle inside her contracting, making it damned hard to move.

Her heart thudded so hard against her ribs the werewolf hiding out in the trees would have to be fucking deaf not to hear it.

The gift drained her, something she'd yet learned to counteract. Reaching for the doorknob to the cabin, she let go of his thoughts, exhaling loudly at the same time. He watched her and she would have to be prepared when he made his move. At least she could get inside before he pounced on her. If that was his intention.

And the thought of all that muscle, that raw power taking her down made her knees weak. Her pussy throbbed almost as hard as her heart.

"The instructions on this disc better be thorough," she grumbled. She hated at times that she had to answer to GWAR.

Instinct ached to take over. Survival was in her nature. A man was out there—more than a man—God, she'd swear more than a werewolf. His body heat, the power that had radiated from him, was stronger than anything she'd ever encountered before—at least in the past five years. And she'd responded to him. Sensing his strength, his intense power, her mind had reached out to him. Hell, she'd almost come for him.

Even after closing the cabin door, there was no protection. Her nerve endings tingled with too much energy. He was a stranger, a fucking stranger. And she didn't know a damned thing about him. Yet all he did was watch her, standing quietly while he carried more strength than most alphas possessed. That had turned her on. Hell, it made her damned horny.

Why was he out there? Who was he? God. She knew who he fucking was. Only one werewolf could come off so strong, heighten her senses and almost bring her to her knees just by inhaling his scent. In all the years she'd been in the States, no werewolf had ever affected her the way the stranger on the motorcycle had the day she left Malta. It hadn't just been his intense "fuck me now, little bitch" persona, but also the words he'd spoken to her. Promises from her sire.

God, she missed her parents so badly, even after so many years. She missed them to the extent there were days she swore they were with her, walking by her side, protecting her like they had the first eighteen years of her life.

Not having answers bugged the shit out of her. She was here for a purpose—granted, she had no fucking idea what that reason was. This was so typical of GWAR. Always dropped off on location and then briefed. As if it took too much of their precious time to enlighten her about things before she arrived. She knew why they did this. And she wasn't the only werewolf who complained. GWAR assignments were tricky, often deadly. Some werewolf, obviously with his head up his ass, had decided their agents worked better if informed of the details once they arrived on location. Supposedly this kept their emotions from being smelled and kept them from bolting when sent into what was often a suicide mission.

She doubted very much that it was to get laid. But she was about to find out.

Her hands shook from too much adrenaline pumping through her as she looked around the simple one-room cabin. There was no light switch, no indication of power at all. Blackness surrounded her, while a cold, morgue-like sensation crawled over her flesh. Her heart already pounded in her chest, her nerves overexcited and anxious, but she gave the rush of energy inside her new direction. Focusing on controlling the change, she allowed her eyes to adjust enough to see in the darkness.

A single bed on one side with a sink and small refrigerator and stove on the other were the basic amenities. A card table stood in the middle of the room. She stared at the new-looking black suitcase. A laptop, hopefully charged, had been left for her compliments of GWAR.

"Okay, let's find out who you are and if you're the reason I'm here." Moira flipped the laptop open.

At the same time the smell of a male werewolf attacked her. Rich and spicy—and so damned strong a cub would pick up his scent.

She froze. Any human would have heard her heartbeat. It pounded so loud. Gritting her teeth, she fumbled with the disc, working to slide it into the computer after booting it up. The urge to pounce, yank open the door to the cabin and attack whatever was out there sent her thoughts into a whirlwind that took some effort to control. She tapped at the keys, waiting for the file to open.

Damn GWAR for not giving her time or information to prepare for this mission.

The male neared the cabin, his scent growing, filling her, creeping over her skin and sinking into her pores. Her breath caught in her throat. She smelled his determination. The werewolf in the woods had closed in on her. And he'd moved silently and quickly. All the power she'd sensed, his raw, intense energy, didn't add up as to why he tried so hard to sneak up on her. He had to know she was alone. He would know she was a female. Most male werewolves would come storming in, making demands before they bothered with introductions.

A menu finally appeared on the screen.

"I'm here to chase down common thieves? Three of them?" she mouthed, not daring to speak out loud.

There was no way the werewolf who'd haunted her dreams and filled her lusty imagination was nothing more than a common thief. Sniffing the air and inhaling his scent so deeply she swore he stood right next to her, she glanced around the dark room. It glowed an eerie pale blue from the light of the monitor. She turned her attention back to the screen, reading quickly while every inch of her throbbed with anticipation.

Two GWAR agents were stationed on the mountain—her and one other a mile from her. Their assignment was to track and capture three criminal werewolves who'd managed to slip through Werewolf Affairs' fingers.

A trickle of sweat dripped between her breasts. Exhaling, she fought nervous excitement that washed over her body. Every nerve ending heightened, her pulse taking off in a rapid beat. Raw power, barely tamed, seeped through the cabin walls. It excited and scared the hell out of her.

A crack of wood popped like a spark from a fire. That was her only warning before the door to the cabin swung open. Even in the dark, his pale eyes glowed, capturing her attention before she was able to take in his large physique.

"We meet again," he said in a disturbingly familiar tone.

"Do we?" she asked without thinking, taking in his scent before dwelling on his physical appearance.

He was a large man, well-built, with shiny black hair and creamy white skin. In a simple black shirt and jeans, he hadn't dressed to impress. His large physique called for caution. As a werewolf, he would be huge and quite possibly deadly. Those eyes though. They were so pale and captivating that she was sure she would have remembered if she'd seen them before.

Of course, she'd never seen his eyes before. Silver reflective sunglasses had hidden how incredibly distracting they were.

"I know you, Moira Tangaree. And I've waited a long time to bring you home." He shut the door behind him, encasing them in the glow from the monitor.

No matter that he'd been incredible masturbation material over the years, she didn't know shit about this werewolf—except that five years ago he claimed she would be his mate. She'd been damned naïve back then. Today, his incredible sex appeal, muscles bulging everywhere and the domination that glowed in his eyes wouldn't make her belly-up.

He moved in on her.

"I don't think so," she cried out, lunging at him. It wasn't the first time she'd acted first and asked questions later.

The first time they'd met, she'd never seen him stand, only sit with powerful-looking legs straddling his motorcycle. He stood head and shoulders taller than she, easily six-and-a-half-feet tall if she had to guess.

Allowing the change to rush through her enough to add a fair amount of muscle, she plowed into him. And hit a fucking brick wall.

He sent her flying across the small cabin. The wooden panels on the wall cracked against her weight and she slid to the floor.

Moira had spent years fighting to survive. Getting the wind knocked out of her only outraged her. Not to mention there was something incredibly enticing in his gaze. Towering over her, his arms spread and hands fisted, he looked more deadly than some of the worst criminals she'd seen working with GWAR. Lust pooled between her legs, adding to the excitement of the fight. His reasons for being here were a mystery, one she would solve later. Right now, taking him on, proving he couldn't burst in and give her orders mattered more to her than learning why he was there at all.

The change roared through her body. She didn't bother with her clothes. Her bones popped, reshaping. Muscles contorted and veins stretched. The sweet pain of transformation took over, a more primal instinct guiding her now.

All dark shadows in the room faded. No longer did human vision hinder her. The chill in the night air disappeared, her long, thick black coat growing quickly as her human flesh became harder, tougher. Hands turned into paws while her muscles reshaped, her body contorting into her purer form.

A growl ripped through her and she leapt into the air, using her gift along with her animalistic traits to take on her intruder.

He changed just as quickly, falling to all fours and lunging on her before she could hit the ground.

You don't know who you're messing with, wolf man.

She twisted under his impact, turning tooth and claw on him as she attacked.

His body was solid steel, even more developed than she remembered him being years ago, if that were possible. And as a werewolf, his black coat, which was not long-haired like the purebred Malta werewolf, covered muscles that rippled like an angry tide. Silver eyes sparked with pleasure when she managed to get out from underneath him. He opened his mouth, showing off a deadly row of long, spiked teeth that glowed as much as his eyes did. The smile he gave her was enough to know he would enjoy taking her down and claiming her as his prize. Fire ignited quickly inside her when she pictured him mounting her. His hair didn't cover his thick, dark cock that even unaroused was larger than anything she'd ever seen before. What would it feel like to be impaled by that?

He lowered his head, growling an invitation, letting her know he'd love for her to find out. She gave herself a quick shake. As though he could read her mind, or something.

Very few female werewolves could win in a fight against a male. Moira gave thanks to her sire, as she did daily, when her gift pumped inside her.

If she relied solely on her werewolf abilities, she would lose this fight. And the last thing she would ever do was go belly-up for any werewolf. Not now or ever.

His mouth soaked her fur as he worked to grip her neck. Not many things could kill a werewolf, but breaking her neck would be an injury she wouldn't recover from.

Instinct called out the gift in full force. The heat that rushed through her veins was so intense that she screamed — not out of fear but from how quickly it worked through her.

You will not take me down!

The room seemed to turn sideways. He'd lifted her off the ground, holding on to her by the flesh at the back of her neck. His teeth pinched her hide, the pain only adding to the intense quickness of her reaction.

You can't defeat what you can't see.

The Powers that Be carry me. Let me use the elements so that he can't see.

Moira knew the instant she'd faded, using the element of air and becoming one with it, twisting into his thoughts and making him believe her invisible. The werewolf could no longer see her. At the same time she twisted furiously against his grip on her neck. Heat rushed inside her hard and so fast she could barely breathe. Her vision blurred briefly. But she fought the strength of her powers, knowing they would consume her, make her pass out, if she didn't control them.

Not too surprisingly, the shock of her disappearing before his eyes was enough for him to let her go, the moisture of his mouth leaving the coat on the back of her neck damp, but he didn't move off her. He could no longer see her, but he could smell her, feel her, find her body if she didn't move quickly. And so she did just that, jumping out of his reach and turning to stare at him.

What the fuck?

She watched him change, his body taking human form. At the same time, he moved forward, falling on top of her while he contorted and stretched over her. What made even less sense was the stunning fact that he remained as strong as a werewolf.

He was human again, yet still strong enough to hold her down. Confusion made it impossible to keep the power rushing through her. He shouldn't be able to see her to find her. Yet he'd changed, mutated back into the shape of a man and managed to hold her in place. Fucking unbelievable. Who the hell was this man? This werewolf who'd claimed so long ago to know her sire, to have worked with him and to have exchanged promises—one of which entailed her.

"Once again, I hold your life in my hands," he said quietly.

Well, fuck me! That moment on his motorcycle so long ago, where he'd crushed her to him, saved her life and then confused her with words that had never left her, returned with enough clarity that it was as if it happened moments ago. *No one holds my life in their hands but me.*

His body was more solid, more filled out, and if possible, even sexier than she remembered. For a second she couldn't breathe, his voice chilling her yet making her blood boil at the same time. Lust filled the air, and when she finally inhaled, it fogged her senses until she couldn't think.

What would it be like to turn and fuck this man? This deadly and impressive werewolf who saw right through the gift?

It would probably bring her more trouble than she could get out of.

Roaring as she reached for all of her strength, she turned on him, sending him flying. The man fell backward, hitting the door, his head cracking against the wood. Moira watched as his naked body slumped to the ground. He didn't move.

Pacing for a minute, she tried to figure out what had just happened. She'd been dropped off on the side of a mountain out here in Bumfuck, Nowhere, and obviously someone other than GWAR had known she would be here. This male had been waiting for her, watching, knowing when to make his move.

The iron smell of blood tickled her nostrils. Lowering her head, she edged closer to him, sniffing the air around him. His heart still pumped strongly in his body. And it was a damn fine-looking body at that. Muscles corded and bulged under his creamy white male flesh. Hair blacker than night fell straight around his face. The same-colored hair sprinkled over his chest, his arms and his legs. And even soft, his cock distracted her, making her think of a predator sleeping that could wake at any moment and pounce.

Her pussy grew damp and began throbbing. He was absolutely beautiful. Every inch of him perfect. And even lying there, his dominating scent made her drunk with need. She could mount him, take him, ride him, making his cock as hard as the rest of his body. He wouldn't stop her. Hell, he'd probably try and control the act. God. He'd be one hell of a damn good lover. With a body like that, rubbing her breasts against his coarse chest hair, digging her fingers into his flesh, nipping at his neck…shit!

She must be out of her fucking mind.

Drooling over a dangerous alpha was not what she needed to be doing right now. Using the elements to control his mind, to keep him from seeing her, drained physical strength. The gift had its drawbacks. Altering someone's vision, using their mind to create images not there, or in this case, create the thought that she'd disappeared, meant entering the man's mind. Slumped against the wall, his virile body relaxed, it was almost like the illusion was now played on her. Moira wouldn't believe for a second that he was as helpless as he appeared.

Praying he would remain knocked out long enough for her to figure out what the hell she should do next, she let the change take over. Suddenly naked, her teeth chattered while damp sweat made her even colder.

She hurried to the table, pulling the chair closer to the laptop. Cursing her trembling fingers, she grabbed her bag, fighting with the zipper. Frantically searching for clothes, she kept shifting her gaze to the man on the floor in front of her although he didn't move. Ripped clothing lay scattered on the floor near him. Worst case scenario, she'd add the destroyed clothes to scraps of wood later to keep warm. If wolf man wanted to share the only roof on this side of the mountain with her, that was his business — if he learned some manners. It was here or finding a cave and curling up in his fur. And she'd kick his tail out in the cold, no matter how fucking sexy he was. No werewolf pushed her around.

The laptop hummed when she opened another file on the disc. Pictures of the three criminal werewolves she was supposed to sniff out appeared on the screen. It didn't surprise her that the male in front of her wasn't one of them.

She glanced over the top of the screen at him. He was a hell of a lot more appealing to look at than any of the three criminals. Even relaxed, long corded muscle twisted under his pale skin. Dark curly hair covered his chest, his arms and his legs and pooled around his cock that relaxed against firm, hard-looking abdomen muscles. If only she could use the gift to make herself think that he wasn't there. Unfortunately, it didn't work that way. Even if it did, too much perfection sprawled out before her. Clearing her thoughts would be damned near impossible.

It dawned on her that he didn't have any other clothes. Unless he had a bag waiting for him outside the cabin door, he'd entered with nothing but the clothes on his back. They lay crumpled on the floor, torn to bits, along with her clothes. Damn shame he'd have to remain naked while with her.

She didn't have a clue what to do with him. Well, other than fuck him silly. He told her he was there to take her home. Whatever the hell that was supposed to mean. Moira no longer had a pack, a den or anything to return to. And he knew that. He wasn't one of her thieves, he'd known she would be arriving here, which was more than she had known. Until she had a clue what he was really up to, it might be best to keep an eye on him. And she sure as hell didn't mind staring at him. Not that she'd get her job done if she continued to do so.

"I really am here to take you with me. Home will be wherever you wish." His eyes didn't open, not a muscle in his body moved.

And he'd just read her fucking mind.

Chapter Three

ഔ

"What did you just say?" Her full, red lips puckered. Perfect for kissing or wrapping around his cock.

"It's been a long time, Moira. Gather your things and we'll leave."

"I'm not going with you anywhere, wolf man. I'm not out here on vacation." Although she had a feeling he knew this already.

"The other agent on your mission had a disc like the one you're looking at. It made it pretty easy to find you."

"What did you do with him?" She chewed her lower lip, searching his face—then looking lower.

It was all he could fucking do to stay soft when she drooled over him like that. What he wouldn't do to have this conversation after they had sex.

He shrugged, pulling her gaze up from his cock and back to his face. "The other GWAR agent will find all of your criminals. I left their bodies together to make it easier for GWAR when they search the mountain. I'm sorry, sweet bitch, that he'll get all the credit for this mission and not you. It has to be that way this time."

"You killed them all?" She stared at him in disbelief and the bag on her lap fell to the floor. She looked down at it, holding clothes in her hands and then shook her head, trying to accept everything he'd just told her. "Then there's no mission."

"Nope. And it gives us an extra day or so to disappear before GWAR starts looking for you."

"Disappear. You think I'm just going to prance off by your side?"

"I've given you five years. You're twenty-three now, plenty old enough to take a mate." And it had been beyond torture waiting. A promise was a promise though. He didn't go back on his word. Bruno Tangaree had known that.

"How thoughtful of you," she snapped, pursing her lips into a fine line while staring at him with dark orbs. "I think I know when and if I want a mate though. Barging in here and hauling me off isn't going to work, wolf man."

"You would have disappointed me if you'd responded any differently."

She ignored him and instead fumbled with the clothes in her hands. Her slender, delicate-looking fingers stroked the material, carefully stretching and pressing the clothing probably without realizing it. If she gave that same meticulous attention to a werewolf's body, he'd have to have her soon. In spite of the throbbing headache he now had from the gash he'd foolishly gotten, it was impossible not to enjoy staring at her.

Skin the color of caramel with long, silky black hair that fell just past her curvy hips to her ass and firm, perky tits—she was one fucking hot bitch. Her arms were slender, as were her legs. Muscular yet thin, with a narrow, willowy look about her. Blood rushed from his head to his cock while he watched her dress.

The teenage girl he'd rescued five years ago had turned into one hell of a stunning woman. Her life had hardened her, made her appear older than she was. A strong smell of mistrust and hatred emanated so fully from her that he swore it was part of her natural scent. Yet she was turned on. Lust swam thickly in the air around them. And it wasn't all from him. She liked what she saw. Hell, she fucking craved it. Remaining naked more than distracted her. His body excited the hell out of her.

Which was a damned good thing.

He moved deeper into her thoughts.

Careful. He had to be damned careful. Just as he'd been five years ago and every minute of every fucking day ever since.

She was her sire's pride and joy. Bruno had been right that she'd figure out the gift on her own. The fact that she was still alive was proof enough. No werewolf would survive the life she'd endured. Unless they possessed the gift. The gift in full force. A gift she'd been born with. Just like her parents. Just like him.

Having lived that life, shielding the gift that coursed through his veins, he understood the battle she dealt with daily. Not being trusted. Being needed. No pack welcoming him. Fear. Aching for a den, a pack, yet fitting in nowhere. He'd done his research thoroughly with Moira. It had kept him busy while enduring the torturous years Bruno put him through waiting to claim her. Introductions at eighteen, allowing her to mature, then seduction. He sure as hell was going to enjoy this stage.

Before Bruno Tangaree's pack had been destroyed, Dante had learned enough to survive. No one knew his connections back then. No one knew his connections today. It had to be that way. Survival instinct ran inside him as powerfully as the gift.

Now the gift would be taken to the next level. He had found her. Moira Tangaree. His destined mate.

When she stood, every thought in his head washed away like a greedy tide had just attacked it. He looked up, focusing on her belly button when it creased as she stretched. What he wouldn't do to lick her right there.

She pulled a knit dress over her head, briefly covering her face. Her dark nipples were hard, eager peaks that made his mouth go dry. Allowing his cock to go hard as a rock would scare her. There was no doubt that she'd attack again. He knew fighting turned her on, made her blood boil with the need to gain respect—and a need to be overcome. Already he respected her or they'd be fucking right now. He would overcome her slowly, watch her submission blossom. The thought made his cock lengthen in spite of his order to himself to remain slack.

For one warped moment he wondered how many changes of clothing she had in that small bag. Couldn't be that many. Force her to change again and he might render her naked—without more clothes to cover that hot little body of hers.

God, he couldn't wait to touch that body, feel her come to life underneath him. He wanted to watch need relax her expression, see her dark eyes fog over with lust.

Her thoughts were shielded. Mingling with them briefly, he receded. The obvious was easy to pull from her. Loneliness—fear. She didn't trust GWAR. Wondered how much truth lay in his words. Plotted possible means of escape. And she thought about his cock.

Dante suppressed a grin. His nudity definitely had an impact on her. She fought her interest toward him. But he smelled it, sensed it. Moira had been turned on by him the moment she'd detected him in the woods. She didn't understand why she wanted him and he doubted she'd believe him if he explained it to her.

We're destined to be together, little bitch. Two halves of a whole. No other werewolf will do for you, so kindly spread your legs and let's fuck. Yeah. That would go over real well.

"How did you find me?" She pinned him with black eyes, like glowing onyx.

The thick, pungent odor of fear faded quickly. Something salty, like irritation, surrounded them. It mixed with a sweeter smell. If the little bitch couldn't hide her sexual curiosity, then she wasn't that scared of him. And she should be. She should be damned scared. He was about to change her life forever.

He kept his muscles relaxed. All of him. He focused on his heart, keeping the beat steady. Her closeness, her scent, her intense beauty — damn, he wanted her. For now, for her, he fought not to appear a threat.

"I never lost you."

"That doesn't answer the question." She adjusted the dress to her body, the knitted material hugging her firm, small breasts, her flat tummy and the curve of her hips.

Sitting down in front of her laptop, she gently ran her fingers through her long black hair. There was no physical resemblance to her sire — something she should be grateful for. Bruno was many things, but for the life of Dante, he never understood why Renee, his mate, continually told him how sexy he was. Females were odd creatures though, and Bruno and Renee's happiness and love for each other made Moira the strong bitch she was today.

"You have connections inside GWAR then?" she asked.

"Yes. But connections can be made anywhere when you have something others want." He stood slowly, watching her gaze drop before she shot it back to his face. There was not a damn thing he cared to do about his nudity at the moment. "I'm afraid you aren't going to get answers to satisfy you completely. What matters is that I have you and GWAR no longer does."

"And now what?" She focused on the screen of her laptop.

"A car will arrive for us soon." He walked to his torn clothing, lifting his jeans and taking the cell phone from his belt. It didn't surprise him that there was no signal. "We'll leave here and go to a place a bit more accommodating."

"I'm not going anywhere with you, wolf man." By no means was she a large woman, yet she held herself with dignity, with confidence. There was no hesitation in her expression. "Act like a mutt and that's how you'll get treated.

Without answers, you can walk out that door and go back to wherever you came from."

"I came from the same place you did," he said quietly, ignoring her insults.

She managed to maintain her indifferent expression. Those dark eyes smoldered though. He saw in them the anger, frustration, curiosity and sexual craving that plagued her. There had never been doubt that she'd be fiery by nature, a bitch willing to fight with tooth and nail. He wouldn't want her any other way.

"You need help getting back there?" She raised an eyebrow, challenging him.

Slowly she crossed one of her legs over the other, doing it on purpose to show him that she didn't fear him. In spite of his human eyes impairing him in the dark cabin, her slender, muscular legs were hard to ignore. She relaxed, cocking an eyebrow, which showed off her alluring eyes. Every bit of her was a weapon. That sexy-ass body of hers would distract any werewolf. And at the moment, she was more than aware she was distracting him. She believed she had the upper hand. Perfect. She had no clue what strengths he possessed. In time she would learn to use her gift to determine the extent of danger a predator could be. The gift was raw inside her. No one existed in her life to draw out its strengths. Until now.

He grinned, pushing away from the wall. Her expression changed quickly and he enjoyed the look of hesitant prey, the way her dark eyes widened and her mouth opened slightly. He focused on those full lips, just slightly damp, and wondered how they would taste as he moved in on her slowly.

"What I need, I take. Pretty simple, actually." He reached for a strand of her hair.

Immediately alert, she jumped from her seat, putting the chair between them.

"If you can handle simple, then handle this—hands off."

The second she reached for the gift, focused deep inside her mind to call forth abilities she'd been born with, he prepared himself. Now wasn't the time for her to discover his secret. Blocking what he possessed, creating a mental shield, he diverted her probe.

But there was no attempt to climb into his thoughts on her part. Instead of entering his mind, she used her gift externally. Interesting. The logical method of attack would be to use the gift to search the mind of the aggressor. Moira didn't do that. She searched the cabin instead, wanting to throw something at him. Attack.

She searched for a diversion, anything to throw him off her scent. Preventing her from learning that he possessed the same powers took more concentration than he'd anticipated. Dante wondered if Moira realized how strong she was. He'd apply his own diversion the old-fashioned way.

"I can handle it simple. Or I can complicate things." He grabbed the chair, tossing it to the corner of the room.

Moira jumped, her body tensing. Her hard nipples poking through her dress were more of a diversion than anything she could throw at him. Her dark eyes were perfectly almond-shaped. They narrowed as she scowled, not daring to take her gaze from his as she took a step backward.

His nudity distracted her. That was one advantage. Fear and anger still presided. Curiosity bested her fear though. And lust remained the strongest scent between them. But Moira was a hunter, addicted to adventure. It was in her nature. Turning her into the hunted changed the pace for her and had her creaming between her legs. The scent of it was intoxicating. That was his second advantage.

"Either way, I'm not interested," she hissed.

She glanced at the laptop, his only warning before it flew through the air straight toward his face. Intercepting her thought, he ducked before she could do serious damage. The dull ache he nursed from her previous attack was sufficient enough. The laptop crashed to the floor, breaking into two pieces as it slid in opposite directions. She growled in frustration, the sound as erotic as it was deadly.

Dante moved quickly and grabbed her arms, her silky black hair brushing against his palms.

"Change and I swear I will too," he snarled, pushing her backward until he pinned her against the wall. "Or do you like to play rough?"

"I'm not playing." Her body physically relaxed but her mind still churned, emotions clogging the room.

Like hell she wasn't playing.

He didn't relax his grip. "Then clear your mind and pay heed to who you're messing with."

"Tell me who you are." She ignored his first order.

"My name is Dante Aldo." He doubted telling her who he was would mean anything to her. Bruno Tangaree had always been very closemouthed. Especially with his only cub. Protecting her meant more to him than saving his own hide. "Your sire wishes for us to be together," he added quietly.

She put on some muscle quickly. Not changing. But bones and muscle contorted against his grip, twisting and bulging under his fingers. Her arms strengthened at the same time she let out a howl, throwing him off her.

"My sire is dead," she screamed, darting past him.

She didn't make it halfway across the sparsely furnished cabin before he leapt on her. Terror and outrage clogged the chilled air. The disgustingly sweet odor of fury mixed with the thick, pungent smell of fear swarmed through his senses, turning his stomach. Ignoring her emotions, fighting to block out their smells, he took her down, the two of them landing with a thud on the cold, wooden floor.

"Let me go!" she screamed, immediately fighting him.

Her long black hair momentarily blinded him. Holding her in place, he raised the top half of his body off her while pinning her with his legs.

"Not on your life," he said calmly.

Calm was the last thing he felt though. Her soft ass moved furiously against his cock, hardening it before he could stop it. She stilled quickly, resting her cheek against the floor while she strained to look up at him. The shape of her eyes had changed, narrowing while silver streaks mixed with her black orbs. Black hair thickened over her arms and bare legs. Her dress rode up high on her thighs. And he knew she wore nothing underneath it. She fought the change, fought her emotions.

"What do you want?" she hissed through clenched teeth.

He'd give her credit for being intelligent enough to realize she was outmatched. She wouldn't escape him. Slowly she resumed her human form, her smooth, silky legs pinned between his.

"You." There was no reason to lie to her.

She didn't say anything, made no attempt to move. Nor did he. Lying on top of her, half of his body draped over hers, he could feel her warmth, her strength, the carnal desire that rushed through her to survive, to understand. Her submission was a far cry away. But he was a patient werewolf. Five years of waiting was proof of that.

"Why me?" Wary and curious, she turned her head to see him better.

Her scent changed, continually altering with her ever-wavering emotions. Suspicion mingled with curiosity. Her soft body underneath him was enough to drive any sane werewolf crazy with lust. Dante never claimed to be better than the next guy. She'd distracted him for years though and he'd managed to keep a level head, keep his tail out of trouble, remain focused. That wouldn't change now.

"Because of who you are."

She tensed underneath him.

"And because of who I am," he added.

Dante had watched Moira over the years, kept a close eye on her track record. She was a damned good bitch — trained warrior, her fighting skills superb, and more beautiful than any other bitch he'd ever sniffed out.

The gift allowed him to read emotions better than many. Smelling a werewolf's scent, burying himself in their thoughts, was second nature. Or maybe first. He'd done it for so long he wasn't sure anymore.

One thing was certain. Her emotions ran too rapidly. The gift was too powerful inside her for her to react to him like this.

Unless…

"And what is so special about you?" She still rested her cheek on the floor, her gaze pinned upward.

Damn. Could he be right?

Brushing strands of black hair away from her cheek, he cocked his head, intentionally digging into her thoughts. He gave her the opportunity to feel him in her mind. Her cheek was warm against his fingertips. She didn't flinch, didn't look away from him. Her thoughts were warmer. So many of them. Rushing at him. Hitting him hard. Memories. Speculations. Fantasies. Fears.

They weren't curbed in. They weren't hidden. Interesting. Very fucking interesting.

She wasn't feeling his thoughts.

He couldn't believe it. All these years. He'd been sure she had the full gift. Would have sworn to it.

But she didn't. Damn it. She didn't know he melded with her thoughts.

"I told you that already." He hid his disappointment.

He couldn't be mad at Bruno, but there was nothing worse than being lied to. Now to figure out why Bruno

119

Tangaree had told him that his cub had the full gift when she didn't.

"Tell me again."

"Your sire and I made a deal," he repeated, giving her all the information he dared for now.

"I don't believe you." She quit trying to look up at him. When she lied she didn't make eye contact.

He lifted his weight off her enough to grab her shoulder and flip her onto her back. Her black hair fanned around her and her look of surprise faded quickly. Tiny silver streaks still laced through her black eyes, her emotions running high. She tried pushing against him but he grabbed her wrists, pinning them to the floor on either side of her. He rather liked lying on top of her naked like this.

"Lie to me again and I'll take your clothes off too," he whispered, loving how her lips pursed into a pout when she turned defiant.

"Threats don't work well with me, wolf man." She twisted underneath him, fighting to get free.

Dante loved how her mind worked when she struggled to clear her head and put the gift to use. He pulled her hands above her head, gripping her wrists with one hand. That was enough of a distraction but for good measure, he cupped her chin. Moving his legs between hers, he thrust his cock up her dress. Fire almost burned him alive when he touched the smooth skin between her legs. Damp and hot, her pussy made him rage to life so quickly it made him dizzy.

"Then don't lie to me." He clenched his teeth, fighting for some semblance of sanity so he wouldn't bury himself deep inside her.

He had the strength, the ability and the desire. Not once in his life had he raped a bitch though. He sure as hell wouldn't start with Moira.

She didn't say anything, didn't look away. Lust clogged the air between them with its rich, sweet smell. At the moment, he'd be damned whether he knew if he smelled her more than his own scent.

"Move," she ordered through clenched teeth. Her heart pounded furiously against his chest and in her wrists. The rapid beat thumped through him, distracting him as badly as her smooth pussy did against the tip of his cock.

His cock thrust upward when she spoke.

"That's not what I meant," she growled.

For the first time she looked away from him, searching the room. Then he heard it too. Heard what had pulled her attention from him.

Lifting her quickly into his arms, he yanked them both away from the door.

It opened quickly, silently, and the tall werewolf who entered the room looked at the two of them and smiled. That way too charming of a grin had always been Juan's trademark.

"Wouldn't it be easier to mate with her if she was naked too?" Juan Anthony, his littermate, asked as his gaze drifted down Moira's clothed body.

Moira had fooled him. Her thoughts had been an open book. Until now. There was no indication in her thoughts of her next move. She tore free from his embrace, changing with enough ferocity to send shreds of her dress flying from her body. Muscles rippled through her, the change embracing her as her roar echoed in the small cabin. Tearing past the two surprised men, she bolted out the open door, disappearing into the night.

"Damn it." Dante barely had the word out of his mouth before he released the beast within him. "Let's get her."

Juan began stripping but Dante didn't wait for him. His heartbeat accelerated, thumping too hard for his human body to handle. Blood rushed in his veins while they hardened and stretched. Muscles grew. Bones popped and contorted as his body changed. Hair poked through his flesh while his spine altered its shape, no longer strong enough to hold him on two legs. He fell to the floor, arching his neck while his mouth transformed. Everything around him grew easier to see. Every sound—the boards creaking underneath his new weight, the breeze outside, leaves rustling in trees around the cabin—intensified and crackled with extreme clarity.

He ignored the biting pain that gripped his body, stealing his breath. It lasted moments, meant nothing. True freedom took over—the ability to see and hear better, smell everything around him and tackle it without hesitation. Tearing at rock and dirt with massive claws, he bounded past the running car that sat outside the cabin, the fumes and exhaust from it blocking his scent of her for only a moment. Leaping over large rocks, he tore up the mountain, following her rich scent as he gained speed on her.

Juan wasn't far behind. She had to know there was no way she could outrun two male werewolves. And in their fur, primal instinct prevailed. He raced after the bitch that would be his. Moira would now be viewed as a member of their den, to be chased down and retrieved at any cost.

Werewolf laws predated time. No matter the pack, the race, what part of the world they came from, the nature of who they were, what they were, ran strong and true. He'd laid his mark on her many years ago, had her sire's blessing. Few knew the truth, but the fact remained. Moira was his and she wouldn't escape.

Cold air soaked his nose but thick black hair covered his hide. Not that he gave a damn about the cold mountain air. Adrenaline pumped through him, stronger than what any human could experience. Emotions turned raw, instinct prevailed.

Moira would be hunted down, captured, claimed. She'd set those boundaries when she took on her fur. Every bit of him hurt just thinking about sinking deep inside her, feeling her muscles constrict around him. He'd waited a hell of a long time, respecting her sire's wishes and allowing her to mature.

The torturous waiting had ended. Charging up the mountain, he ached to capture her, mate with her, make her his for life.

The crisp scents on the mountain heightened his senses. Not that they weren't already on overdrive. He ignored the smells of nature around him. Paid no heed to the small animals that scattered in terror. Moira consumed his thoughts.

Halfway up the mountain, he spotted her. Tearing over the rocky terrain, running around thick clumps of trees and underbrush, she raced with no direction. There were no houses up here, no humans, no roads leading to any town. With nothing more than the full moon glowing down on them, she'd set up conditions for primal emotions to surge to their fullest.

Slow seduction no longer mattered. He would take her hard and fast. She'd belly-up and submit. His carnal side dominated. The harder he raced after her, blood pumping through him while his muscles worked to climb the mountain, the more determined he became.

And in his animal form, determination had a narrow focus.

Capture and fuck her. Claim what had been given to him. Make Moira his.

The Malta werewolves, with their long black coats, were at the top of the predatorial chain. Viewed as extinct by most, an endangered species by a few, the inability to spot them at night, their large size and incredible speed made them the most dangerous werewolves on the planet. Dante was about to prove that very true.

Mine. The primal announcement roared past his lips. *You're mine.*

He leapt over a large boulder with ease. A clearing lay ahead, the sound of cold rushing water nearby. Dante slowed, aware of Juan closing in behind him. Night vision and a full moon made it easy to see around him.

Moira had disappeared but her scent prevailed. It was everywhere. On every blade of grass, every limb of every tree, in the air, in the dirt. There were no smells other than hers.

But he didn't see her anywhere.

His heart pounded furiously, need rushing through him, hardening his cock while the dampness in the air clung to his fur. He turned slowly, studying every inch of his surroundings, his ears twitching while he heard every minute sound. A leaf falling, a twig popping, dirt scraped from the earth by long claws.

His littermate stood like a statue next to him, his instincts on full alert as well. Neither of them moved.

The little bitch couldn't have just disappeared.

Disappeared.

Fuck!

A growl rumbled through him, understanding slowly taking life. Juan cocked his head, his ears twitching while his black eyes glowed against equally dark fur.

Damn the bitch for her cleverness. If he weren't so suddenly pissed off he'd have a good laugh over it.

Disappeared is exactly what Moira had done, using the gift, the powers that he'd begun assuming didn't run as strongly in her as they did through him. She'd used the elements against both of them, determined to escape.

Turning to race back down the mountain, another thought hit him as if he'd just run into a brick wall. Juan had left the fucking car running. Getting stuck on the side of some damned mountain didn't appeal to him at all.

The brief amusement that had trickled through him disappeared even faster. If that little bitch took off in the car, leaving them stuck there, he'd have her hide.

Whether Juan understood or not mattered little. He stuck to Dante's heels, matching his stride as they raced back to the cabin. Headlights glimmered ahead of them and began moving just as the two of them approached the car.

Nice try, little bitch!

He leapt onto the hood, landing with a loud thud just as Moira started accelerating. The car lurched to a stop, which was all the time he needed. The change ripped through him, stealing his breath, pinching muscle and tendon, burning through his veins. Ignoring the sensations that made it suddenly harder to see in the night, that made the cold air attack him like a brutal enemy, he ripped open the driver's side door, almost yanking it from its hinges.

"I'm driving," he barked, his voice still too husky to clearly form the words. He reached inside and slammed the vehicle into park.

Moira shot to the passenger side, letting out a squeal when Juan opened that door.

"It would be nice if you'd allow me time to get my clothes." His usual charm had a hard edge to it.

Moira swallowed a scream, turning the sound that escaped her lips into a frustrated grunt. She had a damn good view of Juan's cock as he straightened, leaving the passenger door open. He gave her a nice ass shot when he walked to the open door of the cabin.

She was either too stunned to fight, or the realization that escape was futile had finally sunk in. There was no resistance when Dante took her wrist, pulling her naked body to his and yanking her out of the car. He was a bit too rough when he opened the back door and shoved her onto the seat, sliding in next to her. She'd learn real damn fast that he could be pushed only so far. Had she succeeded in leaving him on the side of the mountain, it wouldn't have been pretty when he caught up with her.

Juan didn't waste time dressing then shut the passenger door before sliding behind the driver's seat. "You two don't do anything back there that I wouldn't do." His usual teasing nature had returned. "And Dante, damn, man. A new hood for this thing is going to cost a pretty penny."

Moira froze. The car pulled away from the small cabin. Dante didn't let go of her and she didn't resist him. Sensing an overwhelming sadness creeping from her pores usually would have had an impact on him, but the carnal side of him hadn't faded yet. Anger, need and primal, determined lust spawned by a hard run in his fur dominated the air around them. Whether she could climb into his mind or not, there wasn't a shred of doubt in him that she smelled his emotions.

At the moment, he couldn't have cared less.

Chapter Four

୫୨

Stale coffee and the aging smell of flour, sugar and fried oil hung heavily as the afternoon wore on. Two more weeks and Rose Silverman's thirty-day notice would be up. She'd served her time and diligently entered data for Werewolf Affairs for over five years. A change was needed. Time to raise her cubs instead of letting some day care service do it.

The mountains beckoned to her as she stared out the window at the end of the narrow office—an office she'd grown to think of as a caged pen. No more artificial air. No more stale smells that lingered day after day in the busy office. Rose couldn't wait to run in the meadows, get more involved with her pack, lay her kill at her mate's feet.

Her computer beeped, indicating she had mail. Rose glanced at it then focused on the clock on the wall that ticked endlessly. No more watching the clock, aching for five o'clock to come around. No more responding to tedious e-mails.

The phone rang. Mattie Wilson, one of the younger bitches in the office, grabbed it. Not a problem. Rose didn't mind letting the others at Werewolf Affairs fight to work their way up the ladder. She was so close to being out of there.

"WA," Mattie said in a cheerful voice.

Rose remembered the time one of the younger secretaries answered the phone, saying, "Werewolf Affairs." A big no-no. Even though humans, for the most part, tolerated the packs in their cities didn't mean that they wanted to hear about werewolves. One wrong number dialed and they'd have headaches for weeks. Very few humans knew about this particular branch of the FBI.

The doors opened into the lobby just past the secretarial pool. For a brief moment Rose smelled the outdoors, the hint of rain coming off the mountains, the many scents carried in on the cool afternoon breeze. The smells faded quickly, aftershave and the thick odor of werewolves taking over. Their masculine scents grew. Rose glanced toward them, noticing two werewolves in suits just past the double doors.

"Rose?" Mattie turned around, her expression puzzled. "I don't know how to do this."

"How to do what?" Rose gave Mattie half her attention.

Outside the secretarial pool, the two werewolves strolled inside like they owned the place. Curiosity hit her.

Mattie smelled her interest in the men outside and frowned. Rose gave her a defiant look. She was a happily mated bitch and didn't give a rat's ass if some other bitch misinterpreted what she smelled.

"What do you need?" she asked stiffly.

"It's someone in Washington." Mattie held up her receiver, her hand covering the mouthpiece. "They want me to pull up a file and delete it. I don't have clearance."

"Put them on hold and transfer it to me." Rose glared at the younger woman for her lack of professionalism. "I'll take the call."

Mattie didn't like relinquishing such an important call. Frustration filled the air, blocking the scents of the werewolves in the outer office. No one had asked Rose to train someone to take her place so she wasn't going to waste time giving explanations.

"This is Rose Silverman," she said politely into the phone. Her attention remained on the two werewolves standing on the other side of the doors to the secretarial pool. She would die to know what they were doing here. "How may I help you?"

"I've got a code zero that I need to send through," the young werewolf on the other end of the line said. He offered his identification number, which she typed in to the computer for validation.

Rose brought up the appropriate screen. Mattie had moved behind her. Let the bitch watch if she wanted. It wouldn't surprise Rose at all if Mattie fought to get her job before she even had her paws out the door.

"Your identification number is verified," she told him, then offered hers and listened while he typed it in.

"You're verified as well." The mundane policy was simple, yet necessary so that no one could pretend to be with the agency and remove werewolves from the system.

Rose clicked on the file. It popped up on the screen, and she read the numbers that the computer gave the file. "Code number is seven, seven, five, three, zero, four."

The werewolf on the other end of the line repeated the numbers back to her. Rose barely listened. Distracted when the two werewolves in suits entered the inner office, she grunted into the phone. Mattie moved around her quickly, all smiles as she quickly asked the werewolves if they'd like coffee. The other bitches in the office all quit working as well.

Once upon a time, Rose would have growled at the bitches in the office for giving a lazy appearance. The last thing they wanted werewolves from Washington thinking was that they didn't run a tight ship here. She no longer cared though. Her days here were over. Just two more weeks and what happened with the government would no longer be any concern of hers.

Before long she'd be with her cubs all day, taking them to school, picking them up. No longer would they be bussed to after-school care, forced to be civil around humans. Rose and her mate, Bruce, believed in raising their den to be respectful of humans. After all, they were a lesser species, half of a whole. But neither of them had ever wanted their cubs to have to deal with humans on a daily basis. Soon she'd be raising her cubs the werewolf way, getting more active with the pack, joining the committees and tending to pack business.

"Okay. Transmitting the file for deletion now." The werewolf on the other end of the phone brought her back to reality.

For now, she still worked here, still had a job to do. A code zero meant some poor werewolf had died on the job. Part of what she did was delete all knowledge that the agent had ever worked with WA—basically doing cleanup. Within minutes, it would be as if the werewolf never existed. Agents for WA, and especially GWAR, the more covert part of the agency, sure got a fine farewell if they didn't make it back from a mission.

Not her problem.

"It's loading now. Approximate deletion time one minute and thirty seconds." It had been policy for longer than she'd worked there that two members of WA had to witness the deletion of a file.

And it made sense. Sort of a checks-and-balances type of thing. The werewolf on the other end of the line stared at the same thing on his screen that she saw on hers. No one werewolf could go around deleting files this way.

She looked up when she heard Mattie say her name and then point to her. Rose raised an eyebrow as the two werewolves in suits gave her their attention.

"A file has just been sent to you for deletion," one of the suits said to her, not making it a question.

"I've got it on the screen now." She didn't know why her stomach suddenly twisted in knots.

"Stop the deletion." The same werewolf gave the order as if it were that simple a process.

"What?" she stammered, staring down at the red bar that moved to the halfway point on her screen.

Forty-five seconds remained until this werewolf disappeared in to the void of Nowheresville.

"It's already in progress." Suddenly she felt as green as some of the other bitches in the office.

The small picture on the top right-hand corner of her screen caught her eye first. Rose remembered the young bitch being in the office just a few days ago. Her caramel-colored skin and long, sleek black hair made her stand out easily. Rose hadn't spoken to the bitch personally, but she'd overheard her say a few words to one of the other agents. The young bitch had a lovely accent. Not an American werewolf. Rose hadn't been sure what pack the agent was from. Too many of the agents with WA, and especially with GWAR, didn't belong to packs. Rose remembered thinking the bitch was so young to be living a life of such solitude.

She glanced at the two werewolves. "I've never seen either of you before."

"Not surprising." The older of the two agents offered no further explanation, instead rattling off his identification number to her.

The second agent did the same.

Quickly pulling up both agents on a separate screen, she looked at the pictures of the two werewolves, which matched the males in front of her.

"Are you sure you want me to stop the deletion?" Rose raced to get her thoughts in order and remember the reversal sequence required to stop a deletion. The werewolf, a tall, thin man with graying hair and equally gray eyes, reached around her desk and took the phone from her before she could react. Placing it quietly on its cradle, his smell grew aggressive.

"Stop the deletion now."

Rose's heart started pounding. She hit the wrong key at first and then quickly struck the backspace key. Twenty-five seconds remained.

"I can't," she began, quickly clearing her voice. There was nothing worse than being intimidated by some werewolf with

131

a God complex. "There is no way one werewolf can reverse this process."

She glared at him, gathering her wits about her quickly. What was he going to do, fire her?

The other werewolf moved around one of the unoccupied desks. "Give me the code."

Rose licked her lips. There was procedure to follow here. At the moment, she couldn't remember for the life of her what it was, but it was clearly written policy somewhere. Nothing happened in WA that wasn't laid out in written policy.

Rose heard herself rattling off the code while she clicked on the file, and then found the abort screen. The pretty young bitch whose picture stared at her shouldn't be wiped out of the system if she wasn't dead. Rose didn't remember much about her, but if they'd discovered at the last minute that she'd lived instead of died on her mission, then Rose would do her part to ensure she didn't go through hell for it. Wiping a werewolf out with a code zero meant they no longer existed. The bitch had been too young to die.

Rose watched the program start to run. She scanned the profile of the young bitch, Moira Tangaree, age twenty-three. She was from the island of Malta. Rose had never heard of Malta werewolves, but there were many breeds out there. She imagined the young bitch's pack were beautiful in their furs.

"It's taken care of," the werewolf at the desk said.

The older werewolf looked down at her and nodded once. "Shut down your computer and come with us, please."

Rose didn't like the sound of that. She glared at him, doing what he asked and ignoring the curious stares of the other bitches in the room. She hadn't done anything wrong. Respect ran deep among werewolves. She wouldn't question the two werewolves in front of the other bitches. But as soon as they were alone...

"Show me your badges, please," she said first thing when the two werewolves closed the door behind them.

She crossed her arms and stared at the suits, managing to keep her heart from pounding furiously in her chest. There was no way they'd smell her nervousness.

"Of course." The gray-haired werewolf moved around the desk.

This was Paul Ortiz' office, her boss. Most of the time he was in the field, as he'd been all week. Rose pretty much ran this branch. The older agent pushed a button on the side of the desk, allowing a small panel to appear. Without hesitating, he punched in the code that secured the office, locking the door and ensuring no recording devices were activated.

Rose's heart lodged in her throat. No one was supposed to know that panel existed.

One at a time the two werewolves showed her their badges. She nodded mutely, noting only the stamped insignia indicating they were official WA agents. She despised the salty smell of nervousness, especially when it came from her.

"Rose. Have a seat." The gray werewolf barely moved his mouth when he spoke.

She swallowed, fighting fear that welled up inside her. She'd done nothing wrong. No matter that these werewolves had the power to destroy a den, a pack, anyone — that wouldn't happen to her. All she did was clerical work. Her review had come back with rave scores. In two weeks she'd be out of here. There wasn't a damn thing to worry about.

Taking the seat opposite him, she straightened, holding her head high. "What can I do for you?" she asked calmly.

The salty smell of her nerves dissipated. She let out a slow breath, calming her still rapidly beating heart.

"We need to discuss the code zero that was just canceled." More than likely his mouth barely moved when he spoke because he'd grown too accustomed to showing no emotion.

Rose nodded. She followed him so far.

"The bitch, Moira Tangaree, isn't dead. We know her abduction occurred while on a recent mission. Our job is to find her. The order to delete her file was false and we're still trying to track where it came from."

The other werewolf stood behind her. Regardless that the three of them were in a sealed office, neither werewolf offered any smells that would allow her to detect their emotions. That bothered her. Werewolves with no feelings, no scent to pick up, couldn't be trusted. After all her years with WA, she'd think she'd be accustomed to it. Instead, it was one of a growing list of things that annoyed her about this agency.

She frowned, not completely understanding. "Okay," she said slowly.

"The bitch whose file you were about to delete isn't dead," he repeated, "but she is missing. Let's say she's been compromised. Tell me what your normal procedure would be under such circumstances."

If he was testing her, she wasn't amused. No way would this werewolf have reached the level he was at without knowing procedure for a compromised agent.

"Their file is pulled and put in hibernation until further orders come through."

"Good." For a brief second, the gray werewolf looked past her at the younger werewolf standing behind her.

She heard no movement, smelled nothing. She didn't like this.

"You'll follow that procedure," he instructed. "With one exception. You'll pull her file, but you won't put it in hibernation. Do you understand?"

She didn't understand any of this. "Sure," she said, sounding confident.

The two werewolves left the WA branch shortly after that. Walking across the small parking lot toward their government-issue car, the gray werewolf, Steve Muller, stared briefly at the mountain range ahead of him.

"Where do you think he took her?" he asked without looking at his partner.

Jeff Brim hadn't been with WA more than ten years. He had a good track record though, and Steve trusted him. The werewolf came from a good den. Hardworking, dedicated and efficient. This wasn't an assignment where any of those traits mattered though. In a case like this one, unique and too damned sensitive, tooth and claw might be required. His younger partner would be put to the test working this case.

"We know she left with two other werewolves from Malta last night," Jeff said.

"Only one of them is full Malta werewolf," Steve corrected him. "And neither of them are natives. Dante Aldo's signature was all over that scene. He's the only werewolf who could have pulled something like this off."

"I don't understand why WA doesn't have him killed." Jeff shrugged. "Although any werewolf who can break into GWAR might be worth keeping alive."

"He's got a reputation, that's for sure. WA would be smart to get him on their side." An opinion Steve would keep to himself. WA didn't like being told what to do.

"Yeah. I hear he can destroy packs. That he's been sought out before when a pack needs help fighting off another pack."

They climbed into the car, closing the smell of their anxious emotions in with them.

"How much of his file have you studied?" He glanced at the young agent sitting next to him. "None of that has ever been proven. Only thing I accept as fact is what I can smell with my own nose. Aldo has connections in high places. That makes him a werewolf to keep off your back. And he's stolen a GWAR agent."

"She's a hot little bitch," Jeff said, chuckling.

"That she is. The whole thing is bizarre." Steve shrugged one shoulder. "We've got a pack leader who was annihilated and his entire pack wiped out for trying to alter the genetic makeup of werewolves and turn them into gods or something. Aldo gets credit for taking them down, which gives him too much power whether there's any truth in it or not."

Steve had spent well over a month researching the Malta werewolves after getting the file. The information had boggled his brain. A pack leader on some remote island in the Mediterranean thought he was a witch or something. And he believed he could make all werewolves have this special gift. Apparently his goal was to turn his pack into super-werewolves—werewolves who could turn invisible, who could run faster, work with the elements. Rumor had it that although most of his experiments had been disastrous, he'd had some success.

It didn't surprise him that his young partner had a hard time letting it all sink in. "Now we've got GWAR agents apparently working with the werewolf who was closely involved with that pack. There's no way he would have gotten his paws on Tangaree otherwise."

"You mean the young bitch." Interest piqued in Jeff's eyes. "I wouldn't mind getting my paws on her. I bet she's one hell of a good fuck."

"And incredibly dangerous." Steve wouldn't argue the issue of her sex appeal. "What's even more dangerous though is that agents within GWAR would sell out their own."

"There's going to be more than one fight before this case is solved."

Steve agreed. And he wasn't too old that a good brawl didn't have its appeal.

Chapter Five

ဆ

The large RV wasn't what Moira expected.

Hours before dawn they pulled into the small camping area, the cold air heavy with dew chilling her flesh. Dante took her wrist, his touch burning into her skin as he guided her to the dark, quiet mobile home.

Mostly humans camped around them, all sleeping, smells of burnt meat, popcorn, charcoal and propane swarming in the air. There was also that stuffy scent that humans carried with them wherever they went. Clogged emotions, too much stress and laziness fueled a smell that made them stand out. Most of them smelled the same, unlike werewolves. She never had cared for their scent although she tolerated it as any werewolf would. For the most part, the species repulsed her. At the moment, the smell of the human campgrounds was more like a stench, turning her stomach. Half of a whole, a line to be put up with when necessary. With no fight in them, their battles holding no honor, they were a confusing species. Maybe Dante thought by hiding among them, the three of them wouldn't be as easily found.

Entering the mobile home alone, she turned, letting her gaze stroll down his naked backside as he said a few words to the dark-haired Malta werewolf. She didn't recognize him though. That was a mystery. The chances of him being from her pack were slim to nil. Even after five years, she would know one of her pack if she saw them. Dante also spoke with a hint of the accent showing in some of his words. But Dante's skin was pale, even though his hair was black as night just like the other werewolf's. Dante was no Malta werewolf. A mixed breed, although not an American mutt. He was also a mystery.

The darkness of the narrow living area shrouded her. The two werewolves spoke quietly outside. Hearing what they said—a casual conversation about supplies the dark-skinned werewolf, Juan, would make a run to get—made the situation strange. The two of them spoke so casually, almost lazily, as if they planned some bizarre humanlike vacation and they were some den, supposed to be together.

But this was no vacation.

They weren't supposed to be together.

She'd been kidnapped.

Her emotions intensified while watching Dante's backside. No matter her order to stay calm, to keep her scent from becoming obvious, imagining dragging her nails over that muscular body made her mouth dry—and her pussy wet. He was an inch or so taller than Juan, his pale skin smoothed over powerful-looking muscles. Few werewolves put meat on before they hit fifty or so, if they did at all. But to be so built up, like he pumped weights or something, distracted her more than she wished it would. A nightly or early morning run wouldn't have him looking that powerfully well built.

Very large werewolves, with muscles harder than rock, were a fantasy of hers. Strong enough that they couldn't be taken down, could defend anyone or anything and were undefeatable no matter the odds. Her life had a habit of getting interrupted. Something always seemed to happen beyond her control that yanked her out of her existence and dumped her somewhere else. A werewolf powerful enough to stop that made her nervous. But it was more like nervous excitement that pumped in her veins at the moment. An energy she feared wouldn't go away until she tasted him, felt him underneath her, on top of her, inside her.

She knew her past made her crave the perfect werewolf who could stop any disaster. She also knew that no such werewolf existed. The closest werewolf to meet that description had been her sire, Bruno Tangaree. Hatred and ignorance had killed him.

Dante Aldo had been there that day. She remembered him on his motorcycle, chasing her down while she ran for her life. He was in her life again. She'd escaped him once. She was older, more experienced—running from him now would be easier than it had been before.

But damn, did she want to escape him? He'd just yanked her out of a life she'd grown very tired of. GWAR would sniff her out, but that was Dante's problem, not hers. In the meantime, what was wrong with enjoying the ride? Or taking him for a ride?

Moira scowled. She was staring at the werewolf, almost drooling over him, fantasizing, when in fact he was the one who had ripped her life out from underneath her. Granted it was a life with GWAR, but that wasn't the point. Still, fucking him would more than likely be the most incredible experience of her life. The way his muscles curved and bulged over his shoulder blades and then trimmed down into a taut waistline. His butt was hard, round, solid. And legs covered with coarse black hair looked like they could kick a wall down. He was perfect. She accepted that fact. But submitting to him would give him power over her that GWAR once had. She didn't want anyone owning her.

She closed her eyes, creating the mental wall the way her mother had taught her. Like hell he'd turn around and catch her drooling. If he did, she swore she'd slap his smug smile right off his face.

For once, she'd like a say on what happened in her world. Dante took her from an existence she'd grown tired of. But he hadn't asked, hadn't planned it out with her first. For once in her life, she'd like to make the decisions.

Juan stepped back into the car. Dante turned, pinning her with those incredibly pale blue eyes, eyes that almost glowed with savage lust. It was as if he looked right through her, knowing exactly what she'd been thinking this entire time. And it amused him. No matter that his expression could have been chiseled on his face, his gaze didn't falter from hers. She was forced to stare back, to inhale his rich, seductive scent with every breath. He had a broad face with wide cheekbones and a sharp, straight nose. The only imperfection was a small scar that interrupted an otherwise firm, hard jaw.

Even that was no imperfection. He approached, corded, hard muscle moving under his flesh, until she noticed a smaller, hairline scar on the side of his lower lip. Not imperfections. Battle wounds, small scars from futile attempts of prey that tried to take on the strength of an invincible werewolf.

Pulling her long hair around her, doing her best to cover herself with it, she turned from him. Partly ashamed of the direction of her thoughts but more pissed that he looked at her like that. Like he knew what she thought and intended to appease her curiosity — again without asking.

Blood burned in her veins as the change ached to rip her apart. Strong emotions brought it on. Taking on a purer, more primal form released those emotions, simplifying them, cleansing her. Holding it at bay, she allowed her blood to pump hard enough to adjust her eyesight, to give her night vision, and marched down the dark hallway.

"Where are you going?" Dante followed her.

"Away from you."

Entering the largest bedroom at the end of the hall, she shut the door behind her. The mobile home was furnished. Maybe there would be clothes. Anything.

"Moira." He said her name with a growl. "There are T-shirts in the top drawer."

Amusement mixed with his desire, his lust. It wasn't at all an unappealing scent. But she didn't like it. Didn't like that he had the upper hand. Didn't like his cocky, know-it-all attitude. And she didn't like it one damned bit that fiery need pulsed inside her, hot and out of control, throbbing between her legs and filling the air around her with primal, hard-core lust.

He pushed the door open, his smell wrapping around her, as powerful and enticing as the smoothness of his muscles under taut skin. Everything about him was strong and unleashed. And with him, a leash might not be a bad idea.

"You don't want to be with me." His low baritone rippled over her flesh.

Intentionally keeping her back to him, showing no respect for his masculine presence, she fished through the top drawer.

"Nope." Her lie smelled salty.

She did believe one thing. He'd stolen her from GWAR. That meant the agency had some serious leaks. Not that she didn't already know they weren't perfect. At an early age, she'd learned there was no foolproof government. Her own sire, respected by his entire pack, was overthrown in a day, wiped out, burned to death.

She bit back her sadness, knowing there was no one she could trust, nowhere to turn. Escape was imperative, although she had no idea where to run.

"I want you, Moira. And you want me too." He brushed his palms down her bare arms, heat and strength belied by a gentle touch.

She fisted the shirt she'd pulled from the dresser, turning quickly to escape his touch. Mere fingers brushing skin shouldn't burn like that. He didn't move, although his presence seemed to be everywhere in the dark bedroom. Moira pulled the shirt over her head, grateful for its size when it fell like a short dress to her thighs.

"Why do I matter so much to you?" She finally met his gaze.

"Your sire gave you to me a long time ago." He said it so matter-of-factly.

Moira laughed. "I'm honestly surprised that you're the first werewolf to come up with that line. Good one." She narrowed her gaze. "Now tell me the truth."

"Know now, little bitch—I will never lie to you."

141

"You're lying right now. I doubt you even knew my sire."

Something about his scent changed. It was anger, raw and unleashed. It was spicy, tickling her nose like fresh pepper. Dante lunged at her, pinching her under her arms when he lifted her quickly. She was pinned against the wall, the cold hardness against her back doing nothing to soothe the quick temper that unleashed inside her. Moira clawed at his shoulders, fighting to no avail.

"I will never be accused of lying. Real werewolves don't lie." His face was inches from hers. Silver streaked through his pale blue eyes, his glare hard and cold.

As quickly as he'd pushed her against the wall, he pulled her from it, tossing her on the bed. Moira moved to all fours, furious.

He'd abducted her. Taken her by force. Stolen her in the night. Her outrage was more than justified.

Furniture quaked in the room, her gift rushing through her and the inner ache to hurl something—anything—at him, battled her rational thought.

He grew while standing before her. Anger clogged the room. She fought not to sneeze, the thickness of the strong emotion making her eyes water, her nose itch as if someone had just spilled pepper everywhere. Muscles bulged in his chest, in his arms, his hands fisting next to his hips. Although not hard, his cock definitely wasn't soft. It was long and thick with black curls forming a line up the middle of his hard stomach before spreading over his broad chest. As outraged as she should be, her emotions tumbled over each other. He looked so fucking sexy standing over her like that, naked and growing harder as she stared at him. He looked fierce, deadly, and like he could take her until she couldn't walk.

And he was tall. Damned tall. Growing up on the island, pale-skinned males had never appealed to her as much as her own, darker pack members. There was something about Dante though. He was different, demanding, enjoyed taking what he wanted, and more than likely almost always got it. Challenging him turned her on and submitting to him might possibly take her over the edge sexually.

What the hell was she thinking?

She licked her lips, her mouth suddenly too dry. Her gaze traveled down him quickly. The dresser drawers had opened an inch or two and the sliding closet doors had opened slightly. Willing the room to quit rattling from her intense emotions, she sucked in a long, soothing breath.

Her mouth remained too dry.

"Tell me why my sire would give me to you." No matter his outrage over her challenging his words, it was too hard to believe she'd be given to a werewolf she didn't even know.

Dante moved in on her quickly. He leaned forward, pressing his fists into the blanket covering the bed. Anger swarmed around him, but there was more in his scent, in his eyes, in the strength that radiated from his body. This werewolf would take a challenge. She sensed that about him. He'd take it, run with it. Something told her he'd fight to the bloody end for what he wanted.

Well, so would she.

Moira didn't back away from him. She dug her fists into the bedspread on either side of her and took on his daring stare.

"Bruno knew he was going down." He spoke slowly, as if choosing his words carefully. "His work was challenged. But the proof existed. In you…" he paused. "And in me."

What proof existed in him? She didn't ask. He hadn't answered her question.

"Your sire knew I'd protect you. Keep you alive."

"I've kept myself alive," she growled at him. His face, inches from hers, invaded her personal space. "No one has helped me. No one's protected me."

The anger had faded. But the intensity of emotions, dominating, strong, challenging, kept her on her guard. Still she didn't retreat. No matter his size. No matter that he probably had ten times her strength, if he thought she'd belly-up to him, he could go to hell.

"The day your pack burned, packs from the other islands and parts of Europe descended and took over," he began, his voice no more than a cold whisper. "You were only eighteen. In that short dress, your scent prime and ripe, any other werewolf wouldn't have ensured you made it to the bay."

The day her sire and mother died. Never too far from her thoughts, but something she'd refused to think about. That he'd bring it up, mention it with such a harsh, bitter tone violated some unspoken law she'd created for herself.

In spite of her determination over the years to move forward, that terrible day flooded her thoughts.

"Okay. So possibly once in your life you were a gentleman. You've shown me that you've overcome that trait."

"I would never take a cub, even if she looked like a woman." He almost sounded hurt. "When I learned Bruno thought he could share the gift he'd been born with, I sought him out."

"Then how come I never saw you?" She never saw her sire when he worked with others. Her parents didn't want her pulled into the intensity of the gift until she was old enough to understand it. As a cub it hadn't bothered her. When she'd grown older, she'd felt left out.

"I know you ached to work alongside your sire, to understand and be closer to him by learning more about what he did." He straightened, moving to his knees on the bed, and took a handful of her hair to push it behind her shoulder. "I told him that more than once, but he saw into my mind too well, knew my interest in you was more than just concern for a cub and her sire."

Suddenly she was eye level with his cock. Thick and long, it straightened as she stared at it. She inhaled his rich, alluring scent. Son of a bitch! It would take nothing to stick out her tongue and taste him, stroke the smooth roundness of the tip of his cock.

"And what were your interests?" she asked, again drawing his scent deep into her lungs.

He continued stroking her hair and she had a feeling if she'd tried to move, he would have pinned her right where she was, her mouth inches from his cock.

"I wanted to know you. Eventually I talked to Bruno about this. He made promises, but also laid down rules."

That sounded just like her sire. Always rules, always ways to make her grow, make her stronger. And if she followed his rules, his promises of what her reward would be made it all worthwhile.

She licked her lips, letting her tongue move out of her mouth and closer to his cock. His fingers tightened in her hair. Good. Misery loved company.

She fought the urge to give her ass a slight twitch, arch her back and shift suggestively on the bed. "What were the rules and the promises?"

Dante chuckled. His cock jerked in front of her, growing while his soft baritone laughter vibrated from him. "He sent me to you for the first time to make sure you got off the island. I had to wait though, and give you time to mature, discover your own path in life and become your own female. And that's where we are now."

She raised her hand from the bed. His fingers were tangled in her hair and she put her hand over his, attempting to free herself from his grasp. His grip on her hair tightened, and he pushed his cock closer. The tip of it brushed over her lips. She tasted him, salty and tempting. Her lips parted, aching to experience the width of him in her mouth, to run her tongue over his soft tip and down the length of his shaft.

Her insides swelled and quivered, need pumping inside her so hard she almost collapsed onto her belly on the bed.

"There's more to your story," she managed to say, her voice raspy and her lips brushing over his cock when she spoke. "You'll tell me everything if you expect anything."

"There are some things you are better off not knowing right now. Trust me, little bitch," he said, sounding just like her sire.

And she'd hated it when her sire spoke to her like that.

Enduring the sharp pain when she yanked her hair from his fingers, she jumped off the bed. For a moment, her leg muscles quivered so hard she worried they wouldn't hold her.

"Treat me like a cub and you can go find some other bitch and fuck with her head." She marched to the door, yanked it open and headed down the hall.

The overwhelming power of a predator, a protector determined to lay claim, wrapped around her, sinking in so deep it stole her breath. Moira gasped, momentarily frozen from the impact of emotions that attacked her.

And they weren't her emotions. Heat, burning with more intensity than she'd ever experienced before. Lust, carnal and raw, rushed through her hard enough to make her legs weak. A pressure stabbed through her, thick and strong.

You aren't going anywhere. She didn't hear him speak so much as she experienced the words shot hard into her mind.

Hyperventilating. Fighting to make her limbs function. Moira's world spun around her. Rising. Movement. A grip so hard on her she couldn't breathe. And then she was airborne, her feet leaving the ground while suddenly air filled her lungs too quickly.

She hit the couch, stunned, fighting her hair that tangled around her face as she looked wildly around the room. Where she would swear he wasn't there a second before, Dante now stood over her. The first thing her gaze locked on to was his large cock, erect, hard and determined like the warrior werewolf it belonged to. Gulping in air, she shoved hair from her face, almost scratching her flesh before quickly allowing her claws to recede back into fingernails.

"What the fuck?" she gasped, looking up at the hard expression of a predator.

Dante lifted her. She was too stunned to react in time. Strong arms pulled her to him, her legs still not cooperating with her as she stumbled and fought to regain control of her actions. He didn't allow her time.

Muscles harder than rock pressed against her, the T-shirt she'd donned far from providing a shield against his body when suddenly she was stretched against him. Strong arms wrapped around her. His mouth captured hers on a breath, stealing it, giving her a taste of pure, raw virility.

Her vision blurred, barely focusing on pale blue eyes streaked with silver as he kissed her. Leg muscle pressed against her thighs. Powerful arms enclosed her against his chest. Corded muscles pulsed warmly along her front.

Moira closed her eyes. Too many sensations, both physical and emotional surged to life inside her.

His mouth was hot, his tongue aggressive and demanding. Long fingers combed her hair, stroking her back. She arched into him, unable to grab hold of her thoughts.

He deepened the kiss. A growl rumbled inside him. His cock throbbed to life, hard and demanding as the rest of him.

One with the elements, carry both of us. Show us all and all we will see.

How the hell did he know the rhyme her mother had taught her?

His voice was right next to her, but he didn't speak, didn't stop kissing her.

His lips pressed against hers. Their tongues intertwined, exploring, thrusting, stroking.

But he had spoken...

Moira whimpered. Her thoughts twisted in a tangled mess, making it impossible to think. Dante had just spoken but he couldn't have. It didn't make any fucking sense. She knew what she heard though. Dwelling on it was enough to clear her head.

He impaled her mouth with his tongue. Again he spoke to her in her mind. *Unless you control your thoughts, no physical action you inflict will allow you to win.*

Moira ripped her mouth from his. Every gasp of air filled her lungs with his scent, his domination, his control of the situation, of her.

She stared at her hand, her fingers stretched over the curly black hair that covered hard, smooth muscle. Strong hands slowly stroked her back. His lips moved over her forehead.

More than anything, she wanted to know how the hell he spoke in her thoughts. Asking would make her sound like a damned fool and admit he possessed a strength she didn't have. No way would she let him see her weakness or her curiosity.

"The gift you have is untamed. And until you understand it, you'll never be able to control it." His breath was like fire against her skin.

And his words didn't make a damned bit of sense.

Nothing did. Too many muscles pressed against her. His hands on her, stroking, caressing, gentle and yet more powerful than anything she'd ever experienced in her life.

Unable to find her own strength, trapped by her own lust, this incredible werewolf who held her created a fire inside her that burned out of control. Her thoughts wouldn't focus. The throbbing between her legs pulsed painfully, building inside her. Need that was riper, more powerful than she could handle coursed through her veins.

She'd been seduced before. The best of them had taken her on. Nothing had ever hit her like this. It didn't make sense. No werewolf got the better of her.

Chapter Six

ഇ

Her dark skin was soft and smooth. Black hair, coarse like raw silk, teased his flesh. Every inch of her was fucking perfect. Dante had known that much for years.

Her thoughts, torn and confused, lust-filled and on fire, threw him off balance. It wasn't too often that he cursed the gift. This was the moment he'd ached to experience for as long as he'd known her, as long as he'd had the knowledge that she would be his. Holding her, feeling her against him, was better than any fantasy he'd ever had about her. And there had been a hell of a lot of those.

Her breasts were full and ripe. Her dark nipples puckered against his palm, teasing the soft part of his flesh when he brushed over them. His hands stroked the curve of her hip, reaching the end of that blasted T-shirt she'd put on. Finding skin again, he gripped her soft ass. He was so close to her heat and her aroused scent that it about did him in. Her small hands, hesitant and warm, rested against his chest. She wanted him. Fuck. He needed her so desperately he was about to explode. But it wasn't finally having her body pressed against his that threw him off guard—and damn, the way she stretched against him brought out a carnal side that he didn't want to control. It was her thoughts, raw and wild. More aggressive than he'd realized they would be. Her loyalty to a pack that no longer existed, to a sire and mother she hadn't seen in five years, was stronger than he'd expected it would be.

That brought him pause. She knew less about the gift than he'd anticipated. It made sense. Bruno never took the time to help her develop it, wishing her to have a normal upbringing. But even Bruno and Renee thought she'd explore her gift more than she had. Yet she'd suppressed it, hiding behind the world of GWAR and keeping damaged emotions hidden, which hadn't given them time to heal. Bruno hadn't made him promise to this, but knowing what he now saw in Moira, he would have to take matters slower, draw out what she had, let her experience what was inside her for herself.

Fucking her would be no problem. Taking her hard, riding her while she screamed—he wanted that more than he wanted to breathe. And she'd let him fuck her. That made it even harder. She'd growl and grumble, show a little tooth and claw, but her hot little body pulsed with hard, raw lust. And he saw that challenging him, taking him on, got her more hot and bothered than submitting and going belly-up. She ached for his cock as badly as he ached to give it to her. Truth be told, her getting riled made his cock swell with need faster than any bitch going docile on him ever had.

"What do you know about the gift?" She asked the question that he knew plagued her thoughts as badly as her lust for him did.

"I know it flows in your blood as strongly as it courses through mine."

The only way she could back away from him was to climb onto the couch. His arms kept her pinned, unable to move to either side, while his fingers stroked that perfect curve of ass right above her thighs. He looked down at the top of her head, at the way her black hair parted over her glowing caramel-colored skin.

As a cub, his pack had moved around Europe, exposing him to many different races. The belief that werewolves should mate with their own still ran strong among most packs. Werewolves were even more antiquated than humans.

Moira appealed to him though. No matter that many would comment on their different races. Neither he nor Moira had strong ties with any pack that would judge them for mating. Diluting the line, some would call it. Bruno hadn't seen it that way—he'd created a new line, having nothing to do with nationality or breed. Dante didn't see it that way either. He saw Moira, spirited, aggressive, taking on the world when it had labeled her extinct. And even though her thoughts at this close range were new to him, her warrior drive, her will to survive, to fight, to challenge and not accept until she was satisfied turned him on more than any other bitch he'd ever met.

She pushed against his chest, a feeble attempt on her part to create space. He dug his fingers into her ass, shoving her against his hard cock. Her entire body jumped. Looking up at him quickly, her lips parting, forming a small circle while a breath escaped her, the need that swarmed in her gaze had his cock throbbing between them.

"If you had the gift then you should have helped save my pack," she said bitterly.

Now wasn't the time to defend his actions or what had actually transpired all those years ago. Already she suspected his ability to grab her thoughts. And yet she wanted a reason to deny that he'd been in her mind. She'd grab on to anything right now to call him a liar again. Well, he wouldn't feed her fire.

At least not the fire that instigated her temper.

"There are many things you don't know," he whispered, bringing his hands up her back, raising her shirt with his movements.

"And you claim to know so much." She lowered her arms, pressing against him to block his path up her warm body. "Your actions belie your words."

"How is that?" He slipped his fingers around her waist.

She didn't have half his strength, probably less than that in her human form. No matter that she tried to control his wandering hands, she was no match. "For all I know, you saw me five years ago, liked what you smelled, and just happened to stumble into my path again," she whispered, her lips barely moving. "Do you really think you're the first to try and play this game?"

Her touch grew hot, too hot. He looked down at her hands, her dark skin making him look pale in comparison. For a moment he saw what she attempted. Smoke appeared around her fingers. The heat from her hands was building. If he allowed it, he would smell burnt flesh, see the flames she cast into his mind as she worked his own thoughts against him to make him believe his arms were on fire.

The parts of her gift that she knew, she'd mastered very well. GWAR would fight tooth and nail to get her back. And he would fight just as hard to keep her. The only difference was that he didn't want to use her, to play games with her. And no matter what she said, she didn't think he wanted to either.

He let go of her waist, giving her what she wanted, but then moved quickly.

He grabbed her shirt and yanked. The material ripped down the middle. Her breasts bounced when he pulled the shirt from her body. He tossed her down on the couch while she let out a surprised yelp.

"What the fuck!" she cried out.

Before she could fight back, he was on top of her.

"So you like to play with fire, do you?" he hissed, forcing her legs apart and pressing his cock against her moist, hot pussy.

Her eyes darkened. The smell of her lust mixed with surprise until she relaxed underneath him, not moving for a moment while she studied his face. Possibly he'd finally pushed her to the point of their sexual battle where she would offer herself to him. The rich smell of hard-core fucking need thickened between them. He took advantage of her astonishment and pressed his lips to hers, tasting her once again.

Her arms moved, her body pinned under his. Adjusting himself, his cock burning from heat that was very real, he grabbed her wrists, pinning them above her head. Second-guessing her took as little effort as breathing.

She struggled underneath him, her breasts brushing against his chest. Nipples as hard as small pebbles tortured him beyond control. Lowering his head, he sucked one into his mouth, tasting her flesh, teasing her with his teeth and his tongue.

"Shit. Oh shit," she cried, twisting underneath him.

Arching against him, giving him free rein, she didn't fight to release her hands. A fog rushed through him, carnal needs surfacing that made it hard to focus on his own thoughts, let alone hers. Her legs glided against his outer thighs, warm and smooth and muscular. Her twisting and squirming underneath him positioned his cock at the peak of her heat, soaked, on fire, willing him to take the plunge.

He held her wrists in one hand, running his fingers down her arm, touching her cheek, stroking her neck. Every muscle inside him bulged, desire that he'd kept at bay for years coming to a quick, furious head. She made it real damned hard to think clearly, something he wasn't used to. His mind burned with primitive drive. Fuck her hard. Fuck her now. It was as if they were in their fur, rational thought having no play in their actions. All thought drained to his cock. Take her. Claim her. Finalize this mating he'd been promised so many years ago. It would hold. No pack, no werewolf government anywhere would challenge him. His cock screamed to dive into her soaked cunt. Every muscle in his body cramped while what little strength he had fought for control.

"Moira," he growled, looking up at her, reluctantly pulling his attention from her perfect breasts.

Her mouth was open, her lips parted as her breathing came hard and staggered. Long, thick black lashes draped over her eyes. When she blinked, opening her eyes briefly, he saw how fogged her gaze was.

"Moira," he said again, barely able to speak, his cock inflamed with more need than had burned through him in a long time.

Her tongue moved, slowly moistening her top lip. She made no attempt to free her hands, as if she'd forgotten they were above her head. Her perky breasts were round mounds that distracted him, her dark brown nipples damp and shining against her caramel skin.

Too much lust, need, clogged his mental vision and his cock was pounding furiously. Blood pumped through him too hard and fast for him to think clearly, see clearly. Unable to control his own mind, there was no way he could see into hers.

"You...you..." she stammered, licking her lips again, her eyes closing and then slowly opening.

Hard breaths made her breasts rise before him. His cock filled with blood, his orgasm pressing hard, building furiously.

"I can't fight you like this," she said, exhaling.

Her admission of defeat hit him harder than if he'd been punched square in the gut. No way could he take her when she'd be giving herself to him on a reluctant surrender. She'd resent him later, pull further away. Without her trust, her lust meant nothing.

Damn if his cock didn't want to disagree.

"Fuck!" he roared, forcing himself backward.

His muscles hardened with enough fury to stimulate the change. Blood rushed through him like bolts of electricity. Every vertebrae in his spine stiffened, the hard pain of change rushing through him faster than he could run.

Letting go of her wrists and falling back on his haunches, he stared at her naked body, at so much temptation lying underneath him. No matter the amount of control he enforced, he almost came all over her.

"There is no battle between you and me," he growled, his teeth pressing against his gums, speech becoming harder as his tongue thickened.

"There is nothing between you and me." She made no attempt to move though.

The rich smell of her lust could be cut with a knife.

Grabbing her legs, lifting her ass off the couch, he devoured her cunt. Feeding on her with his half-changed mouth, he was careful not to cut her tender skin but more than aware that his teeth scraped over her.

"Fuck you." She squirmed against his mouth, but her legs spread farther apart. "Oh, hell yeah!"

His tongue wouldn't form words at the moment, but not a damn thing was wrong with his taste buds.

He growled his approval.

Dipping into the heat that his cock ached to be a part of, he watched her through hazy vision.

Moira cried out, grabbing the side of her head, thrashing it from side to side while she pulled her hair. "You are so damned good. Shit, Dante."

Muscles rippled and hardened her belly, her body tensing as he sucked and nibbled and watched her come. She exploded for him. She thrust her hips the best she could in the position he had her in, soaking his mouth, his cheeks and chin.

Pain tore through him, taking over every muscle, every bone, while he fought his own release. His mind remained in a fog while he watched her thoughts clear. Surprise mixed with intense satisfaction spread over her face. She stared at him for a long moment, her black hair falling over her breasts and fanning around her over the couch.

When her gaze dropped to his cock and her tongue slowly moved over her lips, he couldn't take it any longer.

"What about you?" she purred, and ran her hands over her breasts, teasing him further, taunting and torturing while her desire to control him sparked in her eyes.

His will was strong, damned strong. It would take nothing to fuck the shit out of her right now. She wouldn't stop him. Her satisfaction ebbed, but he didn't doubt for a moment he could bring her heat to a boiling point and push her over the edge harder than ever before.

"Is that all you can do?" she teased.

He sensed her confusion, her wonder at why he didn't fuck her.

Standing quickly, the act making him lightheaded while all blood still resided in his cock, he grabbed her arm, pulling her up with him.

"What?" she asked.

But words weren't there for him right now. He stalked down the hallway, fighting his every movement when all he wanted was to slam deep inside her. Not letting her go until they reached the bathroom, he flung her inside, moving in quickly behind her and closing them in the small space.

"We're showering." His voice was still garbled but his thoughts slowly cleared.

His cock seemed to weigh a hundred pounds. It was swollen and grew even more uncomfortable when he moved. His balls itched, tight and drawn up, craving release.

He wouldn't fuck her—not yet. There was no trust, and without that he'd be forcing himself on her. That wouldn't happen tonight. He didn't let go of her arm while turning on the shower, testing the water and then pulling her into the bath with him.

She reached for him. He grabbed her wrist.

"Not tonight." He let go of her wrist, afraid he'd hurt her. "Just stand there and I'll take care of things."

Water streamed over her, draping her long hair over her breasts and her hard, flat tummy. She didn't answer but he knew she wouldn't move. His actions confused her and she would damn well live with that.

Sticking his head under the jets of pounding water, he used it to clear his brain. Grabbing his cock, he stroked it, pulling hard and long, bringing his own release. She didn't watch. He wouldn't give her that privilege. Not yet. Not until she understood. Her scent wrapped around him though, weighing heavy in the steam that collected, trapped by the shower curtain. Blood pounded in his brain while he stroked and breathed in the smell of her.

With his back to her, he jacked off. Refusing to look at her, his eyes closed tightly, didn't keep him out of her mind. He just didn't have the strength to leave her thoughts alone. Her anger nipped at him. She was angry that he'd attacked her, gotten her so aroused, and although he'd allowed her to come, he hadn't finished what he'd started. That confused her, but it was her own denial that put her in that state. Refusal to believe him. Until she did, she was little more than what she professed to be—his prisoner, kidnapped and stolen. That bit at him harder than the unsatisfying orgasm that released his muscles, allowing him to relax somewhat.

* * * * *

Juan immediately noticed the heavy smell of sex in the air when he returned some time later.

"She as good as you'd dreamed she'd be?" he asked, grinning at Moira while she scowled in return.

"He has no idea," she answered before he could say anything. "Dante doesn't seem able to finish what he starts. Maybe he knew he wouldn't measure up to my standards."

She said it to piss him off. But her challenge rang loud and clear. Juan laughed, unloading supplies he'd returned with.

"That doesn't sound like Dante," he told her, then handed her several bags of clothes. "I guessed on your size," he said sheepishly.

Moira licked her lips, smiling although there was hesitation in her eyes. She looked at him and her smile faded. Dante moved into her mind while his gaze hardened on her.

For a moment she regretted her cocky response, worry seeping through her that she might push him too far. As her thoughts changed, so did her stance. Straightening, her gaze narrowing on him, she let him know she wouldn't be bullied.

Dante almost smiled. Just that small amount of determination rushing through her brought his cock to life. Then she surprised him.

Don't think you're getting a second chance, she said to him, staring directly at him, raising one eyebrow slightly.

It was the first time she'd moved into his mind, joined their thoughts and communicated with him without speaking. He wanted to jump for joy, grab her and swing her around the small living area and shout with excitement that he knew she could do it. But she played coy, teasing him. He would share thoughts with her and let her know what waited for her.

My dear little bitch, it is you who will get the second chance. He could get used to sharing thoughts with her like this, communicating on such an intimate level.

Moira turned quickly, her thoughts leaving him. Tossing her long black hair over her shoulder, she didn't give him her attention again. When he tried, somehow she'd managed to put a wall around her mind to the point where he swore he saw it when he tried moving through her thoughts.

Damn impressive. Moira was a quick learner.

Chapter Seven

Moira watched the two werewolves work preparing the mobile home to leave. Humans moved around the trailer park but Dante and Juan paid no attention to them. There was a bond between the two, as if they'd known each other a long time. Juan was darker-skinned than Moira, and Dante paler, almost appearing black Irish in descent. The two men's movements were a lot alike and both were built similarly. And other than casual comments, they worked in a comfortable silence like they'd done this task many times before. In spite of different skin color, she'd swear the two were from the same den. And that made no sense. Werewolves didn't interbreed — not in Malta. Possibly they had different sires, or maybe different mothers. Either way, her guess was that they were definitely related.

The sun shone through the tall, narrow pines while they wound their way along the narrow mountain roads, heading south.

"I take it you got a hold of your friends in Albuquerque?" Dante sat in the large passenger seat, his broad shoulders visible on either side of the chair.

"Yup. Figured we'd do better mixing with the packs down there. Less questions."

She didn't know what questions they were leery of — there could be so many. Reclining on the couch in the living area of the mobile home, she tugged on the dress she'd chosen to wear from the outfits Juan bought her and stared at the endless blue sky outside the large window. With no clue where they were headed other than, obviously, New Mexico, or what plan the two werewolves had devised, she ached to ask questions.

No way would she open her mind to be searched though. Whatever tricks Dante possessed, and possibly Juan as well, it involved being able to read her mind. No one got that close to her. Someone climbing inside her, hearing her thoughts, terrified her worse than being kidnapped.

Lying there doing her damnedest to think about nothing was harder than she thought. Especially as the hours rolled by. A nap sounded damned good. Storing up energy for whatever lay ahead of her would be smart. There was no way she could control her dreams though.

The quiet rumbling of the engine lulled her to sleep. Dreams quickly haunted her. Dante, large and powerful, touching her, stroking her, making her come with a predatory look. Hands so warm and strong spread her legs, gripping her thighs while his tongue probed her, released her juices, until she begged him to fuck her.

Then there was his cock. Like steel, throbbing, promising her satisfaction like she'd never experienced before. She saw him in her dream, toward the front of the RV. If he walked to her, he did it without her noticing because suddenly he was there, in front of her, looking down while she dreamed. And it was a dream. Even as it happened, as he grabbed his thick shaft with long, powerful fingers and began stroking, she had no doubts she slept.

Her pussy swelled, eager and ready. She sat up, reaching for his cock, smelling his sex wrap around her like a thick, warm blanket. All she wanted to do was taste him, experience that rich scent inside her. He'd deprived her of it before, and after working so hard to seduce her. It pissed her off, leaving her horny and anxious.

She lapped at the tip of his cock, its smoothness swelling against her tongue and lips. He growled over her, showing his approval. Her mouth stretched over his thickness. God. He was fucking huge. Dante would be damned flattered that her mind created such a huge cock for him. He wasn't that big in real life. But her lips stretched and she struggled to wrap her mouth around him.

He was salty. His taste appealed to her and she stroked him with her tongue, working him farther into her mouth, which was no easy task. He grew the more she sucked. Her jaw would split in two if she tried taking much more of him. She let her lips slide back and they tingled when he was no longer in her mouth.

Moira gazed through blurred vision up at him. His pale blue eyes glowed as if electrified. Set against creamy white skin and hair so dark it was like a midnight sky, the contrasts heightened his incredible good looks.

The rich smell of his lust mixed with a tangy, clean smell. Satisfaction and happiness were like a mixture of fresh oranges, just cut with their juices flowing, and a beautiful day, clean and washed free of all clouds and turbulence.

I promise I'm even better in real life. His growled words vibrated in her mind, unspoken, but as clear as if they were.

Waking disoriented, her hair tangled around her, she stared at her surroundings. She lay on a couch built into the side of the RV. The engine rumbled with confidence underneath her. Her body tingled, every inch of her charged with sexual energy. She licked her lips, swearing she tasted Dante on them.

That dream was too damned real. And it left her craving, throbbing, dying to experience more of him. Suddenly she was grouchy and sick to her stomach with the reality that she might not even be in control of her own dreams. She scowled at the two men sitting in the captain chairs with their backs to her. They drove in silence.

She didn't like being seduced in her dreams. Somehow she knew that's what had happened. If she jumped up right now and hurried to look at Dante's crotch, she'd bet he was hard as a rock. Her stomach twisted even more while a hot, damp sensation crawled over her skin. It made her uncomfortable realizing that for five years she'd craved her freedom, the knowledge of where she was going, what she would do next. Here she was, yanked out from under GWAR's teeth, and still in the same damned predicament—and by a werewolf she was lusting after. Fucking great. Straightening, sore muscles cramping from sleeping on the couch, she stayed put and attempted combing her hair with her fingers. Maybe it had just been a dream stemming from his aggressive seduction earlier. And maybe she wasn't ready to find out.

Dante drove now. The two-lane highway, a dark burnt red from the natural resources it had been made from, curved around rugged hills and sandy ground. A soft blue sky spread endlessly in front of them. The view was incredible.

"Where are we headed?" Still groggy, she fought to create her wall around her mind.

"The Sandia pack. I've stayed with them before." Juan gave her the once-over, his expression and scent one of curiosity and interest. "Want some coffee?"

Before she could answer, he stood, taking her arm and seating her in the passenger seat then moving past her toward the back of the trailer. Within minutes the rich smell of coffee reached her nose.

She dared to look at Dante. His profile burned its image into her mind. His jaw set and determined, his look focused. Black, straight hair shone against the bright sun coming through the windows. One hand rested on the steering wheel, the other relaxed on his leg. He wore a simple T-shirt, faded jeans and boots. The plain clothes didn't look so ordinary adorning the body of a powerful warrior. Muscles leapt out at her from every inch of his body. There wasn't a damn thing simple about him. With that one quick glance, memories of how controlling, how powerful he could be reminded her to be on her guard.

"I'm better in real life," he mumbled under his breath so only she could hear him.

Heat raged over her cheeks and down her neck. Embarrassment attacked too quickly for her to hide its tart smell. She gawked at him, unable to speak, while he stared ahead at the road, a small smile playing at his lips. Full lips — kissable lips.

God. She was fucking losing her mind.

Albuquerque traffic quickly distracted her, the smell of humans strong enough to detect through the glass and metal of the RV. Dante maneuvered the large vehicle with ease until they'd reached a quiet, suburban area. Similar homes, made from white stucco and looking like any comfortable American suburb trailed on either side of them. The few people she spotted in yards and at their cars in driveways stopped what they were doing, watching the mobile home drive by.

Dante's expression didn't change. Juan reclined behind them where she'd napped. She didn't smell any emotions on either of them that clued her in to why they were being watched intently as they drove by.

"It's the next right," Juan said from behind her.

"I know where we're going," Dante grumbled.

"Where are we going?" she asked again.

"I'm sure the accommodations will suit you," Juan said.

"Don't mock me." Moira glared at Juan. "You take me from my life and then we hit the road. I have a right to know where the hell we're going."

"I can't imagine working for GWAR was such an incredible life. At least now you're free and with Dante." Juan straightened, running his hand over thick black hair, looking at her as if he believed she'd always wanted to be with Dante. "The Sandia pack has a nice resort outside of town. I'm sure neither WA nor any other pack you've run with have treated you as well as what you'll see here."

He raised an eyebrow. Juan had his charm. More than likely bitches rolled over for him on a regular basis. She met his gaze, not missing what he was trying to do.

She wouldn't give him any clue about which packs she'd been with. For the most part, there hadn't been any. But if they didn't already know that, it was none of their damned business.

"Why is it that you're treated so well by this pack?" she lowered her voice, turning in her chair to give him her complete attention.

Where Dante was a closed book, Juan appeared easier to read than a billboard.

Juan ran his tongue over his lip. Something in the way he looked at her matched Dante's expressions. And in his scent, definite interest. She'd smelled that same pungent smell last night from Dante. Not that she hadn't smelled interest and lust on plenty of werewolves before. It was more than that. These two werewolves smelled the same, like they were from the same den. She glanced at Dante. He kept his attention on the road, slowing the RV and turning right.

"I can't take credit for the red carpet treatment," Juan said, stealing her attention.

"Red carpet treatment?"

"Enough," Dante growled.

Moira tilted her head at his sudden scowl. "Is that why everyone turned and watched us arrive? Are you famous somehow?"

Juan snorted. Dante adjusted his grip on the large steering wheel, relaxing his hands and then tightening them. Muscles twitched in his arms. Something dangerous lingered in his expression although he let off no scent to reveal his thoughts. She didn't trust a werewolf she couldn't smell. Having the ability to hide feelings to the extent that they couldn't be smelled made a werewolf unpredictable—dangerous.

"WA shouldn't keep its agents in the dark so much," Juan muttered.

"I said that's enough."

Moira tore her attention from Dante, knowing he was irritated even though she smelled nothing. He didn't frighten Juan. If anything, the werewolf behind her seemed very relaxed, continuing to smell amused. She glanced his way and he winked at her.

She would have questioned him further, pried information from him, but they pulled into the parking lot of a large mansion. The place was almost surrounded by jagged white rock, climbing high, inviting her to run, explore. The natural enclosure hid the place from the neighborhood they'd driven through. And it was well hidden. Mountainous cliffs climbed toward the pale sky all around them.

Run. Claim your freedom. Escape, she thought to herself.

It would be damned hard for someone to chase her in these mountains. All she'd have to do is find a phone, make a quick call, and WA would pick her up. Or maybe not, maybe for the first time in her life, she could be her own bitch.

Dante got out on his side, and fresh, cool air wrapped around her. The front doors of the large mansion opened and two werewolves walked out toward them.

Moira glanced at their concerned faces.

Run and I'll catch you. She stilled, Dante's words so clear in her head it was as if he'd spoken them.

She turned her head, staring into his distracting blue eyes. They were so pale and bright, probing, his attention riveted on her. She tossed her hair over her shoulder, strengthening that damned wall she'd allowed to slip for one fucking minute.

Damn him. *You needed the help of someone inside a government agency to catch me the first time. Like you'd have a chance in hell on your own.*

Her fingers fumbled with her door but she opened it, managing some grace as she slid out on her side.

I dare you to try.

No way she'd honor his thought in her head with a response, spoken or otherwise.

"Your rooms are ready." A tall werewolf with short black hair almost shaven against his thick, round head and noticeable tattoos on stocky, muscular arms focused his attention on Dante. "Will you be with us long?"

"Not sure yet." Dante headed toward the doors of the mansion, the others following suit.

One of the werewolves stood to the side, letting her enter before he followed, pulling the two solid doors shut behind them. Aggravation seeped from him—or was it fear? Keeping her expression blank, she quickly took in his dark skin, black eyes and short, stocky build. A Mexican werewolf, possibly born American. There was no way to know.

Remembering Juan's comment earlier on how they'd fit in better here, it was suddenly clear what he'd meant. Dante was the only one among them with white skin. The two werewolves were both as dark as her and Juan. To anyone not paying attention, she might appear to be one of them.

Obviously Dante didn't feel a need to blend in. He moved to the center of the rather large foyer. A long, winding staircase flowed toward them, widening as it reached the white tile. Their footsteps tapped against it, making a hollow sound. Dante's boots clicked harder than the rest of theirs. Broad shoulders stretched his T-shirt hard against solid muscle. He stood a good couple inches taller than the other werewolves, dwarfing them with his presence.

"Darrell Martinez is our new pack leader. He'll join you for supper once you are settled in." The werewolf led them up the stairs, the other pack member bringing up the rear.

Moira stared at hard, packed buns of steel as she followed Dante up the wide staircase. Bulging muscles flexed and long, thick legs moved with the grace of a deadly predator. Her mouth went dry watching and she forced her gaze from the too enticing view. No matter that this werewolf had stolen her from her life, the sight of him did some damned unnerving things to her body.

She fought to maintain focus. *Clear your mind. Block your thoughts. Use all that fucking training you've worked to master over the years.*

His all-male scent, still devoid of any emotion, tangled with her senses as they reached the top of the stairs.

"Give us a couple hours and I'll meet with your new pack leader." Dante put a possessive hand on her lower back, a small gesture claiming loudly to the other werewolves that she was his.

The action wasn't ignored. Both of them glanced at her and then looked away. She smelled respect and fear. Yes, fear. The smell of the emotion was almost overwhelming.

"The servants are here if you need anything," the werewolf who'd done all the speaking told them.

The other werewolf opened three doors in the hallway, inspecting each room with a glance and then standing back so they could enter.

"Well, I'm showering." Juan entered his room, looking over his shoulder. "I just know the feast you'll have for us will be magnificent. Can't wait to chow."

The two werewolves backed away, leaving them without further comment. The whole thing seemed rather strange. They were being treated like pack leaders. Yet the strongest sensation rippled through her, telling her that they wished the three of them weren't here. Moira headed toward the one room opposite the other two.

She reached for her doorknob, ready to close herself away in a private sanctuary and regroup her thoughts when Dante put his hand against her door, quietly pushing it open farther.

She fought to silence her thoughts and keep him out of her head.

Damn, that was hard to do when thousands of questions rushed through her.

Telling him to leave her would be a waste of words. Stepping to the side, he entered before her. When she thought of how many times she'd snuck into rooms, broken through doors to enter rooms, charged into rooms in full attack mode — the thought that these werewolves wanted to inspect where they put her seemed almost laughable.

"I expect you to run." He didn't ask her. It wasn't a question.

Dante pulled heavy curtains away from shiny glass, inspecting each window before letting the heavy fabric drop over the brief light that filled the room.

"Is that an order?" she mocked him. Cocking her head, watching his body move like a fine-tuned machine, she almost let her jaw drop when she smelled his amusement.

It was a rich, enticing scent, mixing so perfectly with his smell that she'd quickly grown accustomed to inhaling.

Apparently satisfied with the security of the windows, he turned, a small curve of the corner of his lips producing one hell of a sexy smile.

"Would you follow an order if I gave you one?" he asked.

"No." She didn't hesitate, although it crossed her mind to add that it would depend on what the order was. She held her tongue though.

"Shut the door, please."

She looked at the door behind her, sensing immediately that the small task was a test. The door being opened or shut would make little difference. No doubt existed that Dante would do as he pleased regardless. But she decided to humor him.

She hurried out the door and shut it behind her, unable to suppress her grin. Crossing the hall and entering the remaining bedroom, she closed the door quickly before he could follow. A small button in the doorknob hardly seemed lock enough to keep him from her.

She pushed it anyway.

Her heart raced in her chest, the fear of being caught any moment making her want to hurry with her actions. But what to do?

There wasn't time to form a plan.

The doorknob turned behind her, clicking, followed by the soft swoosh of wood over carpet as it swung open. She'd locked that door. Aggravation rushed through her and she turned around quickly, shoving her hair over her shoulder.

"It's polite to knock," she said, scowling.

"This is my room," Dante said, closing the door behind him. "But I have no problem sharing."

"Why is this your room?" She didn't see anything different about this room from the one they'd just been in.

"Because you're here," he said quietly, his hushed tone filled with promise.

He moved toward her silently, seeming almost to float rather than walk. He cleared the distance too easily. His deadly gaze, that body rippling with too much muscle, and the strong smell of lust that she was sure he intentionally allowed to cloud the room, left her breathless.

He grabbed her hair, tugging until her head fell back. Gripping her bodice between her breasts, he twisted the fabric in his fist, pulling her to him and lifting at the same time. He forced her onto tiptoe and captured her mouth.

A growl rumbled through him, not quite a human sound. It didn't matter that she'd let her guard down. Her mind was complete mush. Not one thought that made a damned bit of sense existed inside her.

She opened to him, unable, or perhaps unwilling, to resist his aggressive seduction. His tongue dipped into her mouth, exploring, probing, thrusting deep. He touched her shoulders, his hands on fire and branding her flesh. His fingers were strong, caressing and kneading her muscles, drawing forth the need in her that matched his.

Her lips were numb and swollen when his mouth left hers and created a hot, moist path to her neck.

"Moira," he uttered, his voice raspy.

Then he grabbed her dress at the shoulders and ripped it from her body.

"Good God!" She wasn't ready for that.

Her nipples hardened painfully, her breasts swelling with need at being suddenly exposed. He left her no reaction time. She stumbled back from his grasp, completely naked. The back of her legs brushed against the edge of the bed.

She said the first thing that came to mind. "You just destroyed my dress."

A minute or so to gather her thoughts, get her wits about her, would be nice. There was no way she'd calm the fever that burned her alive though. She wanted Dante too fucking much.

She shouldn't. He'd abducted her. He tortured her with his seduction. It was wrong to crave mounting and riding that hard cock of his.

He pulled his shirt over his head, giving her an eyeful of his strong, hairy chest. She about drooled.

"I figured it would slow down your escape attempt." He tossed the shirt behind him and reached for the button on his jeans.

She watched his long fingers move along his zipper and then push his jeans down his thighs. She swallowed, her throat suddenly thick and dry. It was hard as hell to keep her guard up with every inch of her throbbing. Curiosity bested her. She wanted to be with him, discover the truth of her dreams.

Damn it. He fascinated and challenged her. No werewolf got the best of her. But she damned sure wanted to see what the best of him might be like.

"A werewolf who can hide the smell of his lie shouldn't be trusted."

His gaze had rested on her breasts and he looked into her eyes quickly. "I can be trusted."

"You tore my dress from me because you want to fuck me, not to hinder my escape. I could run from here in my fur as easily as my feet."

"I could fuck you without taking off your dress." He stepped out of his jeans. "But I like how you look naked."

All thoughts of arguing with him disappeared when his magnificent cock appeared between them. She swallowed, her mouth way too dry.

It was hard as hell not to tell him she liked how he looked naked too. "Chasing after me with your cock that hard might prove a bit painful."

"Sounds like I'm going to have to do something to convince you not to run from me." He lowered his head as he spoke and then nipped at her lip.

A shiver rushed from her head to her toes. He nibbled his way to her chin, then down her neck. His cock throbbed between them, hardening and demanding attention. Her hands were on him before she thought about it. Hell. She wasn't thinking. That simply took too much effort at the moment.

She let her head fall back. Her hair brushed over her ass, tickling her. Later she'd deal with the consequences of her actions. For now, he'd created a fire inside her that burned out of control. His offer to extinguish it was too powerful to fight.

Moira fell back on to the bed. Or maybe she floated. Everything around her blurred. His hands were on her, taking control, and she wanted to enjoy it. She would enjoy it.

Besides, Dante wouldn't stop pursuing her until he had her. Once he did, possibly his guard would lower and then she could figure out what to do about him.

Chapter Eight

&

Moira stretched out on the bed, her hair falling over her dark skin, parting around her breasts and fanning across her belly. She put her arms over her head, gazing up at him with dark eyes. Tiny streaks of silver almost made them glow. Lust dripped from her so much it intoxicated him. Her smell was sweet, rich and stronger than it had been since they'd been together.

He didn't sense her blocking him out. If anything, she was more relaxed. But there were no thoughts to pick up. His own brain was stuck in overdrive, need coursing inside him at a dangerous speed. His heart thumped loud enough it surprised him the walls didn't shake.

"I'm not going to just fuck you." He had to know that she understood. "You are my mate."

He moved between her legs, standing at the edge of the bed, and leaned over her. Moira moved underneath him, twisting slightly while she reached for the headboard. She was fucking sexy as hell when she lazily raised her lashes. Looking up at him, it was as if she'd left him, her mind gone to some distant place and only her body stretched like an expert seductress underneath him.

"Wolf man, I might change my mind in a second," she murmured, her voice raspy and rough.

"There will be no going back." Something hardened inside him and he fought a stab of pain at the thought that after all these years she had the right to reject him.

The urge to let the subject drop and enjoy the moment irritated him.

"Tell me something I don't know." Her eyes fluttered shut and she lowered her arms, running her hands over her breasts and down her tummy.

He moved closer before he thought about it. He ran his tongue over her breast, swirling around her hard nipple and then capturing it between his teeth.

She arched into him, crying out and then grabbed his hair. Her fingers dragged over his scalp and pulled, drawing his more carnal side forward.

"Mate with me," he whispered, her breast filling his mouth.

"Are you asking?" She held his head to her breast.

Although he could force his head away if he wished, her grip tightened, his scalp stinging as she pinned him to her chest. The acute pain forced his heart to pump quicker and the blood to flow faster in his veins. His skin tingled, prickling from tiny hairs that popped through his flesh. The pressure in his jaw, in his gums when his teeth lengthened caused a ringing in his ears. He scraped his teeth over the tip of her nipple and she jumped from the sensation.

"Are you?" she persisted, pulling harder on his hair.

"Yes. Moira. Be my mate." He moved to her other breast, squeezing it and forcing her nipple to poke up, eager for his mouth.

"Then I'll think about it."

She wanted that power. He saw through her suddenly. Wherever her thoughts had gone, they suddenly returned. Pushing up her body, enduring the pain when she pulled harder on his hair as he moved from her breasts to her mouth, he devoured the taste of her. When she couldn't keep his mouth where she wanted it, she ran her hands down to his shoulder, scraping her nails over his flesh. Electric charges spurred the change to life inside him.

She'd fight for control with tooth, claw and her hot fucking body. Whatever it took, warring with him, distracting him with pain, with sensuality, she'd go to that extreme not to let go. Once, she'd lost everything. He saw into her mind, her torment and confusion. Submitting to him meant losing it again. She wouldn't let that happen. She fought for power over him.

For years, he'd dreamed of the day she'd belly-up to him and mate with him.

Moira couldn't give that to him.

Pain attacked his body.

Fighting it, he warred with her tongue. They moved around each other, swirling slowly and then with more fervor. Not only could he smell her lust, but it tasted sweeter than anything he'd ever imagined. He meant to distract her with the action but she kissed with so much passion it made it hard as hell to move into her mind, to see what she'd hidden behind clouds of lust a moment before.

She wanted him, needed him, ached to have him fuck her. A pressure grew painfully inside her, throbbing with a fury that matched the need flooding inside him.

But that was it. For now. He sensed her satisfaction with him asking for the mating. But she needed more. He should have known this about her. It made sense.

Moira needed love, knowledge that her commitment to her mate would be filled with happiness. She craved a den, a place of her own, an escape from the life she'd led since she'd escaped Malta.

Damn it. Why hadn't it occurred to him that Moira would want a place to settle down and call her den? She'd been a bitch on the run with no pack, no normal life, for all of her adult life. Dante was the last werewolf on the planet to offer a bitch a normal life.

His heart swelled, suddenly aching worse than his cock. Her fingers stroked his flesh, continuing to feed the fire burning inside him. She traced lines down his chest, reaching between them, and then wrapped her hands around his cock.

He broke the kiss, his teeth extended and puncturing his lip. The taste of blood fueled the beast inside him further. Lights sparkled before him like a thousand fireflies dancing before his eyes. He howled, feeling the bed shake underneath him, and pulled from Moira's mind quickly when the elements tore at his soul.

"I dreamed about this." Her voice sounded so far away.

But her touch, her fingers rubbing his shaft, was pulling all the blood from his body and making his cock swell furiously. She lifted her legs, clamping down against his outer thighs and raised her hips. She offered her pussy to him.

And damn it, he was just a werewolf. For years he'd believed Moira was his. *"When she's old enough to mate, you may have her. But you must seduce her, gain her willingness to be yours."* The old werewolf's words had hung heavy in his mind like a dark mantra over the years.

Werewolf tradition remained stronger in Europe than in America. Even over here, he'd believed once he'd convinced Moira of her sire's words, she'd accept it. He'd never had a moment's doubt.

Yet in these past few minutes, something had changed. He'd wanted more than sex from her—a commitment. And all she wanted was a good fucking. With all energy draining to his cock, he couldn't focus on what had altered in his world.

Hot, wet flesh brushed against his cock. Fire, needy and demanding, burned him to his soul.

Fuck Moira. Give her what she wants.

He fisted his hands on either side of her, holding himself up while his arms straightened and shook from the energy tearing at him. He pushed his cock against the entrance of her pussy, feeling her moist heat and almost dying from it.

"Yes," she whispered. "Please. Now."

That was all it took.

He glided quickly inside her, entering fast and hard, burying himself deep while tiny muscles constricted and caressed him in farther.

Every muscle in Moira's body spasmed. She screamed, grabbing his shoulders, digging her nails into his flesh and drawing blood as she scraped them over his back.

"Moira, damn it." His mouth didn't want to form words.

Moving quick and hard, his thrusts were met by anxious, hot muscles that almost suffocated him. She was fucking tight as hell. Tiny muscles vibrated and quivered around his cock. Her long, thick lashes fluttered over her partially changed eyes, which glowed with silver streaks as she looked up at him.

"Fuck me, wolf man," she purred, enticing and seductive.

"Believe me, little bitch, I plan on it." He straightened, using the sting from her nails to help clear the fog from his brain. "Who has fucked you before me?"

She stroked his back, his shoulders and his arms. Moving under him, she gave him a way to go even deeper, experience more of the intoxicating heat she offered. No bitch had ever been so tight, so on fire. She fit him like a glove—like she'd been made, designed, just for his cock.

She smiled, taunting him with her silence. A bit of sanity had returned to her brain as well, clearing her thoughts and allowing him to move inside her head. No image of another formed in her mind. There was no one she longed for. Damn good thing too. He didn't want her dwelling on another while he was buried deep inside her.

"Are you going to tell me the name of every bitch you've taken?" she asked finally, her voice strained.

"There is no one else," he muttered.

No one else mattered. Moira was here, underneath him, the sweet smell of her sex rising between them. God, she smelled good—fucking perfect.

Reaching for her legs, he spread them, holding her in place as he lifted her. He slowed the movement, focusing on how fantastic his cock looked covered with thick, white cream as it slowly slid out of her pussy. Her dark skin contrasted perfectly against his lighter skin. Her small body, every muscle tense, was an image of beauty—of a lost paradise he'd spent a lifetime finding and now had to claim as his own. She took quick breaths, her breasts rising and falling while her dark nipples puckered and formed small circles.

God, he could take her like this for hours, sliding in and out of her heat, feeling her muscles constrict and pulse against his cock.

When he slowed, dwelling on her heavy breathing while he fucked her, she managed to block his thoughts again.

"Don't," he growled and slammed into her with enough force to push her against the headboard.

Her pussy clamped down around him so hard it almost squeezed the life out of him.

"Oh fuck!" she screamed, reaching for him but grabbing air when he impaled her.

A rush of thoughts—need, excitement over how he made her feel, what he did to her—flushed through him. She'd let down her wall but stared at him wide-eyed, confused and unclear about what it was he didn't want her to do.

He'd make it real clear.

His cock was so swollen that moving slow blurred his vision. He gritted his teeth and endured it so he could speak. "Don't close me out of your mind again."

"Then I want in, too."

This was part of the commitment she needed from her mate. And it was no less than what he demanded from her. Trust. The only way to get it was to offer it.

He pulled out of her, his cock instantly cold and craving the wet heat again.

"Come here." He grabbed her, yanking her off the bed and flipping her over. He gripped her hips and pulled her to her hands and knees. Without hesitating, he thrust deep into her cunt. Fire burned him alive. "Fuck!" he screamed and pounded hard into her hot, wet pussy. "Enter my mind, sweet, adorable bitch," he whispered against her shoulder. "Feel my thoughts even without seeing me. Know who I am and let me know you."

Her ass was covered with her come, shiny and wet. He knelt behind her while her black hair streamed down her narrow back and fanned over her like a magnificent cape.

"You think you already own me," she gasped, slowly raising her head, arching her back farther, while she made an effort to look over her shoulder at him. "But you never will, not even if I agree to be your mate. Know that now, wolf man. We are equals on all levels."

Words of sharing, thoughts of trust, were as wonderful as fucking her was. But the meaning behind all of it would only come with time. And they would have that. He admitted that he hadn't thought it through when he'd demanded that fucking her would bond them for life.

"As equals, we will own each other." He slid deeper inside her, feeling his cock threaten to swell.

Her entire body began shaking and her arms gave out underneath her as she howled. Charged sensations like electrical currents ripped through his body when she convulsed underneath him. Moira made the most incredible whimpering sound when she exploded, her orgasm hitting her hard and tearing through her.

Traditionally, in the eyes of any pack, they were now mates, although tradition wasn't held on to as strongly over the past century. Few entered into mating as virgins. Nonetheless, there were no marriages like humans performed. The ceremony consummating a mating was private, between werewolf and bitch. Although it was a tradition so many werewolves ignored these days, making love was enough to mate two werewolves. And he knew in Moira's heart, he now held a rank and position that hadn't been there before. But the true bond, the dedication to each other for life, hadn't been formed. Not yet. And simply because she'd said as much, that she hadn't agreed yet to the mating. In his heart they were mated, but she demanded equality, and truth be told, he wouldn't want his demanding little bitch any other way.

That's why when his cock swelled, preparing to trap him inside her, he pulled out, depriving both of them from the awesome aftermath of damn good sex. He left her heat, feeling like he'd deserted her when she needed him most.

This is what she asked for though. And it was no less than what he demanded. A commitment. A mating. She wanted trust, love, a den to call her own. It would take some work to give that but she'd get what she wanted. As his mate, Moira would know happiness. And that's why he spilled his come on her back, loving how the thick, white cream dripped over her caramel-colored flesh. Its salty smell mixed with the smell of their lust.

Moira would commit to him, submit and openly say the mating stood. But until then, he wouldn't sanctify their mating by coming inside her.

She collapsed on the bed, not saying a word and not blocking him out when she mentally praised him for fucking her so well.

* * * * *

Darrell Martinez was a tall, well-built young Mexican werewolf. Barely out of the den, the pup was hyper, anxious to show how he'd taken control of his pack. Dante didn't find a lot in the werewolf's mind. He was all brawn and little brain.

"So you're the pack destroyer." Darrell spoke with a thick accent and his thoughts were in Spanish.

Dante bristled, facing the pack leader on the large brick terrace outside the back of the mansion. Darrell's two men who'd joined them outside gave him the once-over, as if putting to memory what a pack destroyer would look like.

"I'm Dante Aldo," he corrected the pack leader. He elaborated. "I haven't given myself that label."

A pack destroyer?

The tiny hairs on the back of his neck and down his spine straightened. Moira asked the question, but not so anyone else heard. She spoke in his mind. He didn't look over his shoulder where she sat. After dining and at the request that they all enjoy the cool evening outside, he'd escorted Moira to the terrace and stationed her at the edge along the brick wall. She reclined in one of white iron chairs, away from the other werewolves, her slender legs draped over the armrest. The only female present, she'd be seen and not heard while they discussed business. With the way she looked, she was most definitely being noticed. She didn't argue yet another age-old tradition, although she didn't hesitate to question him clearly in his head.

"You grace us with your presence. I suppose now is when we learn why?" Darrell was pushy, more than likely a bully who'd wiped out the other alphas to gain control of his pack.

He pissed Dante off with his sarcastic tone. And he did it on purpose, foolishly thinking with his omnipotent youthful attitude that he could take Dante on.

"We need a place to stay for a few days without a lot of attention." Being clear and straight to the point would work best with this werewolf. "Your pack and this location works well for me."

He ignored the low growl of disapproval that rumbled from one of Darrell's mutts who hovered behind him. Sipping his beer, Dante walked past them, staring at the white cliffs that provided natural protection from the rest of the world. And he knew they'd left little to no trail that could be sniffed out. After a few days he'd sniff around, get a feel for how GWAR and WA were reacting to Moira disappearing.

Then they'd make their next move. Already Juan worked the streets of Albuquerque, learning what he could about what gossip might be drifting through the werewolf grapevine about them.

Darrell muttered something in Spanish to his werewolves who immediately rumbled their disapproval. Darrell wanted to speak with Dante alone. Neither one of the werewolves wanted Darrell to approve their stay. They feared Dante. A common reaction he got out of most packs. Darrell growled louder, hissing his order for them to get the fuck out and let him speak to Dante alone. The two of them stomped off the terrace, entering the home like two pups throwing a fit for being sent to bed early.

Darrell stared at Moira, definitely enjoying the view. She wore a sleeveless shirt and no bra. Her narrow shoulders and long, slender neck showed off how petite she was. She'd found her way downstairs after he did, joining them to eat. She'd twisted her long, thick black hair into a knot behind her head. Silky strands drifted around her face, highlighting her regal high cheekbones. She was the daughter of one of their kind's greatest leaders, purebred royalty—and by right, completely his.

Moira raised the corner of her lip and growled at Darrell, giving the pack leader absolutely no respect in his own territory. Darrell took a step toward her and Dante moved forward. Darrell hesitated, finally looking away from the bitch and focusing his attention on Dante.

Although he'd made no formal announcement that Moira was his mate, he knew his scent was on her. Darrell would prove even more stupid than he'd originally thought if he made a move on Moira.

"Why are you here?" Darrell puffed out his chest and fisted his hands on his hips. There was no fear on the young punk. The werewolf didn't trust him though.

"We're deciding what part of the country we'll settle in. A few days here should be long enough for us to decide if this place suits us."

Moira raised an eyebrow and her mouth parted before she closed it quickly. She stood and moved to the low brick wall bordering the terrace, brushing her hand over the smooth surface before plopping her cute ass down on it. Darrell didn't turn to give her any attention so he didn't notice Moira's surprise. She looked down, wiggling her toes through her sandals and stared at them.

He won't accept you in his pack. Her words were like music in his mind, warm, wrapping around his own. And she'd kept her end of the deal so far not to close her mind to him. She was obviously enjoying her newfound talent of mixing with his thoughts. *And what do you mean by settle down?*

"And what would you do in this pack? I won't have any pack destroyer in my territory."

"Your pack is safe from me as long as you don't do me wrong."

What a bully. She chuckled, the sound dripping through him like a sweet, torturous drug. May she never learn what her thoughts in his head did to him.

Darrell glanced over at Moira then turned from both of them, pacing the length of the brick terrace and then back. He crossed his arms over his chest, a silent statement that he knew Dante wouldn't attack him. His body language showed all signs of confidence but his mind was a whirlwind of doubt and animosity. The only problem was that he thought so quickly in Spanish that Dante could barely keep up. The predominant message was clear—he didn't trust Dante.

"You may stay in this house for two days," he decided, staring Dante in the eye. "I'll have no trouble—none. Is that clear?"

"Offer none and you'll get none," Dante told him honestly.

Darrell moved quickly, jumping into Dante's face. "Disrespect me and you won't be here two hours," he growled, his Spanish accent thickening as the putrid smell of anger laced the air.

Dante glared at him. "A title doesn't gain a werewolf respect if he acts like a fool."

The glass doors leading into the house flew open at that moment. Dante didn't take his attention from Darrell when the werewolf spun around, startled and wired enough to leap at the disturbance. His two werewolves almost fell through the door, Juan with them. The three of them let out a spew of profanity, yelling and growling at each other until Darrell yelled at the three of them.

"What the hell is this?" he demanded.

Juan jumped away from the other two werewolves. Shrugging to straighten his shirt, he glanced toward Dante. His comical expression would fool many, and although he didn't possess any of the gift, he was damned good at covering hostile emotions with amusement. Which more often than not in the past usually had the two of them in fights.

"He insisted on coming out here," one of the werewolves told his pack leader. "We told him you were in a private meeting and if we couldn't be out here, neither could he."

Juan turned to Moira. "No one keeps me away from a beautiful bitch," he said gallantly and moved to stand by her side.

Darrell pointed a thick finger at Dante. "Two days," he told him and then moved faster than Dante would have guessed his thick, short legs could travel as he stalked into the house.

Hostility and outrage lingered in the air after the three werewolves left them on the terrace.

"I don't think we should stay here for two days," Juan said quietly the second the glass doors closed behind the werewolves.

Moira leaned on the four-foot brick wall that surrounded the terrace, her hands flat on the smooth surface on either side of her. She didn't look up but stared at the concrete ground in front of her, long, silky strands escaping the twisted knot behind her head and drifting over her shoulders with the breeze. They blocked a clear view of her face.

Dante quickly searched his half-brother's thoughts. Juan had learned something when he'd begged off after dinner to return to his room for a shower before a late-night run. The werewolf was damned good at snooping and enjoyed doing it. Most of the time he didn't get caught.

His thoughts were muddled, overlapping each other, which was common for Juan.

"Why is that?" Dante asked, tilting his head to try and get a better view of Moira's face. She continued to focus on the ground.

"Someone has contacted WA asking about you. We've got trouble headed our way. I can smell it." Juan kept his voice low. "No matter your reputation, you can't fight off all of WA."

Chapter Nine

ಐ

Moira moved through strong emotions, which made the air feel tighter. She fought to concentrate. Leaving her body alone on the terrace with Juan and Dante out there wouldn't be safe after a few minutes. She gave the werewolves credit for having enough sense to figure out something was wrong with her if she didn't move or speak for long.

The moment the glass doors banged open, she'd picked up bad vibes. She smelled them, felt them, knew something wasn't right. With all the commotion and testosterone hanging heavy in the air, she'd leapt out of her body and sped into the house, searching for information—anything. She'd left the shell of herself sitting out on the terrace, a very dangerous act with so many werewolves around, but something she had to do. Staying out of her body for too long could prove deadly if Darrell or one of his mutts came back and tried talking to her. But she needed answers.

And it hadn't taken long to find them.

The large mansion was either the pack leader's den or a central location where he and his mutts hung out. Either way, there were a hell of a lot of werewolves on the premises. More than she'd realized at first. The walls were thick and large and potted plants had been chosen intentionally for their strong aromas, making it harder to smell out who might be in the next room. A clever ploy, and one she doubted that numbskull of a pack leader she'd met had anything to do with.

Moving through walls disoriented her. She preferred not messing with molecular structures and risking getting her own thoughts all screwed up. But once she was in the house, hurrying from one room to the other, it hadn't taken long to find a small group of werewolves huddled in an office full of computers.

"Darrell needs to just kick them all out of here," a short Mexican werewolf said. He leaned on a cluttered desk, looking down at the monitor while a younger werewolf typed with obvious expertise.

"You don't just send Dante Aldo packing." The younger werewolf sniffed the air, glanced around at the three other males lingering behind him and then looked back at the monitor. "He makes me nervous though. Everyone has a record of some sort and I can't find shit on him."

"Don't waste your time. He's like a ghost."

"He destroys packs. And more than likely with WA's approval," the fat werewolf said.

"Watch how loud you say that," an older werewolf, his silver hair falling in strings over his weathered face, scowled at the lot of them and glanced toward the door nervously.

Moira hovered toward it just in case he decided to close it. As much as she ached to hear more about Dante, she didn't want to end up trapped in here with her body out there with Dante. That would be bad.

"He destroys more than packs." A fourth werewolf, who wasn't half bad-looking in his muscle T-shirt with tattoos covering his thick arms, kept his voice at a whisper and glanced over his shoulder before going on. "He wiped out an entire race of werewolves over in Europe. Then he comes here and goes wherever he's needed, destroying packs who get out of line."

"That's just not possible." The younger werewolf at the computer tried another search engine, typing in something and waiting for the site to load. "No one werewolf can take out a pack. I need proof."

"You can smell the power on him, Jorge. Not all proof is in your computer there. They say he's more than a werewolf. *El es magico*," the older werewolf said.

"Well, I've got some proof on at least one of them. Check this out. That little bitch out there is with GWAR."

The werewolves moved closer, hovering around the screen. She ignored the crude comments they made about her.

Moira backed out of the room slowly, then turned and flew through the house. She wouldn't risk trying to go through the now-closed glass doors but found an open window in the kitchen. Hurrying around the house toward the brick terrace, she sank into her body, instantly feeling the hard pounding of her heart. She almost coughed on her first breath.

"Is that a yes or a no?" Juan laughed and nudged her arm.

Moira stared at him, not having a clue what the question was. He was quite amused by her, his grin adding to the thoughts of envy and curiosity as to how far Dante had made it with her and if she would be Dante's mate or not. She sucked in a breath, unable to do anything more than stare into his handsome face. Holy shit! His thoughts had spilled out of him as clearly as if he'd just spoken to her. Before Dante, that had never happened to her before. She swallowed, and closed her mouth, realizing it had been gaping open.

"I'm not sure," she mumbled, more than disoriented by Juan's thoughts and the knowledge she'd just gained.

Apparently Juan had it in his head that she was supposed to be Dante's mate. That backed what Dante had told her, although at the moment that was the least of her worries.

How the hell could she mate with someone who was known for destroying her pack?

For the life of her, even though she hadn't known Dante that long, she had a hard time believing it was true. It wouldn't be the first time a werewolf took a false rumor and built on it to make themselves seem more than what they were. But if Dante had done that, allowed packs to believe he'd destroyed the Malta werewolves, how could she lay her kill at his paws?

It wasn't the first time she'd despised the fact that GWAR made it a point to keep its agents in the dark when it came to common pack knowledge. The only information she was supposed to have in her head was facts about the mission she was on. GWAR believed its agents would work at their best if they had no outside knowledge that might sway their opinion on how they were supposed to do things. She'd been trained to act on orders and let WA worry about the rest of the world.

"Don't believe everything you hear," Dante said quietly, pulling her out of her panicked thoughts.

"What did she hear?" Juan looked around the terrace. He frowned at Dante and then looked at Moira. "Do you want to go on a run now or not?"

For the moment, the three of them were alone. Moira didn't look at Dante but glanced at the windows, then up at the walls searching for any surveillance equipment that wouldn't be easily sniffed out. A camera was fixed to the wall just above the windows at the edge of the terrace. More than likely it was equipped with a microphone too.

She wouldn't insult Dante by implying he had no idea what she might have heard. She stood, straightening her shirt and moved away from both of them.

"I'm going to my room."

"It's almost dark. You can join us on a run and then we'll go to our rooms." Dante didn't make it sound like a question.

She finally met his gaze, reaching out to his thoughts. More than anything she wanted to find proof inside him that everything she'd just heard was wrong.

He locked on to her gaze, seeming to pull her into his head as if he greeted the opportunity for her to see what was in his mind. She remembered watching pack members turn to watch the RV when they'd drove into town. They all knew about Dante Aldo, knew who he was. Quite honestly, she'd never been matched up against such a powerful werewolf before. And it didn't help that his scent did a number on her insides. Just staring at him increased the heavy thud of her heart, made her pulse pound between her legs.

God. If she weren't careful, the smell of her lust would drown all three of them out.

"Let's go," Dante stressed, taking her arm and guiding her toward the edge of the terrace.

When they reached the edge of the yard, Dante wrapped his arm around her waist, pulling her against his hard body while they slowed their pace.

He looked down at her. "Maybe you'd like to talk about what you just learned?"

"What did she find out?" Juan asked, surprised. "She was on the terrace or with you. When did Moira learn anything?"

Dante held his hand up, silencing Juan. He continued to stare at her. She had half a mind to play stupid and second what Juan had just said. But she demanded trust from him. And she would give him what she expected in return.

His pale blue eyes turned fluorescent as he stared at her. Heat burned her insides. He knew she'd moved through the house. Obviously, telling her how he knew didn't seem important to him. If her body had given away the absence of her spirit, then Juan would be wise to it as well. Yet he wasn't.

What she wouldn't do to learn the extent of Dante's abilities. He knew how to read her thoughts, knew when she left her body—what else could he do? Besides turn her into a puddle of boiling hot need and lust.

She looked past him toward the house. They were probably out of earshot from any werewolves who might be outside, and she didn't smell any. She chewed her lip. Trust wasn't something she knew how to give.

"I don't know anything, really," she said quietly without looking at either one of them. "It bothers me that you're known as a pack destroyer whose claim to fame is destroying my pack."

"I didn't destroy your pack," he answered without hesitation.

Silence grew between the three of them. Long, dark shadows stretched beyond the surrounding cliffs. A breeze picked up, too warm to cool her face. The shrubbery and flowers planted around the large house had strong scents, which would easily distract anyone from a werewolf's scent unless that person paid close attention.

"He didn't destroy the Malta werewolves," Juan added with emphasis. "They aren't destroyed."

She looked up at Juan quickly.

"What he means is that there are still members alive. I've been searching, working to reunite us." The way he said *us* broke some barrier inside Moira.

"How many are alive?" She relaxed against his steely body, looking into those intense pale blue eyes that seemed able to drag her mind into his.

He shook his head slowly. "I honestly don't know."

"Well, I know that Darrell Martinez contacted WA. A couple of their agents are headed this way." Juan turned his attention to Dante.

"Moira and I will head out from here in our fur," Dante decided. "I want you to take off in the RV. No one will question you driving away right now alone. Tell them you're heading to the bar or something. We'll meet up at the Colorado line."

"So we're going to run." Juan wasn't pleased with the idea. His dark eyes pierced her, his disapproval smelling sour. "You've never run from anyone, brother. I hope she's worth it."

"And you've never doubted me." Dante's tone turned harder than stone.

Moira stared from one werewolf to the other. So much alike, yet so different. Juan met Dante's gaze, not backing down although he didn't have half the strength or confidence.

He trusted Dante though. Juan was confused. The questions he wanted to ask were so easy to read it was as if he'd spoken them out loud. She bit her lip so that she wouldn't remind him that she hadn't asked to be part of this little trio.

"That's because you've been a levelheaded bastard. Now I wonder if you're thinking with the right head."

Dante growled, stepping into Juan's personal space. Moira took a step backward without thinking, smelling the animosity that somehow she knew wasn't a common scent for these two to display toward each other.

"Go get the fucking RV," Dante growled, growing before her eyes. Anger seeped from him, making the air so spicy she fought the urge to sneeze. "And if you walk into that den down there with the smell of doubt on you, they will be on to us in a heartbeat. Do you feel me on this?"

"Whatever." Juan backed down, turning without looking at her and stomping back toward the mansion.

Moira let out a slow sigh and then shook her head. An electrical charge attacked the air around her. Something raw, untamed and bordering on violent crackled around her. It raised the hairs on her arms, made the back of her neck tingle.

She stared after Juan until he bounded up onto the brick terrace and then disappeared through the sliding glass doors into the mansion. The animosity that had clogged the air moments ago was drowned out by the electricity that almost raised the hair off her shoulders. She rubbed her arms, glancing sideways at Dante.

"The last time we were here, there was a different pack leader. He had my back." It was the only explanation Dante offered before placing his hand on her lower back and guiding her away from the house.

"Do you really believe we can outrun WA?" She reached out, but the charged air made it hard to search his mind for the answer before he offered it to her.

And he didn't answer right away. They walked in silence until she knew without looking that no one from the mansion could see them.

"I know with some effort I can convince them to leave you with me," he said finally. "That is, if they find us."

The meadow they'd walked through had turned rocky. Almost on hands and knees, they climbed a rugged hill until white rock surrounded them. He stopped, long shadows ready to fade into nightfall making his brooding expression border on dangerous. His eyes glowed almost silver while a slight breeze lifted his black hair from his neck. He stared down at her, not speaking but searching her face.

His touch forced the electricity out of the air. Her skin still tingled but no longer from an unknown source. He brushed her flesh, his rough fingertips making her insides flip-flop as he stroked her cheek then ran a line along her jawbone. Heat scoured her in spite of the cooling temperature as nighttime took over.

She didn't want to lust after him, didn't want to crave his touch elsewhere on her body. Her breasts swelled and her pussy throbbed. She fought for control, though, and wrinkled her brow as she concentrated on not letting him make her yearn for him to fuck her again.

"Why do you allow everyone to call you a pack destroyer?" she asked, nibbling her lower lip.

"Moira. Not once have I given any impression to any werewolf that I destroyed the Malta werewolves. The rumors grew from my ability to help packs in the States who were being pushed around, or who couldn't get WA to help them when they were almost wiped out. More than anything, I've fought to make sure no other pack would lose everything the way your sire's pack did."

"Then why do werewolves think you destroyed my pack?"

Dante shrugged. "It came with the territory. I doubt you'll hear any werewolf with any knowledge suggest it's true. It took several packs united to bring your sire down. No one werewolf could have ever taken him out."

He grabbed her arm so that he pinned her in front of him. Pulling her closer, his mouth was just over hers and his gaze devoured her as he spoke.

"The wrong people had learned about the gift. Bruno made the werewolves of Malta strong. He accomplished his dream and offered it to everyone around him. Your sire was the greatest werewolf I've ever known, selfless and powerful. But he saw what would happen. I was there—with both of them. Your parents knew the gift would be abused and would destroy our kind—but once they realized this it was too late.

"Moira, if I could have saved your pack, believe me, I would have. We were simply outnumbered by too many packs—packs backed by the government to destroy something they couldn't control."

"So you've used this misguided reputation to help others when they've been bullied or attacked by surrounding packs?"

"That and the gift," he told her, brushing his lips over hers.

His cock hardened between them, lengthening against her. It stole her breath, reminding her of how he'd made her feel. Not that she'd been able to forget the way he'd fucked her—and had pulled out—robbing her of complete satisfaction. It had also been a silent assurance that he wouldn't bond them together until she agreed with what he claimed already to be the truth.

He let go of her hair, releasing his hold on her, but didn't move away. Instead he stroked the sides of her head, petting her. He was too damned good at making her pant for him.

The desire to belly-up, to surrender to his will and beg him to soothe the fire he'd started inside her took over her ability to think straight. He no longer kept her pinned to him, yet she didn't move. Their bodies touched, heat climbing between them as the night grew colder. She stared at the top of his T-shirt. His neck was thick and his skin creamy white. If she stared long enough she was sure she'd see his veins pulse with life under his skin. Dante was strong, powerful and confident in the knowledge he possessed. And he didn't run without purpose, without direction. No one gave this werewolf orders. Dante did what he wanted.

How long had she craved a life like that?

Trust me, little bitch. His words floated to her, inside her, consuming her.

"I want to," she whispered, answering his thought out loud.

"Moira." He said her name on a growl and goose bumps made the hair on her body stand on end. It wasn't from some electrical charge in the air though, but rather how he said her name. He pushed his thumbs under her chin, tilting her head. "Look at me."

She did. His eyes were like rare jewels in the darkness. Black eyebrows bordered their light color, making him look even more intense. Other than his physical appearance, the way he spoke and touched her filled her with hot sensations, had her teetering on the edge. Desire, anticipation and fear swam around inside her. She fought to clear her mind, to stare up at him and see inside and beyond the sexy package displayed for her.

"Imagine you and me working together to reunite the Malta werewolves, make them stronger and respected once again."

"Is that why you want me as your mate?" she asked, her tummy suddenly twisting.

She sensed his answer before he slowly shook his head. Emotions strong enough to once again charge the air around them made her tingle from head to toe.

"No," he whispered, his voice cracking. "At first I wanted you because I believed you more beautiful than any other bitch I'd ever seen. As the years dragged by and I watched you from a distance, that craving grew because I saw your strength, how damned good you were at everything you did. Now that you're with me, I want you because you're better than anything I've imagined. And honestly, Moira, I'm scared to death you'll refuse me and leave me."

Shit. If his emotions peaked any harder, the sparks in the air would ignite into flame. Her cheeks got hot and the flush spread over her neck then filled her body. No werewolf had ever spoken such words to her. Dante was an intense alpha, strong enough to guide packs instead of simply leading just one. And that he'd humbled himself, spoken out loud his feelings instead of relaxing his mind and letting her dig through his thoughts to find them, made him an even stronger werewolf.

She fought the urge to cry, to wrap her arms around his neck and let him know how good he'd just made her feel. She cleared her throat quickly. "Why didn't either one of them tell me that they'd agreed to a mating?"

"Would you have accepted it if they had?"

She shook her head immediately. "I would have told them to go to hell," she said sadly, her heart breaking that they weren't with her now so she could yell at them and then privately confess they'd done a hell of a job in finding her one of the sexiest werewolves alive. Well…maybe she would have told her mother that. Definitely not her sire.

"I wanted to be the one to tell you." He stepped back from her and removed his shirt.

Black, curly hair covered bulging muscle. Her mouth went dry as she stared at his naked torso. But Dante didn't undress for sex. His movements were methodical, precise. He put his shirt right-side out after pulling it from his body. Then he folded it and rolled it tightly. Next, he reached for his belt.

He undressed in order to change and prepared his clothes to carry while he was in his fur. She watched him strip until he stood before her naked. She made no attempt to remove her own clothing.

"Undress," he ordered, ignoring her as she stared at his rock-hard cock which thrust toward her.

Magnificent and terrifying, even naked as a human male, Dante moved with more confidence than some of the best-trained agents she'd worked with. His body was sculpted perfection. His arms and legs were thick with muscle and he was tall—so damned tall.

But his cock. The way it stood out, proud and strong. Dante didn't hide how turned on he was. It didn't bother him a bit that his raging hard-on distracted her to the point where she couldn't move. He stood there, tying his clothes together until he'd created a collar out of them and then tied them around his neck.

"You're going to have a hard time keeping up with me in your skin," he said, not looking up.

"You'll fuck me in my fur." Animal instinct prevailed over human rationale.

"Probably." His arm muscles bulged when he adjusted a knot behind his neck and secured his clothes to him.

She tried swallowing the knot in her throat. It struck her at that moment that they prepared to run for their safety—for her freedom. Yet until this moment, worrying about any of that had been the last thing on her mind. All of her attention focused on Dante. His past, what he'd done, what he would do—that's what mattered. Fear for her life or what WA might do hadn't crossed her mind.

And that's because she was safe. Beyond a shadow of doubt she knew that while she was with Dante, there was nothing to worry about. Well—maybe what he might do to her. But even then, that didn't make her nervous. It sent a chill of excited anticipation rushing from her head to toes.

She did trust him.

And she wanted more knowledge, wanted to know every little detail about him. Not the rumors, but what was in his head. His thoughts, his plans, his intentions.

Slowly she pulled her dress over her head, hoping her body would distract him as much as his nudity made her crazy. She stepped out of her shoes, standing still so the rocky ground wouldn't puncture her human feet.

A cold breeze attacked her flesh, hardening her nipples while she shivered almost uncontrollably. She fought to focus on the breeze. In her mind, she visualized it carrying her thoughts so that they would blend with his.

"Let me help you with that." Dante was closer than she realized and she jumped, shrinking back into her mind.

Dante took her dress from her and ran it through the straps of her shoes. Then twisting the material, he created a collar for her. His gaze locked on to hers as he wrapped it around her neck.

"Your trust in me will never be betrayed," he whispered, lowering his head to hers and brushing their lips together.

He'd been in her mind. When she'd hoped her body would distract him, he'd taken the moment and explored her thoughts.

"I hope not," she said, her voice thick with need.

His cock throbbed between them, hard and ready. Her insides swelled. Lust made the air thick and sweet and blew around them with growing energy. He nibbled on her lower lip and then sucked it into his mouth while his fingers stroked and tickled the back of her neck until he had her clothes secured. Carefully, he pulled her hair free from the bun it was in, lifting her thick, long strands off her back and then letting them fall. Her hair tickled her back, swaying against her ass. She inhaled the mixture of their raw, carnal desire and shivered. God, it was all she could do not to beg him to fuck her right now.

And more than likely he was in her head, knowing what she ached to have before she even voiced it.

"Change, little bitch," he said, and his teeth grew, scraping her lips.

This time she followed his instruction, needing out of her skin. Her mind was a whirlwind of thoughts, swimming into each other. Releasing pent-up energy, becoming whole and strong, allowed her freedom to let go of worries and uncertainties that would make her nuts in her human form. Changing into a werewolf freed her of her limitations.

The sweet pain of change. What a wonderful gift.

A gift as blessed as the one her parents had given her. The hard rock underneath her bare feet, the cold breeze that wrapped around her body and the fire that consumed her insides along with the rushing sound in her head, like water, combined all the elements before her.

One with the elements, carry me. Show me all and all I will see. She repeated the words her mother used to say, words meant only to help Moira learn how to use her gift. Little did her mom know that whenever Moira thought of the simple phrase, it brought her mother back to her—sometimes with so much strength she swore Renee stood next to her, smiling confidently and nodding that everything would be okay. And for a moment, while the change boiled to life inside her, she swore a dark shadow leapt to the side of her, gone before Moira could focus on it.

Dante roared as the change took over him. She blinked, too focused on her muscles contorting, her bones popping and her vision altering while blood rushed hard and fast through her veins. His barrel chest grew even thicker while his arms became shorter. Thick black hair covered his bare flesh and his spine changed until he could no longer stand on two feet.

Grabbing hold of the moment, she relished her body transforming and released her mind to the wind. Before her eyes, Dante changed into a deadly and ferocious-looking creature. He was stunningly beautiful in his fur, captivating.

Her tongue thickened when she ran it over her shrinking lips, tasting hair instead of flesh. As she fell forward, the skin of her hands thick enough that the hard, rocky ground didn't hurt them, she leapt into his mind, aching to experience him in his purer form.

Strength, clean and pure and in its rawest state, closed in around her. Confidence, untamed and aggressive, exploded when her thoughts became one with his. She witnessed Dante naturally, uninhibited. What made him a man coexisted with the ferocious werewolf who towered over her. She wanted more than his primal instincts. She found intelligence and intense satisfaction that all around him would submit to his will. Daring to reach further, she relaxed into his thoughts, struggling to hear what was on his mind.

Safety – protect Moira – cross the state line – gather the pack – protect – make Moira mine.

His last thought hit her as if he'd whispered it into her ear, tickling her insides. Quickly she gathered her own thoughts, retreated into her body and sucked in a breath that captured every scent surrounding them. No longer did darkness shroud them. Her sight strengthened, making her able to see into the night. She picked up smells around them, wildlife, every plant growing, every emotion coming from Dante.

A wild energy coursed in her veins. She wanted to run, to fly, to relieve herself of the emotions and sensations that attacked from every direction. Her heart beat inside her, matching the throbbing between her legs. Her need smelled rich, creamy, hanging heavily in the air between them.

He growled. The rumble made the ground shake underneath her. Lowering his head, he pierced her with silver eyes shaped like almonds. They glowed against his thick black coat. He looked like her in his fur, giving proof that their heritage was similar. Thick, straight black fur covered his barrel chest and fell from his body, although not to the ground as hers did. They were beautiful creatures. Her heart constricted knowing her breed now was labeled as extinct. But they weren't. She stood before Dante, proof that her kind lived. And there were others. They would find them together. Living extinct, yet strong and powerful and ready to take on whoever might get in their way.

He nudged her, his long, thick tail swaying behind him, and then leapt up the rocks. Moira followed, infatuated by his scent, feeling the power inside her grow as they picked up speed and tore over the rocky ground. Muscles rippled under shiny fur. The moonlight glowed over his coat, making his black hair look like it was smoothed down with some kind of gel. It glimmered as roped muscles glided back and forth under his flesh. She was transfixed, unable to do anything else other than race after him, following him over rocky inclines and through meadows.

At least several hours later—she wasn't sure of the time other than by looking at the moon which now hovered high above them—Dante slowed, panting heavily. When he sniffed the air, stretching his neck and searching their surroundings, his profile looked strong. He was a predator who would conquer and take all that he felt was his.

Her heart thudded heavily in her chest. After running for so long, she'd never been more invigorated. Energy burned inside her. She watched Dante and lust took over. Wherever they were, they were very much alone. Mountains surrounded them. The air was crisp and clean—other than the growing smell of her need.

Mate with Moira. His thought still tumbled around in her mind. She knew what fucking him in her fur would mean. They would be bonded—for life. No other werewolf would touch her. Dante's scent would enter her, brand her, make her his bitch. And he would be her werewolf.

I already am yours and have been for years now, my beautiful, precious bitch.

She willed her heart to slow, looking up at his silver eyes that glowed as powerfully as the moon, and saw the truth of his words there.

A low rumble, not quite a growl—more like a promise—sealed his thoughts. Slowly he circled her, giving her all of his attention. Obviously he'd determined this location was safe. And now he would have her. She'd have to put up one hell of a fight right now, more than likely change, in order to prevent him from fucking her.

She ran her tongue over her long, sharp teeth, turning her head to keep him in her sight when he moved around her. He circled her and then ran his thick tongue over her coat. Rough and wet, he stroked her fur, tasting her. First the side of her face, then her shoulders. He licked her side and then pushed his cool, wet nose under her tail.

She lifted it for him and he pressed into her heat. Then his tongue stroked her pussy. Sensations flooded her insides. She yelped, feeling silly but praying he'd do it again.

Tingles tickled her hide. His thick, long tongue tortured her cunt, robbing her ability to think straight. She panted while energy that continued to build, to create a pressure deep inside her, ached to break free. He hit her most sensitive areas, spots in this form that had never been touched before.

Her legs weakened, turning shaky. When he penetrated her, thrusting his tongue deep inside her tight little hole, she fell forward.

Shit. Oh shit! she yelped, rolling over quickly and spreading her legs. She offered her belly. Dante grinned down at her, his large fangs glowing in the darkness.

You honor me with your submission. His words were rough in her head, more like a growl. She panted so hard, unable to move, to stand, to do anything but look up at the glorious creature who had just told her that he was honored by her actions.

And all she'd done was fall on her ass.

Honor me and give me more. She swore he laughed at her words. When he lowered his head, pressing his rock-hard skull against her pelvic bone, she shivered, anticipation making her giddy.

His tongue worked magic on her pussy. He lapped and stroked, probed and licked. Those long teeth scraped over her, adding to the thrill of the moment. Nothing had ever felt so incredibly wonderful in her entire life.

He lifted his head, his muzzle soaked from her juices, and moved over her. Long, thick black hair made it harder to see his cock. When he lowered his mouth to hers, running his wet tongue over her face, she managed to glimpse between his legs.

Oh damn!

His cock hung hard and long, pointing at her, almost looking more like a deadly weapon than something that would give her pleasure.

It took him a minute to position himself. The tip of his cock pressed against her pussy. Her juices helped moisten him and he thrust inside her with eager energy that almost sent her sliding across the ground. His front paws, on either side of her shoulders, stopped her escape, and he buried his cock deep inside her heat.

She howled, surprised at how big he was. She took him in though, all of him, and instantly he hit the spot that needed him most. Wave after wave of pleasure surged inside her, building and crashing as it took her over the edge. The rich smell of sex, intoxicating and pungent, wrapped around them. She wanted more.

She couldn't move, but Dante had no problem taking over and building the momentum. She held her paws in front of her face, wishing she had hands to hold his face.

Relax, little bitch. The first time will be quite an experience for you.

She didn't understand why he warned her. They'd fucked before, and although she'd never fucked a werewolf while in her fur, she didn't see what difference it made. She already knew he was one hell of a good lover.

But then something happened. He changed inside her. She'd heard the stories over the years. Moira knew what happened when werewolves mated. She wasn't ignorant or stupid. Just for some reason, up until that moment, she hadn't thought about the fact that he'd grow even larger, almost twice his size, once thoroughly aroused and inside her.

Her insides stretched, a sudden burning stealing her breath. Instead of slowing and giving her time to adjust, Dante built up speed, pounding her hot, wet pussy as he filled her, opened her up to him, stretched her so that she would take all of him in his new form.

The burning turned into heat, raw and explosive, and it flooded her insides. Pressure grew, tearing her apart from the inside out. He moved faster, harder, impaling her again and again until she was sure he'd cause permanent damage.

I can't… Something exploded inside her. *Oh God! Yes!*

She came like she'd never come before. Barely able to focus on him, she did her best to watch when he threw back his head, howling at the moon, while his cock shook inside her, his orgasm tearing through his body and hardening every muscle inside him.

He was the most gorgeous, most beautiful creature she'd ever laid eyes on.

And he was hers. For life.

Chapter Ten

છ

Steve Muller didn't often get the leash taken off these days. At least that was how it was starting to feel. WA had gotten a bit too stuffy over the years, insisting its agents remain clean-cut and give off a professional smell wherever they went. He preferred the days when he traveled the country in his old pickup, wearing nothing more than jeans and a T-shirt when in his skin.

The agency wouldn't kill his spirit. He'd seen it happen to some damn good werewolves. They'd get so wrapped up in the fucking bureaucracy that they'd start acting like humans and forget about being whole. If you asked him, that defeated the point of WA. Keeping his nose to the ground, ensuring werewolves were treated right and lived as they should live— that was the point of WA. Chasing after this cute little bitch was the first decent case he'd had in a long time. Moira Tangaree was fucking hot. Her track record with GWAR was impressive. Secretly, he couldn't help but wonder if she'd staged her own disappearance, used this "pack destroyer" werewolf to help her disappear. If that were true, he really didn't blame her. No matter the branch of WA, working for them could start to smell like a prison. And being caged wasn't natural for any werewolf. Not even a bitch.

Another year at the most and he'd retire to his den back in Missouri. Finally, he'd be done with WA. God, he couldn't wait to settle onto his land, maybe find a bitch to keep him warm at night.

He gave himself a mental shake. There was no point dwelling on the decisions he'd made in life. Sixty years old and still a single alpha with no pack to call home. It had been a good life and he wouldn't howl about decisions he'd made.

He looked away from the car window and glanced at his partner, also dressed in similar attire. Jeff looked a little less relaxed as he parked the car in front of a prestigious-looking home. Damn shame too. His partner was too young to be so uptight. WA could do that to a werewolf though. He stepped out of the car, leaving the overcharged air conditioning for the waves of heat that swam around them.

Damn, it was hot as hell in Albuquerque. Too bad they couldn't wait for nightfall to work. Temperatures were known to drop drastically once it got dark in these parts.

"The Sandia Pack leader has one hell of a den." Jeff blew out a low whistle, staring at the large mansion spread out before them.

"Their previous pack leader traded information. From what I heard, he ran on both sides of the fence." They'd used the pack leader a time or two themselves, since the old werewolf had connections that ran throughout the country. Steve had liked the guy. "Less than a year ago some young punk took him out. He's pack leader now and I'm willing to bet you he's not going to be a lick of help."

"Then what are we doing here?" Jeff glanced around the large, well-manicured yard. "And do we have to lay on the horn to get this pack's attention? You know they can smell us."

"It's an old trick." And a rather overused one. "They let us sit out here and sweat while they watch and sniff us out. Some werewolves think that gives them the upper hand."

"You wouldn't think they'd want to get on our bad side." Jeff put his hands on his hips, glaring at the house. "Not to mention they howled for us, not the other way around."

"Kissing tail probably. It doesn't mean they view us as alphas." Steve reminded himself how young Jeff was. His partner still had that omnipotent attitude that WA often gave a werewolf.

"I don't give a rat's ass how they view us. They're going to show some fucking respect." Jeff marched across the circular drive to the front door.

Steve shook his head and followed Jeff toward the mansion. His partner banged on the door, adrenaline hanging heavy in the heat. Barely a minute passed before a young werewolf, possibly in his early twenties, opened the door.

"You're from WA?" he asked, cocking his head and squinting at the two of them.

"I'm Jeff Brim and this is my partner, Steve Muller." Jeff unclipped his badge from his belt and flashed it in the young werewolf's face. "We're here to see your pack leader."

Jeff believed the same thing Steve did. This pup wasn't their leader. The young werewolf reeked of nervousness—definitely no alpha. He backed away from the door, holding on to it as Steve followed Jeff into the well air-conditioned home.

There were other werewolves inside. Steve quickly sniffed out the scent of several of them farther inside the large den. Nervous energy filled the high-ceilinged alcove. Either a heated argument had recently occurred or the pack members were worried about something. He guessed it might be a bit of both. Either way, it didn't smell good.

The large entryway opened into a sunken living room, and the hallway in front of them disappeared toward the other end of the house. There were several closed doors, all painted a glossy off-white. The house was clean, almost too clean. More than likely this place was used for meetings and no one actually lived here. He glanced up a long, wide staircase before turning his attention to the young werewolf.

"Is your pack leader here?" he asked.

The werewolf closed the door, shutting out the suffocating heat. He gave Steve an apologetic look and shook his head.

"I thought he'd be back by now, but he's not. The werewolves we contacted you about have disappeared and Darrell has organized a run to search for them."

"Who are the werewolves you wanted us to know about?" Steve asked. Another thing he didn't like about WA was being sent across country with no more information than to contact this pack about renegade werewolves. Like running in the dark kept them more passive.

The young werewolf glanced from one of them to the other and then scratched his chin. He hesitated and his thick black eyebrows met together under his wrinkled brow while he gave something some thought. Steve watched him closely as the salty smell of nervousness grew in the air.

"Darrell would want to tell you himself. But you're probably in a hurry or something, right?" It was as if he'd fought for reasoning to explain the situation to them himself.

"Wasting WA's time doesn't go well for a pack." Jeff puffed out his chest and glared at the young werewolf.

The young werewolf shifted from one foot to the other and then cursed under his breath. His nervousness smelled like rank sweat in a dirty locker room. Steve frowned, thinking the hot air outside would be better than this.

"Okay. Follow me."

Steve was damned glad they were getting out of the entryway. As they headed down the hallway, leaving the stench of nerves behind, a variety of other smells tickled his nose. Someone was eating a pizza somewhere. The scents of a couple of werewolves and what smelled like a bitch lingered behind one door. Exotic plants in ornate pots were at a crossway in the hall. Their sweet scents temporarily drowned out any other aromas from the house. This was a damned good ploy from someone who wanted to distract guests from gathering too much information by smelling the place out. A ploy he doubted the new pack leader would have had the sense to think of.

Heavy footsteps sounded on the stairs behind them. The three werewolves turned at the same time a large, well-built Mexican werewolf appeared behind them. His anger put Steve on red alert.

"Jorge. I need to talk to you now!" The werewolf grew in size as he spoke, his black eyes flickering with silver.

"Nick, these are —"

"I don't give a rat's ass who they are," Nick growled, not giving either of them his attention. He cleared the distance between them and Jorge stepped backward. "Did Darrell go after that Aldo werewolf and his bitch?"

"Dante Aldo?" Jeff asked.

Nick narrowed his gaze, glaring. He stood several inches taller than Jeff and sized him up with a quick glance.

"Who the fuck are you?" he snarled.

"Jeff Brim with Werewolf Affairs." Jeff had never bellied up to any werewolf, no matter their size.

Nick didn't look impressed — not in the least. He glared at Steve and then back at Jorge.

Steve needed confirmation of who the bitch was with Dante, but he smelled the truth. The back of his neck itched with excitement that they were closing in on Moira Tangaree. It would have been nice of WA to let them know they had a lead on the pretty bitch. But he'd wait it out, see what else they learned as this oversized werewolf lost his cool with Jorge. He'd gathered more information over the years staying patient than he had jumping in with all four paws.

"Darrell's a fucking pup to let Aldo escape. You realize who that bitch was who was with him, don't you?"

"I have my suspicions." Jorge was impressive with his calm tone.

Nick looked like he would break the pup's neck without a moment's notice. Jorge managed to look around his pack member and nodded at Steve and Jeff.

"In here," he said, opening the door next to him.

There was some impressive hardware in the room. Security monitors were lined on shelves on one wall, images of the front, side and back yards displayed. Steve noted several computers, and one that appeared not to be hooked up, sitting on the floor. Jorge pushed a chair to the side and leaned over a desk littered with wrinkled fast food bags and empty paper cups with straws that had been nibbled to an unusable point at the end. He moved the mouse to wake up the screen and then typed in a password quickly.

The smell of nervousness had faded. Jorge was obviously in his element in front of the computer.

"Here are pictures of our guests," he said, glancing over his shoulder at Steve but then looking back at the computer. "They asked to stay with our pack for a few days, so I don't understand why they ran."

A rush of excitement made Steve's bones tingle. He stared at the pictures of Dante Aldo and Moira Tangaree on the computer screen.

"I know why they ran." Nick walked over to the window, his broad back blocking what little light streamed through the almost-closed blinds. He parted them with his fingers and peered outside. "Darrell just got an e-mail from one of the werewolves up north that he used to run with. How much is the bitch worth to you?"

He turned around and pinned Jeff and then Steve with a hard stare.

"You read Darrell's e-mail?" Jorge asked, his jaw dropping.

Steve learned a long time ago that when a werewolf wanted to barter, trying to play him for a fool was more of a waste of time than it was worth. Nick's hardened expression told him enough about the werewolf. Whatever beef he had with his pack leader didn't matter. It was none of Steve's business. What mattered was that the werewolf had information, possibly enough to end this chase and allow him to put in his paperwork for retirement from WA.

"WA doesn't make deals." Jeff stepped in front of him, staring the large Mexican werewolf down. "If you know where Moira Tangaree and Dante Aldo are, it would be in your best interest to tell us now."

"Oh really?" Nick drawled. "I don't do threats, little pup."

"And I don't play games." Jeff pointed a finger at Nick. "Now you're going to —"

"Jeff. That's enough." Steve figured if he didn't intervene, his partner risked losing his finger. "I'll handle this."

Outrage filled the room quickly. Jeff was a good werewolf, but like the Mexican werewolf whose teeth grew while Steve watched, he'd jump into a fight that would get them nowhere.

Jeff turned on him, growling from a mixture of humiliation and anger that he was too young to control.

"We could put him on a chain for talking to us like that," he snarled.

Steve nodded. "Yup." He looked at Nick. "That pretty little bitch who was here could be in trouble. That's why we're here. I don't know what you know about the werewolf with her, Dante Aldo."

"I know plenty," Jorge spoke up, quickly switching screens and then pointing at Dante's image when he turned and looked wide-eyed at each of them. "He doesn't run with a pack, but if he's called in, he can wipe out a pack that is causing trouble. There's a list here of all the packs he's wiped out."

Most of which were probably urban myth. Steve wouldn't argue the point though. At the moment, it served his purpose.

"And the bitch with him isn't running with him by choice. He stole her," Steve told them.

"She didn't seem too unhappy to be with him from what I smelled," Nick offered, his mouth twisting into what might be a grin. Steve wasn't sure.

"Trust me on this. Her pack and den are frantic about her." It was a lie but he relied on these werewolves to have some sense of duty and loyalty in them.

He wasn't off base. Nick straightened, giving Steve his attention. "She didn't give any indication that she was anything but happy. But then she never said that much and some females always smell like that."

That wasn't good news. It hadn't occurred to him that Aldo might want her for a mate.

And he'd been an idiot not to consider the possibility before now. Maybe the agency had gotten to him more than he'd realized. Maybe years and years of dealing with backstabbing werewolves had made him callous. Was it possible that the rogue werewolf simply found a female that appealed to him so much he was willing to steal her from GWAR?

He looked at Nick. "It's worth a lot to us to find her. What can you tell us?"

"Earlier today we got word from the pack leader to the west of us," Nick said and then paused, glancing at Jeff as if he didn't trust him.

"And?" Steve prompted, bringing the werewolf's attention back to him.

"Word was out that Dante Aldo was here and it didn't smell good to them. I told Darrell he was an idiot to let the werewolf stay here. He reeks of trouble." Nick crossed his bulky arms over his chest, scowling.

There was no love lost between this werewolf and his pack leader. Again, not Steve's problem.

"Then just a bit ago, a pack up in the Rockies sends word that they got trouble with another pack pushing into their territory. They heard Dante Aldo was in these parts and wanted him."

"What pack was this?" Steve fought to keep his excitement at bay. He could smell success just around the corner. Another day at the most and he'd have the little bitch in his paws.

* * * * *

Rose Silverman sat quietly until the pack meeting ended. None of this sounded good. None of it. The tension and testosterone filled the room enough to make her gag. The way most of the bitches shifted in their chairs around her let her know they didn't like this either. Almost all of the cubs, who were usually restless by this point, sat quietly and stared at their sires and the pack leader while plans were made.

"Why do you have to go on the run too?" she asked her mate after the meeting ended.

The sound of chairs moving and conversations breaking out filled the room with noise, making it easy for her question to not be heard by anyone other than Bruce Silverman. He looked down at her with exasperation.

"Would you have me look like a coward staying with the bitches?" he hissed.

"Of course not." She wished sometimes he would be more of a coward. But not her Bruce. Anytime there was a problem, he always jumped in with claws extended. More than once she reminded herself that was what made her fall in love with him. "It sounds like there are a lot of those *lunewulfs* though. If they are attacking our territory..." She was howling at a brick wall and she knew it. Her mate's eyes were already streaked with silver. Determination added to the worry lines around his mouth. He couldn't wait to get out there with the rest of them and fight for their land. That was her Bruce. "Just watch your tail, wolf man."

He pulled her into a rough hug, his massive warm body still making her hot with need after all these years. Her heart ached for him, though, and he hadn't even left her yet. Werewolves would die tonight. Over half the males in her pack were headed out on a run to defend the land they raised their cubs on. Their own little corner of the world. She'd been whelped in these mountains, and so had Bruce. Most of them had. It was gorgeous country and worth fighting for. Those *lunewulf*s had no right sniffing their way into her pack's territory.

Rose watched Bruce toss their son into the air when they walked outside with the rest of their pack. A cold breeze came down off the mountain, full of the fresh smell of pine. The scent that always lightened her mood did nothing to ease her nerves tonight. Rose scanned the crowd, searching for their daughter, when a couple caught her eye.

More specifically, the young bitch of the pair grabbed her attention. She wasn't the only one who noticed the male and bitch leaning against a car across the street from Dee's General Store. Curiosity filled the air. There were strangers in their midst. And they weren't American werewolves, or at least she wasn't. It wasn't too often another species of werewolf prowled their way into the mountains.

Most of Valle, the town where she and her mate lived, were werewolves. The few humans who stayed out of sheer determination looked the other way or simply didn't care when the street outside Dee's store was lined with cars after hours for their pack meetings. Dee had a large back room behind the store. It worked well for pack meetings as well as parties and anniversaries.

Headlights began beaming up and down the street. Rose squinted to get a better look at the pretty young bitch. The female's dark skin made her stand out. Whispers around her tickled Rose's ears but she ignored them. It wasn't just the dark skin and long black hair but the expression, her firm, toned body—Rose knew she'd seen her before. And her heart constricted.

The agent with GWAR who'd been declared dead. Rose hadn't forgotten the agents who'd made her reverse the program, who'd kept her from wiping the young bitch out of the system. It had been a week ago and she'd wondered about it ever since. No matter how hard she fought to get work out of her head, to focus on the fact that in one more week that job would be history, she couldn't quit worrying about the young bitch that possibly was in trouble. And GWAR didn't always take care of the young bitches who ran on missions for them— at least Rose didn't think they did.

"Bruce. Let me talk to you for a minute." Larry Shank, one of the alphas who worked closely with their pack leader, sounded stressed. He nodded his greeting to her. "This involves you too, Rose. Let's talk over at your truck."

Rose didn't like the anxiety that filled the air. She picked up on a slightly salty smell too. A wave of discomfort twisted around inside her. Her hands shook as she got their cubs into their seat belts and then stood with the passenger door open.

"How many do we have on the run?" Bruce was anxious to get started. Already he'd untucked his shirt and worked his belt out of the belt loops. He fingered the long leather strap while giving his attention to the other werewolves who'd joined them.

"There's about twenty of us," Larry told him.

He stepped to the side when Ollie Grayson, their pack leader, strolled over to join them.

"Is Rose okay with it?" he asked, looking from Larry to Bruce.

"Am I okay with what?" she asked, her tummy twisting in knots. God. It was bad enough her mate was leaving on a dangerous run. Ollie walking up and asking a question like that didn't sit well with her at all.

"Haven't asked her yet." Larry shrugged.

Ollie muttered a greeting to Bruce and Rose dropped her gaze to their hands when her pack leader shook her mate's hand. The act seemed tense, a preamble to something she knew she wouldn't like.

"I didn't mince words during the meeting," Ollie told Bruce. He ran the hand through his closely cut, dark hair.

He was a short, thick werewolf and pack gossip had it that every single bitch whined loudly when he'd recently taken a mate. Personally Rose didn't see the appeal. But then, Ollie looked nothing like her Bruce, who stood well over six feet and had thick, curly blond hair, perfect for running her fingers through. She scowled, wishing more than anything that Bruce was heading back to her den with her.

"Tonight's run will be dangerous," Ollie continued, giving all his attention to her mate. "I put a call out for some help and he's shown up tonight. He has his mate with him, and we need a den to put her up in while we take care of business. I thought maybe she could stay with your Rose."

"We'd be honored," Bruce told him, not even looking at her to see what she thought.

Another bitch in her den? Something told her that Ollie meant the dark-skinned bitch. Panic soared to dangerous levels inside her. She sucked in a breath, her mouth suddenly too dry to say a word. The werewolves looked at her for the first time and she swallowed the lump forming in her throat, certain they all smelled her fear.

"Your mate will come home to you a hero," Ollie told her, misunderstanding the emotions he smelled on her.

She nodded, not trusting her voice. He didn't say whether Bruce would return to their den alive or dead.

Chapter Eleven

ജ

A shower had never felt so good. Moira's damp hair stuck to her back through her shirt as she stared at the ceiling and walls of the small room. The den was simple, small and clean. Rose Silverman didn't want her here, but was friendly and polite. Moira didn't blame her. The bitch had a perfect den, so cozy and filled with warm and happy feelings that seemed to float permanently in the air. This place was everything Moira had dreamed of having.

After a week of being in her fur, staying in the mountains with Dante, she was more than certain a quiet life like the one Rose had would never be the life for her.

Her heart swelled, yearning for what she ached to have.

Which was stupid.

She rolled over, punching the thin pillow Rose provided for her and kicking off the blankets that were more of a bed than she'd had in a while. She stared at the black sky through the window. Rose and her cubs slept upstairs. Moira sensed Rose's restlessness and smelled the bitch's worry. Her mate fought with the rest of the werewolves, protecting their territory. A fight Moira would much rather have been a part of than being stuck here.

Something else lingered in the air. It didn't come from the den, but it was near. She stood quietly, doing her best not to let the floorboards creak underneath her, and walked to the window. The males weren't back yet but an unease grew in the air. The tiny hairs on her body prickled. God. She hated that feeling. The unknown—potential danger.

Lying back down on the twisted blankets on the floor, she straightened her body and focused on her breathing. She had to relax, slow her heartbeat and calm her thoughts. Only then could she leave her body in the appearance of sleep while her mind explored the land around her. If there was danger, she had a duty to protect this den that had taken her in.

One with the elements, carry me. Show me all and all I will see.

Slowly her soul parted from the weight of her body. She rose, lighter than air, and floated out of her skin. Simply separating body and spirit renewed her, lifted all the worries from her and cleared her mind. No longer did she focus on her heart beating, or her damp hair against her skin. The limitations of her body always preoccupied her — how fast she could run, how high she could jump, how much she could hear or how quickly her heart beat. None of that mattered now. The gift was a blessing she'd never abuse and always use to make her stronger. Just as her sire had willed it.

She'd intentionally left the door to the guest room open. Moving through the quiet, dark den, she left the small room and headed toward the open window in the kitchen.

But she wasn't alone. When had Rose come downstairs?

The female stood in the living room, her back to Moira, and stared out the front windows. She wore a long, thick bathrobe and her auburn hair fell loose halfway down her back. She was a pretty bitch, possibly ten years or so older than Moira and in good shape considering she'd whelped a couple of cubs.

Right now, worry and fear clung to the air around her. It was too easy to sink into Rose's thoughts, feel her emotions as if they were her own. Naturally, she was terrified for her mate. But there was something else — something Moira hadn't expected to feel. Rose was worried for her too. Rose knew something.

Moira pulled on those thoughts, drew them out and sorted through them with disbelief. The bitch worked for WA. She searched her own memories, recalling entering the WA office prior to flying out to the cabin in the mountain where

Dante had found her. There had been several bitches working in the WA office. Moira hadn't paid much attention to any of them. She vaguely recalled one of them looking like Rose.

There had been no indication in Dante's thoughts that he knew Rose worked for WA. Rose had seen Moira's file with the special agency, GWAR. Moira searched Rose's thoughts and learned she'd been assigned to delete Moira from the system. And she'd been approached by agents and asked not to do it. Now the bitch worried those agents would show up here, looking for Moira.

She put Rose and her cubs in danger by staying here. Yet Rose had accepted her into her den graciously, providing her with a hot shower, blankets, a pillow and a room to sleep in. Moira almost felt the tear that streamed down Rose's cheek as she fought with her emotions and struggled to remain brave while her mate was gone. The terror that gripped Rose over what might occur with Moira under her roof caused the change to tremble inside her.

Rose would kill to protect her cubs. As any good bitch would.

This was wrong.

Moira searched deeper, realizing Rose hadn't shared with her mate what she knew about Moira. She didn't like discussing work when she was home. She ached to be a good mate, a good mother, and keep her den a happy and loving place. And she couldn't wait to be free of WA and to no longer have any knowledge of anything other than what it took to help raise her cubs and see to her mate's happiness.

A phone rang somewhere in the house and Rose jumped. Her nerves were on edge. Moira dove out of the female's mind, feeling jumpy right along with Rose. Although she had intended to search the land around the den, Moira hurried back to her body and got up quickly.

"Hello," Rose said quietly from the other room as Moira walked toward her. Rose turned, smelling her as she held the phone to her ear. "Thank God. Yes. Thanks for calling. No, you didn't wake me up. I love you, too. Bye."

She hung the phone up slowly, hesitant about what to say to Moira. Without even trying to move into her mind, it was obvious by the stressed look on her face that the bitch didn't want to be rude, but she didn't really want to talk to Moira either.

"I promise I'll protect you and your cubs as long as I'm here." Moira decided she'd give Rose the impression she already knew what the female had learned about her.

"Where is your den?" Rose turned on the kitchen light and began opening cabinets and pulling items from the refrigerator.

"I don't have one. And you already know that." For some reason she wanted Rose to know she wasn't her enemy.

"What do I know?" Rose wouldn't make this easy. Her hands shook when she pulled a long knife out of a drawer and began slicing raw meat into strips to fry.

"You know who I am. I know you almost deleted my file. Who are the werewolves that are looking for me?" More than likely they were GWAR agents, or possibly even WA. Would she be able to fight them off if they found her while Dante wasn't with her?

Rose had her back to Moira. She slammed the knife onto the counter, slicing a large, raw steak in half. The tangy, sweet smell of the fresh meat made Moira's stomach growl. It was a natural reaction. She doubted she could eat anything right now.

Rose put the knife on the counter and turned around, licking juice from her finger. Her thick hair fell over her shoulder, tumbling past her breast and curling at the end. Anger glowed in her green eyes. She crossed her arms against her chest and gave Moira a level look.

"My mate gave his consent for you to stay here." Her tone was quiet and controlled. "He doesn't know anything about you. And it will stay that way. He doesn't need the extra stress."

"That's fine. But you didn't answer my questions."

"Nor will I. Like I said, my mate said you could stay here, not me. I don't want trouble brought to my den."

Moira fought to keep her emotions under control. She was on Rose's territory and had no choice other than to submit to the female.

But damn it, any information she could gather might save her life. She lowered her head, showing her submission to the bitch of this den. Her heart beat hard with frustration but she fought it, not wanting Rose to see how hard it was to belly-up to her.

"Forgive me for upsetting you," she said quietly. She pushed forward carefully, focusing on the linoleum floor while keeping her tone soft and hopefully sounding sincere. "I'm accustomed to gathering information." She glanced at Rose's pensive expression. "And to protecting dens and packs. I promise no one will hurt you or your cubs."

Rose let out a sigh, nodded quickly and then turned to the raw meat. She yelped when someone rapped at the back door. Moira cursed. She'd been so focused on controlling her own scent and narrowing in on Rose's thoughts that she hadn't smelled a werewolf at the door until he knocked. And here she was bragging about her ability to protect.

Rose moved and put her hand on the doorknob. "Who is it?" she asked.

"Juan. Juan Anthony. I need to see Moira," he said through the door.

Rose turned an accusatory look on Moira.

She held out her hands, willing the bitch to calm down. "It's okay. I know him."

"He's not your mate."

"He is a good werewolf—a friend of Dante's." That he was here, at this den, made no sense. Her heart pounded while possible scenarios instantly plagued her.

Rose opened the door slowly and Juan filled the doorway, his dark skin and hair fading into the blackness behind him. He didn't enter. But then a lone werewolf would never enter a den unless the male of the den permitted it. Having spent a week playing in Dante's mind, Moira had grown accustomed to moving around in thoughts other than her own. She reached past Rose's mind, instinctively searching out Juan's, struggling to learn what brought him here before he spoke.

"I mean no harm to your den, bitch." He showed his respect, keeping his attention on Rose. "I simply carry a message that Moira can give to her mate. Will you allow that?"

Rose nodded her head quickly, her curiosity outweighing any fear.

Tiny hairs rose over Moira's arms as nervous energy spiked inside her. Juan was on red alert, his expression as intense as the feelings she picked up from him. He'd recently been in his fur, the smell of earth and something wild lingering around him. Not to mention his shirt was untucked and slightly twisted on his torso. He didn't want to be here. And it bugged the shit out of him that he had to humble himself in the doorway of an unknown den.

"Two werewolves from your pack are in this territory. They heard that Dante is here and seek him." He kept his head lowered, not looking at either of them. Again an attempt at respect.

But that wasn't the reason. There was trouble. She was in danger. And so was Dante. His thoughts sprang forth like a fresh spring, rushing toward her and bombarding her with fear and frustration.

"I'll tell Dante," she said quietly. No way would she let her feelings surface. Rose already didn't like any of this. If she kicked Moira out of her den, Dante wouldn't be able to find her.

"How can we reach you?" Moira asked.

"My cell phone will be on." He turned then, mumbling his appreciation to Rose and disappeared into the darkness.

Rose almost jumped at the door, shutting and locking it then leaning against it as she faced Moira.

"Your pack no longer exists," she hissed. Her eyes widened and silver streaked through them as she digested the possibilities of Juan's message.

Moira didn't like any of the possibilities that crossed her mind either. She turned from Rose, too many thoughts attacking her to allow her to use the gift.

"You're right." She walked into the dark living room, Rose on her tail.

"You are from Malta," Rose said behind her.

Moira nodded, brushing her hair over her shoulder. She tugged on the long T-shirt she wore, suddenly very uncomfortable.

"My pack was burned to extinction when I was eighteen," she said, needing to think this through. Rose was the only one here to talk it out with.

God help her if the bitch kicked her into the night.

Rose walked around to face her, crossing her arms over her chest and staring her in the eye. There was determination masking the fear Moira smelled on her.

"Obviously that isn't true." Rose searched her face, and something that might have been compassion added to the worry lines around the bitch's eyes. She let out a sigh, staring at Moira and taking her time deciding what she would say next. "Two weeks ago, two men from WA entered the office where I work. They told me not to terminate the file of a GWAR agent who had been scheduled for deletion. That sort of thing doesn't happen every day. They made a big deal out of it. I could smell the secrecy on them. When we arranged for the file to stay active, they made me promise not to tell anyone what I did."

"Yet you're telling me now," Moira prompted, needing to know anything this bitch could tell her to help her figure out what might be getting ready to happen.

No way would she break eye contact with Rose. If she kept her breathing slow, relaxed her thoughts so as not to spook the bitch in any way, maybe she would learn more. At the same time, she focused on the night surrounding the den. Any sound, any indication that someone entered or closed in around them, and she had to be ready. She guessed from Rose's phone call that the males would be returning soon. But if members of her pack were out there, sniffing her out, sniffing out Dante, she had to know if they were closing in before it was too late.

And members of her pack! Good God! Dante had said there were others and that they would find them. Who had survived? Would she know them? Her heart lunged and she fought to keep emotions on a tight leash. She had tried on her own time, with what limited resources she had through GWAR and WA, to find any Malta werewolves who might be hiding in the States. Their reputation had been destroyed, their race feared. If they were in the States, they'd remained hidden. Not once had she heard word that a Malta werewolf existed anywhere among any of the known packs. And over the years and the packs she'd visited while on assignment, she'd never spotted a member of her pack despite the fact that she knew several had survived.

Damn the government anyway for keeping her so in the dark while they used her again and again to serve their own purposes.

"If I ran without a pack, I can only imagine how lonely that would be," Rose said quietly.

Her words quickly dissolved all of Moira's efforts to keep her feelings hidden. Her eyes burned and she looked away from Rose, focusing on the front door. All was quiet outside. Juan had disappeared without a sound. Other than the nightlife searching for food and the gentle, occasional breeze rustling through the pines, all remained still beyond that door. Unlike the emotions fighting to rage to life inside her.

A salty smell filled the air between them. Nervous and confused, Rose bit her lip, capturing Moira's gaze again and staring at her with glowing green eyes sparked with silver.

Rose lowered her voice even further, barely whispering. "I know a little bit about Dante Aldo," she said, almost mouthing the words as if afraid to voice knowledge she viewed as close to terrifying.

Interesting that he had that effect on werewolves, as if speaking his name might bring them harm.

"WA is looking for him and no pack leader will deny him anything. My mate knows this and has his tail. Our pack leader called him here and we're very loyal to him. But you would know if you were with Dante when Ollie called him. For that reason, you are safe in my den." Rose's breathing came harder, her fear getting the better of her. "According to WA you were stolen. You don't appear to be with Dante Aldo against your will."

Moira shook her head. "I'm not. Dante came to me because he is my mate." There was no reason to elaborate. Besides it was the truth. They were mated.

"And they are coming after your mate. Will you fight by his side or defend your pack?"

For the past week she'd run in her fur alongside Dante. It had been a bonding more primitive and raw than could possibly occur in their human form. Although little discussion occurred while they stayed in the mountains, a union formed between the two of them she couldn't deny. They'd moved as two animals, incredible predators that feared nothing and commanded the wilderness they'd claimed briefly. During that time, they'd hunted together, bathed together, slept wrapped around each other. Sex had been raw, primitive and aggressive. It made them one.

In the high altitude with very few resources, they would have struggled to survive in their skin. But as werewolves, isolated and free to roam the Rockies, she'd fallen hard for the mysterious and powerful werewolf—an alpha without a pack, feared and respected by every pack leader on the planet.

"I am Dante's mate. But I will hear why these werewolves from Malta seek him out."

Rose nodded and some of her fear broke. She straightened, her gaze gentle as she met Moira's. For the first time since their conversation started, Rose's expression relaxed, understanding in her eyes. A good bitch would stand by her werewolf.

A sound outside tickled Moira's ear. She focused on it, tuning out all other sounds. Two cars approached on the quiet street outside. Rose heard it too and moved to the window, parting the curtain far enough to peek outside.

"My mate is here," she said, sounding more than relieved.

She hurried to the door, pulling it open and running into the yard. Moira stood in the doorway, sniffing the air when car doors opened. Dante's scent surrounded her like a warm blanket. Her insides responded, heating quickly while her heart thudded in her chest. The electrifying energy of his presence filled the air. How could they all not notice it?

Dante was more werewolf than any other male she'd ever been around. He moved silently, his broad shoulders swaying while his long legs carried him to her. Without a word, he wrapped powerful arms around her, yanking her to him. She collapsed against steely muscle, her body turning to fire, need bursting into flame inside her as he crushed his lips against hers.

He smelled of earth—a tangy, slightly salty aroma that excited her even more. Rough hands grabbed her ass, pushing her into his hardness. A growl tore through him, aggressive and demanding. Claiming her all over again, as if they hadn't fucked several times daily for a week in their fur and he couldn't wait to be inside her.

For a moment she forgot her worries over her pack members. Nothing bothered her when Dante's body pressed against hers like this, touching her everywhere, giving her strength that assured her all problems of the world were easily conquered.

Dante tore his lips from hers, licking and nibbling at the side of her face and then her neck. "What is this message Juan has for me?" he growled against her throat, his hot breath torturing the sensitive spot at her nape.

She should have known he would search her mind, demanding to know all that happened to her while away from him the second he returned to her side. He had her in such a fog of lust she fought to learn what happened while he was away from her without as much success. She still wasn't as good at moving her thoughts into other werewolves' minds as Dante was. If her own emotions flared out of control, she had a hard time moving into someone else's mind. Dante, on the other hand, never seemed to be out of control. She took a calming breath, determined to mix with his thoughts before answering him. He stared down at her patiently, beckoning her inside him.

Blood, death and frustration tormented his brain. She sucked in a breath, retreating quickly in spite of her need to know what he'd been through.

"Members of my pack…"

"Are looking for me," he finished for her.

Taking her by the arm, he pulled her from the den. She almost ran to keep up with his determined gait as he guided her toward the truck and the other two werewolves.

"You honor me by taking care of my mate," he said seriously, nodding to the other werewolf.

Rose had her arms wrapped around her mate. She gave Dante a worried look, and then met Moira's gaze.

"Our den will always welcome you, Aldo," Bruce Silverman said. "You fought with the strength of ten werewolves tonight. Our pack is in your debt."

She watched the two werewolves shake hands. Dante opened the passenger door for her and then moved around the truck, looking more powerful than she'd seen him even in his fur. Muscles rippled under his T-shirt and his blue jeans hugged his long, thick legs like a second skin. And damn—talk about buns of steel.

Need crawled over every inch of her flesh, burning to life inside her, making her wish they could just disappear for a few hours. Adrenaline from fighting dripped from his skin. She smelled his energy, sensed it coursing through his veins. She wanted him more with every breath, ached for him to fill her, to appease the throbbing pressure growing inside her with every passing second.

She willed the driver's side door to open for him, wanting to smell him, to have him next to her as quickly as possible. Dante slid in and wrapped strong fingers around the steering wheel. He looked at her with pale blue eyes that were so unlike any other werewolf's eyes she'd ever seen. They glowed in the darkness against his creamy white skin and black hair. Black stubble shadowed his chin and reminded her how rough it felt against her. She almost cried out just staring at him from the sexual charge he ignited. Chills rushed over her, but it wasn't from the cold night air.

"Will you not shut the door for me too?" he asked, his voice a low growl, his thoughts dwelling on the swell of her breasts and not the damned door.

"Watch your fingers." She matched the gruffness in his tone, keeping her gaze locked on his as she willed his truck door to close.

The door shut next to him, trapping his virile scent in the small cab of the truck. He grabbed a large portion of her hair and yanked her face to his. His roughness turned her on even more and she almost drowned in the intense smell of her lust that filled the air around them. Dante's expression showed his approval.

"These pack members from Malta will find me. They believe as many do that I had a hand in destroying your pack." His mouth was so close to hers. He wouldn't allow her face any closer but kept them a breath's space apart. "You will honor any decisions I make concerning them. Do you understand?"

And at that moment she did.

She craved him physically. The sexual bond between them consumed her. Yet there was more to mating than just good sex—or even damned good sex. Trust. Honesty. Believing in the decisions her mate made and backing them. All of that was needed for a successful mating.

However, even with all of those feelings for him intact, none of them would weather the test of time without love. In their fur, the words hadn't been spoken. They had shown each other through their actions how they felt. Bringing her kill to him, lying relaxed while he bathed her meticulously, finding the freshest of mountain water to drink and bathe in—they had shown each other their growing love.

Voicing those simple words proved harder to do. "I might know these pack members. I want to see them."

He growled, letting her know she hadn't answered his question.

Enduring the pinch when he pulled her hair, she leaned into him anyway, nipping at his lower lip. "Whatever decisions are made, we'll make together, wolf man."

"And if the choice is that it is their lives or mine?"

"If they want you dead then they are misinformed, as I was. They will be offered the truth. If they don't accept it, then I will take them down myself."

His gaze bore deep into her soul. "You would kill for me?"

"Yes," she told him honestly.

"Why is that?" he demanded.

"I think you know." Her heart thudded so hard she couldn't catch her breath.

"I want to hear it."

"Because I love you," she whispered.

His grin showed her what he must have looked like as a cub, all emotions on display, content and happy with the world around him.

"Little bitch," he breathed. "I've waited years to hear those words. I love you, too."

His satisfaction and pleasure had never smelled so good. Holding her close to him, he started the truck and then shifted into gear with his left hand, unwilling to let her go. The truck's headlights burrowed through the darkness ahead of them as he pulled away from the curb.

"How do we reach Juan?" he asked after a bit of silence passed between them.

"He said his cell phone would be on."

More than likely her mind was too rattled after admitting her love for him. She didn't feel him in her mind and gave him space as well. Dante moved his arm from around her shoulder and pulled out his phone to quickly call Juan. Roped muscle stretched in his forearm when he put the phone to his ear. A few minutes later, they pulled up to a dark, small motel built on the side of the mountain. Any other time she might view the place as cozy. Dante's frustration fueled the adrenaline already coursing through his veins. He was wired tight and dealt with it by not saying anything. He opened his door and grabbed her arm, keeping her close to him when he slid off the seat and pulled her out on his side.

A motel room door opened in front of them, shedding light over them. She froze at the unbridled love she saw in Dante's face.

The werewolves draw nearer. His baritone caressed her and she searched his expression, which didn't change. She dug into his mind so she would know what he knew.

"You two don't have to fuck alongside the truck," Juan said jovially, leaning against the motel room door. "I'm more than willing to share my room."

His tone was light, but when Dante turned her and guided her inside the room, she saw tension gripping Juan's handsome face. His dark features were compelling. His features were so similar to Dante's, yet he was such a different werewolf. Standing and holding the door, he waited until they'd entered and then closed it quietly behind them.

The first thing Moira noticed was that for a simple-looking motel, the room was spacious, clean and rather nice. Two king-sized beds took up most of the room, and a large television sat opposite them, set to a weather channel. Several pillows were propped up on one bed and the indention showed where Juan had reclined prior to them showing up.

He returned to the spot, wearing only boxer shorts, and stretched out, filling the length of one side of the bed. Black, coarse hair curled over his muscular legs and arms. There was a fair amount of hair on his chest too. Several scars puckered the dark skin along his collarbone and over his stomach. Otherwise, Juan was damned close to a perfect specimen of werewolf. And although she'd never known him before meeting Dante, he looked very much like the males from her pack. Someday when she knew him better and was more comfortable asking, she'd learn about the pack he'd actually grown up in.

He is from Malta, although not raised with your pack. Dante's voice rumbled in her head and she jumped, catching Juan's attention, but she ignored him and turned to face Dante. *Does he appeal to you, little bitch?*

In the light, Dante's hair was ruffled and stuck to his head from dried sweat. She ran a finger over a scratch on his cheek. It would be gone before morning. A werewolf's metabolism was accelerated, even in their human form.

Only you appeal to me, wolf man.

Dante's eyes glowed with satisfaction. *Juan thinks I'm one lucky son of a bitch.*

You are. She leaned into him, kissing his chin while moving around in his mind. The intimacy of sharing their thoughts was almost as hot as fucking him. *Juan also wonders if I'm as sexy without my clothes on as I am dressed.*

Dante straightened, his gaze shooting over her head as he glanced quickly at his littermate. A slow, dangerous smile appeared when he looked back down at her. *Maybe we should satisfy his curiosity.*

"You need a bath," she said out loud, quickly trying to distract his thoughts. The direction of their mental conversation was hitting dangerous waters. Her voice was a bit huskier than she'd expected.

"Maybe in a little bit." He grabbed her, pulling her to him.

She collapsed against steely muscle and one thought went through her head—actually two.

He was going to fuck her now—and he was going to let Juan watch.

Chapter Twelve

Moira got better at hearing his thoughts daily. Her gift was raw but would grow quickly. Every day they were together, he saw it blossom further. She also had grace, intelligence and a beauty that made her the best bitch he'd ever laid eyes on.

He was blessed to have her run by his side.

When he felt her take in Juan, note his sex appeal, but then turn and look at him with more love and lust than any female had ever graced him with, he knew he was one lucky son of a bitch.

"What are you thinking, wolf man?" She ran her fingers over the curve of his shoulder, her caramel skin glowing with nervous excitement.

The smell of her lust, the desire that pumped in her veins, made him hard as a fucking rock. She knew damned good and well what he was thinking.

Just in case, he'd make it real clear. *Juan wants to see you naked. I have no problem showing off my most cherished possession.*

"The smell of your sexual need will draw the strays in faster than anything else," he growled, vocalizing their conversation for his littermate's sake.

She blushed so beautifully he knew he wouldn't last long inside her.

"You got that right," Juan growled from behind her.

"We need to get some of that scent off you," Dante told her, wrapping his arms around her waist.

"And how do you plan on doing that?" She batted her eyes at him, teasing while she rubbed herself against him.

"Get on the bed." He watched her mouth open then close.

Slowly she moved from him and crawled on all fours to the middle of the bed.

Only if you're comfortable with this. He watched her ass twitch as she moved and situated herself.

Fuck me, wolf man. She didn't want to think about it too much. That much was clearer to him than she wished him to see.

Her lust ripened, the rich, musky scent stronger than any drug or alcohol could ever be. He got drunk just inhaling it.

Juan watched wide-eyed behind Moira, his cock jutting up like a pole making a tent out of his boxers. He was the open book he'd always been to Dante, completely unaware of how easily his older littermate had always read him. Juan couldn't believe Dante would fuck Moira in front of him, but he was ready to enjoy the show, barely breathing as he gazed with open appreciation at Moira's sensual body.

More than anything, Dante wanted to rip her clothes from her body, hear the material tear as she cried out and came from the aggressive act. This time he restrained himself. Soon he'd lavish her with a wardrobe deserving of her natural beauty and grace. Tonight she'd need the clothes she wore.

His muscles twitched when he moved onto the bed with her. When she touched him, he shivered, need rushing too quickly inside him. She held on to his shoulders, staring up at him with lust-filled black eyes. He reached for the bottom of her shirt and her lashes fluttered, stealing his breath. His knuckles scraped against her flesh, so smooth and silky, so warm and enticing.

"If only I had all night to enjoy every inch of you," he whispered, his voice rough, the change threatening to take over.

He buried his face in her hair, inhaling her scent, and pulled her shirt up her body. Her fingers dug into his neck and she murmured something incoherent. She trembled, apprehension and fear momentarily mixing in with her lust.

Dante understood. Malta werewolves, very much from the old, if not ancient, school didn't share their bitches. A true alpha claimed and protected his female, cherishing her higher than any other possession.

Maybe it was from growing up and moving from pack to pack. He'd never share her with another soul. But there was something about Juan watching, growing more and more excited, that made him ache to fuck Moira even harder than usual.

He would undress her in front of his littermate. Juan's rich scent, indication of how turned on he was, mixed with their scents. The room quickly was heavy with the thick smell of lust, rich and creamy, like sweet syrup.

Know now, little bitch — you will always be mine and only mine.

Will you share me with him?

No. And he doesn't expect it. He'll have no problem getting a piece of tail later.

He continued to pull her shirt up her body, exposing her breasts. She held her arms over her head, allowing him to remove it slowly.

She needed to see his strength, but also his security in the moment. She needed the kind of trust where her heart wouldn't be broken, where all thoughts would always be on the table, where no matter where they ran, she would know he'd always be by her side.

She needed his love. And she needed to know beyond any doubt that he'd never hurt her, never destroy their life together.

As it had happened once already in her life.

It was one hell of a large order.

Are you werewolf enough to handle it?

His little bitch had climbed into his thoughts, experienced every worry and concern he had about making her happy.

I swear that I am. He wasn't ready for the amount of emotion that hit him when he gave her his promise.

His fingers trembled at the top button of her jeans. He undid them and peeled them off her. She lay naked on the bed before him, her dark skin glowing from the lamplight that spread across the room. Her long black hair shrouded her, parting over her slender shoulders and curving over her small, firm, round breasts.

He sucked in a breath, unable to move for a moment. All he could do was stare at the beautiful bitch he'd waited so long to call his own.

"You're so damned beautiful," he growled, pushing her hair over her shoulders.

Her fingers shook when she pulled on his shirt. She bit her lower lip, her gaze moving slowly up his body. "And you're fucking gorgeous," she told him, her voice husky with need.

He ran the back of his hands down her front, brushing his knuckles over her hard nipples. Her heart thumped quickly in her chest and she began panting. His shirt scratched his skin and he almost tore it getting it off his body. Blood drained out of his head. Every inch of him burned while his cock roared to life. It was so damned hard he worried he'd break the zipper on his jeans if he didn't get out of them soon. Movement was damn near impossible.

Moira glanced over at Juan, who'd moved to the edge of his bed, his feet on the floor and his hand covering his swollen cock.

"Have you ever watched him fuck before?" she asked him.

"Not with him knowing," he told her, his smile turning mischievous.

Moira laughed, the sound reaching Dante's heart. Juan had eased the tension for her, relaxing her in his presence.

Her dark eyes glowed and black hair fell like silk to the bed, when she returned her attention to him. He moved over her and she spread her legs, lifting them and gripping his outer thighs. The rich smell of her pussy was like a strong drug, fogging his mind and taking over his body.

She licked her lips, her tongue gliding over them like an invitation. God, he swore she glowed with desire.

"It's going to be hard and fast, little bitch. I need you to take all of me." If he could have formed the words in his head and shared them with her more intimately he would have. But at the moment, his mind was mush. "I need you to take every inch of me now," he told her, wanting her ready for the level of energy that pumped inside his veins.

You better make me come or you'll have to do it all again. Her thoughts drifted into his fogged-over brain. A small smile twitched at her lips and she leaned back, straightening her legs and then spreading them.

He couldn't form a fucking thought. Words escaped him. Moisture clung to the smooth flesh between her legs. Her scent captured him, took over his ability to do anything but see to her demands. He moved over her, aware that Juan had propped the pillows and gotten comfortable on the bed next to theirs. He'd pulled out his dick and stroked it to hardness while watching them.

Moira reached for Dante and ran her fingernails down his chest. His world turned into a haze, everything around him fading. The only thing clear in his vision was her, stretched out underneath him, her legs spread far apart as she touched him.

"God. Moira." He could barely move. His cock was so fucking heavy between his legs it weighed him down.

"Fuck me," she ordered, moving her hands to his hair and pulling his head to her breasts.

That's all he wanted to do.

He sucked her nipple, lapping at it with his tongue and then nibbling the hard puckered flesh between his teeth.

"Dante," she purred, grabbing his hair hard enough to hurt.

Juan growled next to them. He didn't move from where he sat, although Dante knew that he wouldn't. Juan respected their space, but also, with his cock that swollen, he probably couldn't have budged if he'd tried.

Dante ran his tongue between her breasts, enjoying the swell of them, the taste of her flesh. His cock jerked underneath him, anxious to be inside her.

Her inner thigh muscles clamped down hard against his sides. "Now, Dante, please."

"Yes. God. I need you." He adjusted himself so that his cock pressed against her moist heat.

She thrust upward, lifting her hips off the bed and dragging him into her hot pussy. He drowned in her quickly, filling her just as he promised, quick and hard.

Moira screamed. Her cry vibrated inside him. She called for his primal side, tearing her fingernails down his arms as he plunged inside her, going deeper, burying himself in her heat.

He wanted every bit of him inside her. Diving deeper, building momentum, all that mattered was getting both of them off. He wanted her coming again and again. Feeling her tiny muscles vibrate against his cock called forth his purer side. She panted while she held on to him tightly.

"It's so good," she said between breaths, her fingers digging into his biceps. "Don't stop. Please. Don't ever stop."

His cock bulged, swelled inside her. He ached to come, to be trapped in her heat where he belonged. All that mattered was Moira.

"I can't hold back," he muttered, fighting to form words when his body craved the change. "Not much longer."

Her mouth formed a small circle, her eyes opening wide. "I feel you. Grow, wolf man. Fill every inch of me."

A small part of him was aware of Juan stroking his cock next to them, his panting almost as loud as Dante's. His littermate jacked off to Moira's beauty, to the hard fucking Dante gave her. That made him even hotter, knowing he was watched. He lowered his gaze, traveling down her body, and watched his cock disappear inside her. As he glided in and out, white cream clung to his shaft. His white body contrasted so beautifully with her dark one. They were a perfect match, an incredible mating. His heart swelled watching her react to how he moved in her.

She loved what he did to her. And he'd never enjoyed fucking anyone as much as he did her. It was more than physical. They'd had that in their fur for a week. Taking her now, being inside her, moved something inside him that could only happen in their human form with all of his emotions on overdrive. Warmth traveled through him that had nothing to do with the change or with how hot her tight little pussy was.

He loved her. A level of compassion for her had existed for years. But now, as he rode her and buried himself in her heat, the feelings he'd had for her had moved beyond possessive. More existed than just a primal need to have her submission. That craving hadn't faded. It had grown, developed into more.

Moira had captured his heart, and he prayed she never let go of it.

She held her breath, blinking a few times and then staring up at him. A rosy hue spread over her cheeks and she slowly smiled, her gaze darting to Juan but then quickly back to him. "Don't let go of my heart either," she barely uttered, and her body spasmed.

She clamped on to his cock, sucking him inside her. She cried out, her fingers running up and down his arms. Tossing her head from right to left, her hair clung to her face while her orgasm convulsed and ripped through her.

It was too much. His brain almost exploded. Her body demanded his release and he no longer had the strength to fight it. His vision blurred, but Moira's beauty and sensual power were clear and easy to see and feel. She stroked his cock with her pussy. Her fingers dragged over his body. The view she offered as she came was too much. Dante pumped his come inside her. He released everything he had. The pressure exploded and flowed freely from his body. Suddenly he was so lightheaded he swore the two of them would float from the bed.

"Moira," he growled, his cock growing and locking them together while he gave her all that he had. "My little bitch, I love you."

She let out a sound that was half cry, half laugh. Her happiness smelled so fucking good mixed with her sex. Like fresh flowers in full bloom releasing their scent after a soft spring rain. Her face glowed and she grinned.

"I love you too, wolf man." She relaxed underneath him, her hands gliding down his arms.

He collapsed, covering her briefly and then moving to the side, pulling her into his arms while their legs tangled together. Still inside her, indifferent to his blurred surroundings, he brushed his lips over hers.

His mind slowly cleared even though his cock remained buried inside her. "Fucking hot," Juan growled behind him. He heard him move quickly, and then the bathroom door shut behind him.

Dante's phone vibrated and then chirped behind them. It was on the floor somewhere, probably in his jeans pocket, or maybe his shirt. He scowled in that direction. His cock was swollen inside her. The damn thing would just have to ring.

"I got it," Juan said, hurrying out of the bathroom with a white towel in his hand. Once again he wore his boxers and hopefully had enough time to clean himself before grabbing Dante's phone. The werewolf smelled like come.

"It's Ollie Grayson, their pack leader." Juan pushed the phone to his chest and let his gaze travel down their intertwined bodies. "Want me to tell him you'll call back?"

She'd pulled part of the blanket over her, covering herself, suddenly shy in front of Juan. Her hair was tousled around her flushed face. That just-fucked look—damn, it looked good on her. He brushed his fingers through her dark silky locks and then focused his attention on his littermate. He had no doubts Juan would be on the prowl soon for a willing bitch.

"Hand me the phone." He held out his hand.

Moira adjusted the comforter over their lower halves since he still rested deep inside her. He allowed her the small act of modesty, deciding not to try and figure out at the moment why it mattered that they were covered when Juan had just seen every bit of them naked. His cock shrank as he took the phone and he slipped out of her, rolling to his back as he glanced at the number on the small screen of his cell.

"Dante Aldo," he said, holding the phone to his ear.

By the background noise, it was obvious the pack leader was outside. Wind picked up as static crackled through the connection.

"Dante, this is Ollie Grayson. Several werewolves claiming to be from Malta have approached me. They demand to see you." Ollie sighed, sounding tired. "You helped my pack tonight and we have your tail, my friend. But I've sent my werewolves home to their mates for the evening. Dragging them back out if there is trouble might be a challenge."

Dante always knew this day would come. Word traveled quickly through packs, and often by the time it had been howled a few times, it came out distorted and inaccurate. Not to mention he'd never bothered to set any facts straight. Having the reputation of a pack destroyer had protected many good packs over the years. The time had come to clear all negative smells from the air. He knew when he shared the truth, suspicion might arise. Some might not believe him. It was knowledge he'd always lived with and would face tonight. Soon he'd know who would howl under the moon with him and who would go for his throat. He glanced down at Moira, who watched him with intent curiosity. God, he prayed she'd always run by his side.

"Where are you?" he asked, wishing more than anything he could lay next to her warm, sated body for the rest of the night.

"Meet me at my den." Ollie told him the address and gave brief directions. "Like I said, you honored our pack fighting by our side earlier tonight. These werewolves demand retribution. If you want, I can hold them until morning."

"No. I will meet with them tonight. It's time to set the record straight. The Malta werewolves deserve that much."

His words brought Moira to her feet. She pulled the comforter along with her, staying wrapped in it. But her long hair, tangled and flying around her face, added to the wild look she gave him as her jaw dropped.

He hung up his phone and stared into eyes filled with confusion and pain.

"What do we deserve?" she asked quietly, gripping the comforter at her breasts.

"Let's get a shower, sweet bitch." He picked up their clothes and bundled them in his arms. The comforter fanned around her like a royal robe as he placed his hand on her bare back and guided her toward the bathroom. Her emotions tripped over each other, swirling around her, and she made no effort to contain them. He turned to Juan. "We leave in a few minutes for the pack leader's den," he told him, offering neither of them any explanation.

The simple fact was, in spite of the years, he didn't have an explanation formed. All he could do was lay the truth on the table. A terrible and gruesome truth that he'd shouldered for years. He was no pack destroyer, but he was no hero either.

The only person he'd saved successfully on that terrible day was the bitch he loved.

By the time they arrived at Ollie's den, a modern-looking log cabin home on the side of the mountain, the crescent moon was high in the sky. Bright stars added light, and the blackness surrounding them was an amazing contrast. The night air was crisp, with the rich scent of evergreen giving it a clean smell. He'd just had damn good sex with the bitch he'd dreamed about for years and loved with all his heart. She stood by his side now as they climbed out of the truck. Everything might have been perfect if it weren't for the knot twisting like a knife in his gut. The reality was hitting him like a brick wall that finally closure would come on one of the deadliest and most destructive days of his lifetime.

Dante glanced down at Moira and she slid her hand in his. Juan came around the side of the truck to face him. For a moment he stared at the pack leader's den, unable to move forward. Her warm, soft fingers gripped his, giving him strength. Both gave him odd looks. It would be the only time they'd see him falter, hesitate. Neither were acts he planned on experiencing often.

He stared at the pack leader's home as an image of Bruno Tangaree appeared in his mind.

He focused on the old werewolf, who in Dante's memory appeared just as strong and powerful as he always had. *"What if they blame me for this?"*

Dante remembered the smell of the Tangaree den, clean and so full of love and happiness. The older werewolf had shared some sound advice during one of the last times they'd spoken.

Bruno stared out of the large window that looked out over downtown. For such a successful werewolf, he and his mate had always lived simply.

"*Rumors will fly no matter what the truth is, Dante.*" The older werewolf turned to face him but then looked at his mate, Renee, and smiled. *He moved to her, stroking her hair, and gave Dante his attention. "You'll know when the time is right to share the truth. And then you'll do so.*"

The time is right, Bruno, he thought to himself. He swore the old werewolf nodded his approval.

Something shifted in the air, like a warm breeze yet nothing blew. The hairs on his arms raised, but he didn't smell any aggression. Looking around quickly, there were no signs of any other werewolves other than the three of them.

Moira's hand went cold in his. She stiffened, looking up at him with an expression he hadn't seen on her face before. She paled as the door to the den in front of them opened.

"My sire," she whispered, and crossed her arms over her chest. "I feel him here."

Ollie Grayson walked up, not hearing her comment but sniffing the air as he stuck out his hand in greeting. "Welcome to my den, Aldo."

Dante nodded, shaking the pack leader's hand. Aggression and fear dominated the scents in the air. He wouldn't take time right now to worry about where the emotions came from. For the most part, probably everyone involved felt a bit of both. There was something else in the air though, something strong and powerful—a scent he hadn't smelled in over five years. For the life of him he didn't understand what he sensed, or experienced. It didn't seem anyone else noticed it but Moira.

"I've cleared out my family for the evening, sent them over to my in-laws' den." Again Ollie sniffed the air, his expression alert.

He was a big werewolf, balding with broad shoulders. For a moment Dante focused on his profile, but then Ollie turned and stared him in the face. There was a lot of respect in the werewolf's gaze. Damn good thing.

"There are two werewolves inside right now who claim to be from Malta." He glanced at Moira and Juan. "They look just like them."

"I was born and raised on Malta," Moira offered, straightening and sticking her chin out. Her pride in her heritage dominated the smell in the air.

Ollie nodded, respecting that fact. "Well, come on in and we'll get this over with. I'll tell you, Dante, I won't let these werewolves cause you trouble."

Two werewolves stood when they entered the den. It was a nice home, rustic, with a definite female's touch about the place. Dante didn't give too much attention to the array of pictures on the wall or the fancy vase with fresh-cut flowers on the coffee table. The bitch of this den wasn't here, but this was her home, her things, and they wouldn't be messed up.

Animosity clogged the air when one werewolf took a step forward. The other seemed slightly more composed but both glared at Dante.

"You are Dante Aldo?" the one who'd moved closer asked. Black hair fell straight around his head, almost reaching his shoulders. He was a tall werewolf, possibly an inch taller than Dante, with piercing black eyes that burrowed into him.

Dante nodded once. The werewolf didn't have the gift. He sensed that immediately.

"Dimitri," Moira whispered, and the werewolf faltered. "Dimitri and Nicolo Spalto?"

The werewolf who'd hesitated came forward, staring at Moira. He rubbed at a day's growth on his chin, which was mostly white and contrasted with thick black hair on his head. Both had the same straight, long nose, dark skin and penetrating black eyes. Dante watched warily, a growl rumbling from his chest when the werewolf approached Moira.

He stopped, looking at Dante. Moira held her hand out, touching Dante's chest. She sent out a calming sensation. It filled the room quickly. Damn her. She used the gift to rob the animosity from everyone in the room. It was late and she'd just fucked him hard. Exerting the effort to calm the situation with her gift would drain her quickly. He grabbed her wrist.

You will not control this situation, little bitch. He made his point very clear and she looked at him wide-eyed, biting her lip so that she wouldn't argue in front of the werewolves. She wanted to though. Her temper spiked, the urge to protect her mate strong. He brushed his thumb over the pulse beating in her wrist.

"You know these werewolves?" he asked quietly, his voice calm.

She nodded, offering a small smile that was only for appearance's sake. He didn't doubt for a minute that she'd have words for him later. Moira turned, glancing from one werewolf to the other.

"Dante Aldo is my mate. What issues do you have with him?" she asked.

"Moira Tangaree. Daughter of Bruno and Renee Tangaree. You live." The younger of the two werewolves gave her the once-over.

Dante growled again. No matter that they were surprised to see her, they would respect his property. Moira looked over her shoulder at him like she wanted to clobber him.

Again a strong presence swept through the room, manipulative and powerful. It took over all scents, replacing it with something dominating, something musky. Moira glanced around the room and then closed her eyes. For a moment Dante worried she'd leave them to chase after the smell of her sire.

And why all of a sudden were they sensing him? How many times over the years had Dante wondered if Bruno's gift was strong enough that he could help Dante even though he was dead? Bruno hadn't come to him—not once had he detected his presence or experienced any words of wisdom in dreams.

"You have the advantage of knowing my mate and me. Care to introduce yourselves and tell me why you seek me out?" Dante knew damn well why they were here. He wanted Moira to remain focused though, to dwell on what happened around her and not on the smell of her sire. Stating to these werewolves who didn't have the gift that they felt Bruno Tangaree in the room would get them all attacked.

Why he was allowing his presence to be felt Dante couldn't figure out.

"I'm Nicolo Spalto," the older of the two werewolves said. "This is my younger littermate, Dimitri. We're here because of your sire, Moira. It's been a long time but we will avenge his death by challenging Dante Aldo and taking him down for destroying our pack."

"You can challenge me if you want." Dante didn't hesitate. "But I'd hate for both of you to die without knowing the truth."

"What truth is that?" Dimitri asked.

"And why would we believe the words of a pack destroyer?" Nicolo grunted.

He knew there was only so much truth he could reveal to them today. He hated the pact he'd made. There were days when he despised it. But Dante was a werewolf who kept his word, even if that meant to the death. He let them glare at him for a moment before starting slowly.

"Ten years ago I agreed to work with Bruno Tangaree. He'd learned how to make werewolves stronger. One werewolf could destroy ten. It was a gift he wished to bestow on his entire pack. And he needed an assistant. I agreed to take the job."

He had everyone's attention in the room. Now to let out the hard part—the secret that had weighed heavily on his shoulders for so many years.

"His work was very successful. There were a few drawbacks, but for the most part, every werewolf and bitch who underwent the experiments came out stronger, capable of so much more. And as always with a gift given to werewolves, there were those who quickly grew jealous, made efforts to steal the knowledge and use it in their own abusive ways. Bruno wouldn't have that. And he fought it. Damn it if he didn't fight it with everything he had."

He reached for Moira's hand, meeting her gaze. She intertwined her small fingers with his and licked her lips as she looked up at him. Speaking of her sire brought her so much pain. He'd do anything to wipe that pain from her. But that damn fucking promise allowed him to say only so much. He looked at her sadly, knowing she needed to hear this more than any of the werewolves in the room.

"Bruno arranged for every pack to escape safely before setting fire to Malta. When we sent out the messengers, giving each den only hours to clear out before wiping out all evidence of his work, we were attacked. Werewolves from the other islands had planted spies. Your sire wasn't perfect, although he was one of the greatest werewolves that I ever had the privilege of knowing. Most of the dens didn't get the message. I fought that day to get you off the island."

Chapter Thirteen

ഇ

"You knew the pack would burn, yet spent your time simply on this bitch?" Dimitri lunged at Dante.

Dante didn't want her swaying their thoughts. But fighting now would accomplish nothing. Years had passed since that terrible day, and she'd much rather hear details she'd never known than watch these two werewolves roll around on the floor in their skin.

He didn't tell her that she couldn't alter her own body. Dimitri's attention was on Dante. Juan and Ollie jumped toward the two werewolves too. Dimitri's anger and hatred, his pain that he'd held all these years, fueled his attack. All he wanted was to take Dante down, release walled-up emotions on the one werewolf he'd blamed for all of his loss.

She had plenty of pent-up anger too. And it was easy to turn it into a raging fire when she attacked Dimitri.

She grabbed his thick arm that he had pulled back in order to strike Dante.

"Ow!" he howled, shaking her free easily enough and then grabbing himself where she'd touched him.

Dante stood tall, an overwhelming presence in the room. *Behave, my sweet bitch. I'd hate to have to send you out of the room.*

The stern expression he gave her was proof enough that he'd act on his thoughts if she weren't careful.

She acted quickly, needing to be part of this discussion more than she needed to breathe. She faced her mate, turning her back on the other werewolves.

"So you're on trial here," she told him, her heart burning when his expression hardened. "Did you try to help the other dens escape on that day?"

The look he gave her didn't change. She felt remorse pumping inside him, but damn him for being such an alpha werewolf that he couldn't show a bit of compassion in front of the other werewolves.

"I managed to get several dens to the bay before finding you. There was chaos everywhere, and I'm one werewolf." He nodded toward Juan. "My littermate worked with me, getting as many as we could to the ship."

"There were eleven of us in our den. Now we're three." Nicolo's words silenced the room, drawing the past forward so that all of them took a moment to see that horrendous day in their minds. Ollie put his thick fists on his hips, taking in everything around him with the quiet authority so common to pack leaders.

Thinking about the many who had died wouldn't change the fact. The pain would simply consume her once again. She had to focus on what was good here.

"I've searched so hard for members of my pack. I had begun to think I was finally the only survivor of an extinct breed." Moira forced her attention away from Dante, although his overwhelming presence wrapped around her even when she turned her back to him. He didn't touch her, but God, she swore the heat from his body sank to her very core. "What pack took you in?"

Dimitri still breathed too heavily. Instead of commenting, he turned away from her, running his hand through thick black hair. Ollie and Juan adjusted their stances, ready if he decided to lunge again. She ignored the charged energy, the adrenaline and testosterone that were thick enough to cut with a knife, and fought to keep her expression calm. She wouldn't use the gift, but she would use her status as a mate to gather enough respect that they wouldn't strike and risk attacking her too.

"The Malta werewolf is feared and despised everywhere. No pack took us in and without a pack, we had no strength. We've moved, traveled in our fur, done whatever it took to stay alive. When word hit us that Dante would be here, we headed here." Nicolo managed to remain a hell of a lot calmer than his younger littermate. He looked over her head at Dante behind her. "There are others, you know. We've had some contact. A few are in packs, but only because they've denied their heritage. We are all out of place until we reunite. The Malta werewolves are different from any other werewolf. The mending won't begin until we can claim territory for our dens and make a pack for ourselves."

"Contact the dens. We'll find a meeting place and work toward settling down." Dante put his hands on Moira's shoulders while he spoke.

His touch burned her skin, and it wasn't from any part of the gift. In spite of how well he'd fucked her less than an hour ago, pulsing need made her pussy wet. She fought to focus on the harsh look that Dimitri gave Dante, just to keep her scent from turning to lust.

"You helped us keep the *lunewulfs* from coming over the mountain, Aldo. Call your dens and we'll offer a secure place for you to meet. All I need is a head count and that all dens announce themselves to me when they arrive." Ollie got everyone's attention.

A few more words were exchanged but Moira had a hard time paying attention. Dante's hands stroked her back, ran down her hair. No matter who he spoke to, he continued to touch her, driving her nuts. On top of that, it sounded like a handful of dens would be contacted. She ached to know which ones. Possibly werewolves she'd run with growing up. There had been cousins, aunts and uncles that she'd assumed perished in the fires. The few who'd escaped with her on the boat had disappeared and traveled to their own safe havens — or places where they thought they'd find safety and peace.

Excitement tore her insides apart. Soon all who were left of the Malta werewolves would reunite.

A strange sensation swept through her. Damn! She swore her sire stood right in the room with them. He beamed at her and then glanced at all the werewolves in the room. His chest puffed with pride before he slowly faded away.

Her heart pounded too hard for her to catch her own breath. *Dad?* she cried out in her mind.

Dante looked down at her, tilting an eyebrow and giving her hand a quick squeeze. She smelled intense determination on him, but nothing else. And her mind was in too much of a whirl to organize her thoughts and hear what was in his mind. She searched the room anxiously, aching to see her sire again, but he was gone.

"We will need some time in your territory while we wait for these dens to arrive," Dante told Ollie. "We've taken enough of your time this evening. You know how to reach me when others arrive."

"I've arranged for all of you to stay at the same motel," Ollie said when Dante led her out the front door into the crisp night air. "It's run by a good older den and there will be no trouble."

"Tell that to your pack destroyer," Dimitri growled. "You'll get no trouble from us. It's him you want to watch. He might have helped your pack, but you know they say he disappears and no one can track his scent."

Dante ignored the werewolf's accusations and turned to shake Ollie's hand. "Give us a call when you're up tomorrow. We'll talk then."

Ollie sized Dimitri up when he turned to him. "I'm not sure how much you've personally interacted with Dante, but I consider myself a good judge of werewolves. Don't cause my pack any trouble."

Dimitri scowled and Nicolo stepped forward. "Our den is very grateful that you welcome us here. You have my word that we'll offer no problems."

"Good enough." Ollie turned and entered his den.

* * * * *

Moira woke up to Dante's cock harder than steel, nudging the soft, tender spot on her lower back. His thick, muscular arms were wrapped around her. She blinked a few times, realizing she used his corded biceps for a pillow.

She stretched, enjoying how his body touched her everywhere. They'd stripped the night before, and that was about all she remembered. She was pretty sure sleep had hit both of them hard the moment their heads hit the pillows. Now, lying naked under the covers next to him felt like the most perfect place in the world to be. She couldn't help twisting her body, rubbing herself against his powerful chest. Their legs intertwined and he raised his thigh until it pressed into her hot, moist pussy.

Instant pressure stole her breath and ripped it from her body. She inhaled sharply, twisting her torso. Her nipples hardened instantly when the covers slipped down her chest. She looked up at his brooding expression, so dark with black hair fanning over his broad shoulders.

"I'd love to lie here and fuck you all day, little bitch." His tone was gravelly, turned on.

"Would you make Juan watch again?" She turned her head quickly, seeing an unmade, empty bed.

"It's almost noon and time to get up. Already Juan is out making contact with some of the dens who've already arrived."

Werewolves were nocturnal by nature. Any decent pack started its workday around noon, allowing pack members to sleep after running during the night. She adjusted herself against his hard, warm body, feeling his erection throb between them. She wanted time to fuck him, and she wanted time to talk. It didn't sound like they'd have time for both. He smiled, reading her thoughts.

"Do you know what dens will be here?"

He shook his head and then lifted her so that they both sat in the bed. "Time to shower."

"Dante," she began when they were in the bathroom. "Last night at the pack leader's den, did you sense anything? I mean, like someone else was there?"

Muscles stretched and bulged in his back when he bent over to start the water in the tub. Black curly hair ran down his thick legs. She took in the view, waiting for him to respond while he adjusted the water. "Who do you think was there?"

"My sire was in that room."

Dante took her hand and pulled her into the shower. Hard, pelting hot water pitter-pattered over her skin, feeling damned good. She tilted her head into the spray, letting it soak her long hair.

"I think he was, too. Moira. Don't get your hopes up. Five years have passed. If Bruno or Renee could come to us from the dead, wouldn't they have done it by now?"

"I forced them out of my mind because I thought it would make me stronger," she confessed. "Last night, right before we got there, I remember thinking that my parents would be proud of us."

Dante ripped soggy paper from the bar of soap sitting in the soap dish. He rolled the bar in his hands, creating foam that filtered with the water and streamed down his body. Steam danced around them, holding the powerful smell of lust captive between them. Her heart picked up pace while she lost herself staring into his powerful gaze. Suddenly the ache in her pussy climbed to unbearable levels. "Little bitch," he growled, lowering his mouth to her neck and nibbling on the sensitive flesh there while he began running the lathered soap over her breasts. "Possibly you have brought them back to us."

She straightened, immediately wanting to ask more. He didn't shield his thoughts from her, but when she explored them, her insides turned to molten lava. All he wanted right now was his cock buried deep inside her. He didn't understand her sire's presence any more than she did.

"Turn around," he growled, and pinched her nipples just to make sure he had her attention.

Moira gasped, inhaling the smell of their mixed need deep into her lungs. She turned into the hot spray from the shower nozzle, closing her eyes and letting it hit her in the face. Dante grabbed her hips, pulling her back quickly. She slapped her palms against the shower wall, needing it rough this morning. Her insides tightened, anticipation coursing in her veins like a sweet drug.

He didn't wait—didn't tease her. That hard, thick cock impaled her soaked pussy with an energy that matched the need ripping her insides apart.

"Oh, fuck yeah," she sighed, taking all of him in.

Every inch of him.

She felt him clear up to her belly button. He broke through her dam of need, crashing into the pressure of lust that consumed her. Her hands slipped down the shower wall, but he held her hips firmly, thrusting again and again while the shower beat down on them.

"Moira. It's so hot, so damned wet." His voice boomed over her, low and predatory.

Dante kept the rhythm steady, not going too fast or too slow. He stroked her inner muscles, soothing and then heightening the need in her all over again. Her hair hung over her face, wet and heavy, providing a curtain that kept the outside world out. If only briefly. But while Dante was inside her, taking her, nothing else mattered.

She closed her eyes, loving him. And then almost fell to her knees when he pulled out without warning.

"Around. Face me." His quick command came out hastily. She turned around, shoving her hair over her shoulder and then grabbed his arms. She was so much shorter than he was that they couldn't face each other and make love easily. But Dante wasn't swayed. He lifted her, pulling her to him, and she wrapped her legs around his waist. That giant, throbbing cock of his slid into her pussy, hitting her in a different spot this time.

She arched into him, letting her head fall back while he kept a tight grip on her.

"What an incredible view," he growled, almost purred, while he thrust his hips, burying his cock deep inside her.

She managed to open her eyes. Movement of any kind proved challenging. Just holding on while he fucked the shit out of her was about all she could manage.

But then she stared into his face. The hardness was gone. The worry lines he'd woken up with had disappeared. Those blue eyes glowed with more emotion than she'd ever seen in them before. There was no way she could look away.

He filled her, releasing everything he had deep inside her. A growl tore from his body so powerful she was sure the walls around them shook. It vibrated through her, making every inch of her tingle. He pulled her to him, swollen deep inside her pussy, and wrapped powerful arms around her.

"I love you, Moira. I never knew it could feel this strong." His mouth covered hers and he fed off her.

Taking and nibbling, devouring her while his tongue swiped the length of her mouth. He crushed her to him, holding her so tight she could hardly breathe. Everything she'd witnessed before, his worry, apprehension, along with an overwhelming sensation of peaceful contentment and yes, love, wrapped around her.

She buried her cheek against his shoulder. Dante was the perfect mate, everything she'd ever dreamed of. Powerful, confident, but not so much that he was stupid. He didn't chase after his own tail. He didn't strut in his fur trying to look better than the other werewolves and not see trouble when it hit him in the nose. He was flawed, but just right for her.

I love you too, Dante.

Enter me, Moira. Make our souls one.

She relaxed against his body, her arms and legs wrapped around him, and slowly moved her mind into his. Raw energy, so strong and electrifying it seemed to lift her into the air, filled her. Dante moved into her mind.

We're one, wolf man.

And we always will be.

* * * * *

Moira stared at the oversized werewolves when she followed Dante into a meeting room at the motel where they stayed. Actually, it was an extension of the restaurant, and at midafternoon, there was no one else around. At least, she didn't smell any humans. There were enough werewolves lingering to make the place look like a meeting she'd have with agents. The same sullen, mistrustful expression was smeared over every werewolf's face.

They stepped through two opened French doors into the designated meeting area. Red carpet and a velvety wallpaper with a red and black design reminded Moira of something out of an old detective movie. The place was in sad need of some modernization. But it was clean. A slight hint of cleaning supplies lingered where windows and tabletops had been wiped down.

That clean scent was seriously bogged down by the heavy, spicy smell of anger, wariness and barely contained aggression. Moira's hairs prickled on the back of her neck. She'd defend her mate to the death. These werewolves blamed him for their losses. And once, she'd believed it too. But now she knew Dante—she loved him. There was no way he was capable of blindly destroying dens, cubs, bitches, no matter the cause. He was the kind of werewolf her sire had trusted with his life, and with the life of what he cherished most—her.

"Is everyone here yet?" Ollie strolled into the room, probably the only werewolf not smelling of animosity. His comfortable confidence came on strong when he walked toward the middle of the room.

A young bitch, around the same age as Moira, stood between Dimitri and Nicolo. Moira remembered the werewolves had come from a large den although she couldn't remember the bitch's name. Her long black hair draped over her breasts and shoulders, partially covering the side of her face and making it hard to read her expression. She looked vaguely familiar but she wasn't someone Moira had run with in her earlier years. The two werewolves stood protectively on either side of her. Moira remembered them commenting they were a den of three now. They would fight and die to protect the female—it was obvious by the protective way they stood on either side of her.

The bitch slowly crossed her arms and focused on Ollie when he spoke. At the same time a chair slid out from under a nearby table. The pack leader would trip over it. Moira glared at the chair, using the gift to push it back under the table. The young bitch's jaw dropped.

Charged energy shot through the air. The bitch uncrossed her arms and fisted her hands at her sides, looking slowly at the growing amount of werewolves in the room. Dante put his hand in the middle of Moira's back, guiding her toward a table where Ollie indicated they should sit.

Even when Moira looked away, the young female's strength filled the room, searching for the culprit who ruined her small prank.

Amazing. Someone else with the gift as strong and pure as hers and Dante's. Moira looked at the other werewolves who strolled into the room. How many of them possessed the gift her sire had wanted to bestow on all of them? And would the gift make them stronger? Or be their curse?

Chapter Fourteen

❧

Ollie didn't appear to have any problem standing in the middle of a room filled with werewolves from Malta. He stood out. Ollie was an impressive werewolf. Dante had gained a bit of respect for him in the short amount of time he'd known him. The werewolf fought like a true warrior. And Dante had never been one to curse a werewolf for mixed blood or diluted heritage. After all, he was no more than a half-breed himself.

"There's about enough of you to make a pack." Ollie didn't sit, but walked slowly among the tables where at least fifteen werewolves from Malta sat and followed his movements silently.

Not many werewolves would exude so much confidence among some of the most notorious werewolves on the planet.

"Amazes the hell out of me that you're still alive, Aldo." Ricardo Montol sat at a table not far from Dante. Even sitting, the werewolf stood out in the room, being a few inches taller than most from his pack. Montol had owned one of the fisheries back on Malta. Dante remembered him running one of the stores downtown. "And I'm beyond stunned that you'd try to bring us back together. You're either the biggest fool that runs in fur or you're braver than I imagined."

"And he claims Bruno Tangaree's cub for a mate," someone else mumbled loud enough to be heard. "You going to try and lead this pack, Aldo?"

"Not as long as I live, he won't," Dimitri piped up, pushing his chair back.

Ollie moved in quickly on Dimitri, his harsh growl and the spicy smell of his temper making his actions very clear.

"Try and fight in this room and I'll kick your fucking ass," he hissed.

Without waiting for a response, he turned his back on Dimitri, showing the rest of them he didn't acknowledge the werewolf as a true threat. Ollie was comfortable in his position as leader.

"There will be no fights in your territory," Dante promised him.

Everyone turned when the glass doors opened and two of the werewolves from Ollie's pack filled the space in the double doorway. Irritation was the prominent smell as they scowled at the werewolves in the room and then focused their attention on Ollie.

"I had to come see if it was true," one of the werewolves said.

Dante didn't remember seeing either of them before.

"I can't believe you'd invite Malta werewolves here. Don't you know why their pack was burned?" The werewolf stepped into the room and then stopped, curling his lip as he looked from one table to the next. "It wasn't meant for werewolves to be tampered with, to be given powers to play like they were witches. Isn't it enough to control the night? You all had to go and tamper with things better left alone. Smartest thing you could do, Ollie, is get rid of the lot of them. WA would probably give you a medal."

Several werewolves jumped to their feet, instantly complaining and howling obscenities. Dante stood quickly, pushing his arm in front of Moira when she jumped up next to him. God. It was broad fucking daylight and they were on another pack's territory. The last thing they needed was for any of these brutes to make a scene when they were this close to reuniting the pack.

Ollie stormed through the room and pushed the werewolf hard enough to make him stumble back a few feet. "And you were the one who wouldn't defend your pack against the *lunewulf*. What was it you didn't like about them? Oh yeah, they were a bunch of fucking perverts who might jump some of our bitches and share them among their males. Was that it?"

The room fell silent although the tension was thick enough it could be sliced easily with a knife.

"This is different." The werewolf's tone had softened drastically. For his size, Dante saw quickly he'd be a werewolf to run with his tail between his legs at the first sign of trouble. He was the one who was pathetic. "The Malta werewolves are dangerous, unpredictable. They can do things. Ask them. See if they can't do magic."

A saltshaker flew off one of the tables, heading with a hell of a lot of force straight toward the coward werewolf.

"No," Moira hissed next to Dante and reached out with her hand.

The saltshaker stopped in midair, crumbling and crashing to the ground, glass and salt spreading quickly while the room grew deathly quiet.

Dante grabbed Moira's hand and pushed it down to her side. *Behave right this fucking minute,* he growled in her head.

I didn't throw it. I stopped it.

Dante looked down into her black eyes. They were opened wide, staring up at him. Her long lashes fluttered briefly over them. She sucked in a silent breath, barely nodding. His insides twisted. He hadn't sensed it. Looking away from her quickly, he glanced around the room.

Bruno. Can you hear me? Do you see what you've created? The gift survives, but we now live as a feared and mistrusted line.

Be strong and true to the gift. There will always be the superstitious. Gain the respect of those who matter and you will be strong again. Bruno's voice was as clear as if he stood next to Dante.

Moira grabbed his hand, almost twisting his fingers in the wrong direction before he stopped her.

"If I'd intended this to be pack business, I would have called for a meeting. Whatever decisions are made in this room, you'll be notified along with the rest of the pack. I don't remember this being a fucking democracy. Now head back to your den." Ollie pointed a finger to the door and the two werewolves backed out slowly.

Ollie barely waited for them to be over the threshold before shutting the doors in their faces. He turned around to face the room, his expression strained with contained anger.

"Many purebred lines have rumors and skepticism that follows them. How you all handle the rumors isn't my problem." He walked slowly toward Dante's table and then pointed a finger at him. "This werewolf saved my pack. My gratitude toward him has all of you here today."

A few whispers tickled Dante's ear, but he didn't bother trying to hear what any of the other werewolves had to say. Like Ollie had so perfectly pointed out, werewolves didn't exist around some fucking democracy. The strongest led the pack. Plain and simple. Whispered complaints or mumbled threats did little to impress him.

"Now there is some land," Ollie began.

The glass doors opened again, this time not as quickly. But every werewolf in the room tensed, ready to jump into action if again threatened.

The mated bitch who'd taken Moira in pushed her head through the door. The smell of terror and fear on her alerted everyone into complete silence. She chewed her lip and a lone tear streamed down her cheek when she began mumbling.

"I know I'm out of line, Ollie. And I'm sorry. I'm so incredibly sorry." She shook and swallowed heavily but forced herself to step inside and ran her hands down her business suit.

That's when Dante remembered that she worked in a WA branch just outside the town.

"Oh shit." Moira stood up quickly, grabbing Dante's shirt and doing her best to pull him to his feet. "The WA agents, they're here. And they're sniffing really hard to find us."

"Oh my God. How did you know?" Rose Silverman's fingers trembled over her lips.

Moira ran around the table, hurrying over to the woman.

"What's going on?" Ollie barked, quite obviously in the dark.

Several of the werewolves at the tables mumbled the same thing. Obviously not all of them had the gift.

"I've never done this before in my life, Ollie. You know I haven't. And I've only got a few days left at the job. I have all the respect in the world for WA. You know I do." Rose cried so hard it was close to impossible to get any sense out of her. "But I had to come. I mean, I planned on heading into town over my lunch break anyway. You know I do that sometimes. WA isn't that far out of town. Please, Ollie, I'm doing this for our pack."

"Rose, if you don't stop babbling and tell me what the fuck is going on, I'm going to call your mate and have him put a leash on you." Ollie's threat had no backing. The werewolf liked the mated bitch. Dante sensed that much in the clogged mixture of emotions piling on top of each other in the room.

Moira turned to face him, her expression lined with worry. "We've got to get out of here. Two agents are on their way into town right now searching for you. They plan on taking me back to GWAR."

"How did she know that?" Rose took a step backward. "I haven't told a soul. I mean, I meant to tell you, but I hadn't yet. It's like you read my mind."

Ollie was quick on his feet. "Head into the mountains where we fought the other night," he told Dante. "We've got your hide covered here."

* * * * *

Moira tore over rough ground, leaping over rock and racing up the side of the mountain alongside Dante. Cold mountain air nipped at her nose. Her long, thick coat kept her warm though. Memories of the first night she'd met Dante popped into her head as she stretched her legs, fighting to keep up the pace Dante set. It seemed such a long time ago. Burnt out on GWAR and frustrated with another mission, she'd raced to escape him. Now she ran alongside him, fighting to stay free and at his side.

Enough daylight remained to see through the thick grove of evergreen trees surrounding them. Dante pushed against her, slowing, when they came to a clearing. He sniffed the air and she pranced around him, antsy, knowing they'd be followed. It was in the air in the calmness that surrounded them.

Dante ran his thick, rough tongue down the side of her face. She stared into his almond-shaped eyes, glowing silver against his black longhaired coat. There was no more stunning creature on Earth. Long, daggerlike teeth pointed dangerously under his lips. His head was thick, his ears alert and twitching as he continually listened for intruders. But his attention never swayed from her. Slowly, he ran his tongue over her fur, stroking and petting her. She rubbed herself against him.

Dante didn't race up the mountain, running with his tail between his legs. Ollie told him about this spot and Dante led their run with purpose. It wasn't by accident that they'd stopped here. She blinked, getting lost in his silver eyes.

His thoughts tumbled into her head. *A den. Territory for the Malta werewolves to call their own.*

They'd twisted their clothes into rope and tied them around their necks before changing. Dante backed away from her, transforming while he moved. She shook her head, yelping her disapproval. They were a hell of a lot safer in their fur. Not to mention, his thoughts faded from her when he started the change.

264

"WA agents won't attack werewolves in their skin while the agents are in their fur. Surely you know policy as well as I do." He began dressing, hiding that glorious body of his with jeans and a sweatshirt.

Moira closed her eyes, letting the change take over. Fire burned in her veins as her muscles contorted and bones popped under her skin. The sweet pain of the change, transforming from the greatest creature ever to walk the earth into her human form, always gave her intense pleasure. She gave herself that moment, feeling every bone reshape, muscles cling and wrap around them, until slowly she straightened and stood on her feet.

Dante helped her untie her clothes from her neck.

"I hear a waterfall," he told her after they'd dressed.

She followed him through the trees and then sucked in a breath at the intense view laid out before them. Water tumbled down the side of the mountain, raw and wild, uncontrolled and free as it bubbled over rocks and raced toward a crystal-blue pool below.

She opened her mouth to ask about the thoughts he had teased her with before changing.

Dante spoke first. "When we first met I worried I'd never be able to give you your dream of a den, cubs and a place to call your own."

She looked up at his hard features. He continued looking at the water tumble for its freedom in the glistening mountain lake below them. His black hair shimmered from the sun.

"I think this would be a good place to set up that den." He wrapped his arm around her, warming every inch of her with his massive body.

Moira's heart almost exploded in her chest. Happiness swept over her so quickly, its clean smell only making the view around her crisper, clearer, as if she'd never really noticed the natural beauty before.

"God. Dante. I love you so much." She didn't want this moment to ever end.

Perfect peace settled between them. The calm before the storm, she thought to herself. Already she smelled other werewolves. Without turning around, she knew it would be minutes before this solitary perfection would be disturbed.

A branch cracked behind them and Dante turned, keeping her close to his side. Several werewolves appeared up the side of the mountain and more followed, sounding like a wild, panting pack. The three slowed quickly, dancing around each other. Behind them a group of Malta werewolves appeared. Their long black coats and large size made them stand out like the magnificent creatures that they were. Incredibly beautiful and more deadly than any other werewolf on the planet. The American werewolves with them paled in their presence. Now they'd live with the reputation the gift bestowed on them. Moira still felt a strong surge of pride as she watched her pack members climb to the clearing and then spread out around the American werewolves.

More werewolves reached the clearing—all werewolves from Malta. The large, black creatures made an impressive pack. And damn, every werewolf from the meeting room had to be there. They circled around each other, forming a line slowly until the American werewolves were surrounded. There were three American werewolves, the pack leader and two she didn't recognize.

Daddy, you'd be so proud.

I am, my sweet little cub. Today you make history. I knew you could do it. Something brushed against her hand.

Moira swore her father's large fingers, always calloused and rough, squeezed hers. She looked down, wiggling her hand, and a tear burned her eye. Quickly she straightened, brushing the hand her sire had just touched through her hair, and faced the werewolves.

The older of the two American werewolves spoke after changing into human form. "Dante Aldo and Moira Tangaree."

A younger werewolf finished dressing next to him. Both of them were obviously WA from the geekish-looking clothes they wore. She never understood WA's desire to make their agents stand out, like they were so damned good they didn't need to worry about their identity.

"It's Moira Aldo now," she corrected him.

A few of the werewolves from her pack looked at her, remaining quiet.

The older werewolf raised an eyebrow. "I see. I'm Steve Muller with WA, and this is my partner Jeff Brim. We were assigned to your case after Dante Aldo kidnapped you while you were on a mission for GWAR."

Moira laughed, carefully hiding the truth deep in her memory so that not even a Malta werewolf, who might have some or all of the gift, would detect it.

She looked up at Dante. "Someday you'll have to share your secret as to how you manage to get so many false rumors started about you." She quit smiling and looked at Steve Muller. "Do you honestly think any werewolf could kidnap a GWAR agent? I'm with this werewolf of my own free will."

"You deny charges that Dante Aldo abducted you while on a mission for GWAR?"

"I ran from GWAR with the werewolf I love, Mr. Muller."

"Call me Steve. And did you?"

"If you have any crime, it is that I left GWAR during a mission to be with Dante."

"No." Dante stepped forward, giving her a hard look before turning his attention to the WA agents. "She won't take the blame for any of this. My reasons for taking her are my own. What you believe happened is the truth. You've caught me, now what will you do with me?"

Juan stepped forward from the line of werewolves behind the WA agents. "I'm the one who chased Moira down and took her in my car away from her mission."

"It doesn't matter what either of them confess. I won't go back with you. If you want to take me away from here, you would have to kill me first," Moira said.

"Lay a hand on her and you'll be the one killed." Dante's growl left no doubt to his words.

Fire burned in the WA agent's eyes. Without even blinking, he turned away from Dante. The werewolf was either braver than he looked or an idiot. Moira studied Steve's backside, moving forward, trying to reach into his thoughts when the agent addressed Ollie.

"How is your pack involved with these Malta werewolves?" Steve asked.

The other agent, Jeff, looked at her pack members. "Do you realize the reputation this pack carries?"

Moira didn't have to climb into Jeff's head to smell his aggravation with the entire situation. It surprised her when she mingled with Steve's thoughts that he had more respect for her than she'd thought. In fact, he envied her freedom. He saw her happiness and her plight. Steve wouldn't do anything to fuck up his remaining days with WA. Moira saw that it pissed him off that he always had to appear the bad guy in front of other werewolves—especially a pack that he'd rather have watching his back than sniffing him out while he slept.

The least she could do was soothe that thought—if she could pull it off. Moving things physically was a hell of a lot easier than replacing angry thoughts with peaceful ones. She'd done it once before and she had to try again. Everything she'd ever wanted was at her fingertips, so close she could smell it, and these two wouldn't prance into her life and fuck things up.

"My pack has no beef with WA. And I don't smell trouble on any of these werewolves." Ollie was a bit nervous. Sweat beaded on his forehead. But he held his own, keeping eye contact with both agents.

"There isn't any trouble with any of these werewolves." Dante grabbed the agents' attention and both turned to look at him. "All they do is search for territory to claim for their pack. WA has always supported a pack's rights to unite and hunt, live as we were meant to live. If I understand correctly, that is the entire reason WA exists, to ensure that we are kept strong."

"You know why we're here." Steve wasn't daunted.

"Yup. And if you need to take me away, then so be it. You will not deny these werewolves the right to make a home for themselves though."

"They aren't taking you away." Moira leapt in front of Dante, glaring at the WA agents.

"Little bitch," Dante growled.

To hell with his damned werewolf's pride. She ignored his silent assurance that he'd come back to her, that he just wanted to get the agents off their tails. A cold breeze picked up around them, lifting her hair off her back. She focused on the two agents.

"I am alive and with Dante of my own free will. Will you charge me with going AWOL from GWAR?" She stared into Steve's gray eyes.

He hesitated and she grabbed on to that emotion. *Convince him to leave. Convince him to leave.* But what could she plant in his mind that would make him go?

Not to mention she'd never done anything like this before.

Her stomach twisted, apprehension making her break out in a damp sweat. Her clothes stuck to her skin and the breeze picked up. Her hair blew in her face while twigs and dead leaves danced at their feet. Too many emotions—anger, fear, frustration—spun around them like mini-tornadoes.

The determination faded in Steve's eyes while she watched. *Malta werewolves will harm no one here.* She prayed to make his mind agree with the thought she'd instilled in him.

Dante grabbed her arms, pulling her back against his rock-hard body. It was distraction enough to break her concentration. Instantly the wind stopped.

Steve looked at Dante and shook his head. "Stay here and claim your territory. WA knows where you are and where she is. If they want you, they can come get you."

His partner, Jeff, looked ready to argue when Steve turned and walked away from the group while the werewolves parted and made a path for him. The lot of them stood silently, watching while the two WA agents headed down the mountain.

Ollie walked toward them, giving Dante his attention.

"You helped protect our territory from the *lunewulf*. I know all of you have your differences to settle, but that is business for your pack, and not mine." Ollie looked around him and then raised his arms, spreading them and gesturing as he spoke. "This mountain and the valley below are unclaimed territory. The *lunewulf* are on one side and we're on the other. The *lunewulf* have fought to gain it for some time now. We'll back you in claiming this territory. Take it for your pack. It's good land."

"And it offers you security from the *lunewulf* trying to attack you again," Dante said.

He ran his hands up and down Moira's arms. The chill she'd experienced a moment ago disappeared. Warmth traveled in her veins. Dante liked Ollie's proposal. He liked it a lot.

Ollie nodded, managing not to smile, and turned to head down the mountain. "Good luck to all of you."

Several hours later, after a hard run from one end of the mountain to the other, Moira curled up against Dante in her fur. Sleeping under the stars, claiming the land where they would build their den, seemed the perfect ending to the day. Hard times lay in wait for them. But they would be happy, fulfilled days and nights. Working alongside her pack members would build camaraderie. There would be fights, challenges, but that was their way. What mattered was that she had her mate. He would lay his kill at her paws and she would bear him pups. And together, they would make it work. Once again, the Malta werewolves would be strong.

I knew you could do it. The soft voice that had lulled her to sleep for years spoke just over Moira. *Your sire and I are so proud of you.*

Mom! Oh my God, Mom! Moira jumped up, almost stepping on Dante while she began wagging her tail so hard the leaves on the ground stirred around them.

Renee Tangaree stood before Moira in her fur. Moira had prayed every night growing up that she'd be as beautiful as her mother. Renee was even more stunning now than she had been five years ago. Moira leapt with unleashed excitement at the bitch and then jumped off just as quickly when she felt fur and muscle and bone.

You're really here? Or am I dreaming?" She shook her head, sniffed the ground, and then turned and stared at Dante who stood slowly.

If you are, we're sharing the same dream, he said, growling as he lowered his head in respect to the queen bitch of Malta werewolves. After all, no new pack leader had been appointed yet.

Don't think your work is done. Her sire's baritone, husky and always sounding like a growl, had Dante straightening in an instant. *The challenges will seem impossible. You'll fight more than once with your new pack leader.*

Challenges? Can you see the future now? Are we doing the right thing? Dante's questions tumbled out of him. *Who will be pack leader?*

Answering your questions won't make your future any easier, Bruno told him.

Take good care of my daughter, wolf man, Renee growled at Dante, but then walked up to them and gently licked him on the nose. She then turned and brushed her warm tongue down Moira's cheek.

She was there, with them. Both of her parents were. Real flesh and blood, not a dream.

Her parents turned, walking into the darkness until they faded into it and were gone.

It wasn't a dream, Dante growled, circling her several times until he pushed her down and then cuddled around her with his giant, warm body. *They've returned, which only assures me that we've done the right thing and that the Malta werewolves will definitely be stronger than before.*

Moira closed her eyes, still feeling her mother's warm tongue on her cheek.

I hope they come back. There were so many things to catch up on, to share with them.

They will, Dante growled confidently.

She rested her chin on Dante's side and closed her eyes. For the first time in her life she fought for what she believed in, not what some government agency told her to. And she was free, truly free. The love for her mate swelled as she drifted off to sleep.

Building a pack from nothing was hard. Rebuilding a pack with the odds stacked against them and animosity still running through some of them would be the challenge of a lifetime. And it was one Moira couldn't wait to take on.

I love you, Mom and Dad, she said silently in her head, and then drifted back to sleep next to Dante.

About the Author

ဢ

All my life, I've wondered at how people fall into the routines of life. The paths we travel seemed to be well-trodden by society. We go to school, fall in love, find a line of work (and hope and pray it is one we like), have children and do our best to mold them into good people who will travel the same path. This is the path so commonly referred to as the "real world".

The characters in my books are destined to stray down a different path other than the one society suggests. Each story leads the reader into a world altered slightly from the one they know. For me, this is what good fiction is about, an opportunity to escape from the daily grind and wander down someone else's path.

Lorie O'Clare lives in Kansas with her three sons.

Lorie welcomes comments from readers. You can find her website and email address on her author bio page at www.ellorascave.com.

Tell Us What You Think

We appreciate hearing reader opinions about our books. You can email us at Comments@EllorasCave.com.

Why an electronic book?

We live in the Information Age—an exciting time in the history of human civilization, in which technology rules supreme and continues to progress in leaps and bounds every minute of every day. For a multitude of reasons, more and more avid literary fans are opting to purchase e-books instead of paper books. The question from those not yet initiated into the world of electronic reading is simply: *Why?*

1. *Price.* An electronic title at Ellora's Cave Publishing and Cerridwen Press runs anywhere from 40% to 75% less than the cover price of the exact same title in paperback format. Why? Basic mathematics and cost. It is less expensive to publish an e-book (no paper and printing, no warehousing and shipping) than it is to publish a paperback, so the savings are passed along to the consumer.

2. *Space.* Running out of room in your house for your books? That is one worry you will never have with electronic books. For a low one-time cost, you can purchase a handheld device specifically designed for e-reading. Many e-readers have large, convenient screens for viewing. Better yet, hundreds of titles can be stored within your new library—on a single microchip. There are a variety of e-readers from different manufacturers. You can also read e-books on your PC or laptop computer. (Please note that Ellora's Cave does not endorse any specific brands.

You can check our websites at www.ellorascave.com or www.cerridwenpress.com for information we make available to new consumers.)

3. *Mobility.* Because your new e-library consists of only a microchip within a small, easily transportable e-reader, your entire cache of books can be taken with you wherever you go.

4. *Personal Viewing Preferences.* Are the words you are currently reading too small? Too large? Too... ANNOYING? Paperback books cannot be modified according to personal preferences, but e-books can.

5. *Instant Gratification.* Is it the middle of the night and all the bookstores near you are closed? Are you tired of waiting days, sometimes weeks, for bookstores to ship the novels you bought? Ellora's Cave Publishing sells instantaneous downloads twenty-four hours a day, seven days a week, every day of the year. Our webstore is never closed. Our e-book delivery system is 100% automated, meaning your order is filled as soon as you pay for it.

Those are a few of the top reasons why electronic books are replacing paperbacks for many avid readers.

As always, Ellora's Cave and Cerridwen Press welcome your questions and comments. We invite you to email us at Comments@ellorascave.com or write to us directly at Ellora's Cave Publishing Inc., 1056 Home Avenue, Akron, OH 44310-3502.

Cerridwen, the Celtic Goddess of wisdom, was the muse who brought inspiration to storytellers and those in the creative arts. Cerridwen Press encompasses the best and most innovative stories in all genres of today's fiction. Visit our site and discover the newest titles by talented authors who still get inspired - much like the ancient storytellers did, once upon a time.

Cerridwen Press
www.cerridwenpress.com